"Are you sure ▮▮▮▮▮▮ **Millie? Just** ▮▮ ▮▮▮▮▮▮ ▮▮▮▮▮▮▮**? We can still be friends and be married."**

He wished the carriage wasn't so dark so he could see her expression better. "I thought things had deepened between us. Can you seriously deny you have feelings for me?"

He heard her soft sigh and felt her sit up straighter on the seat. "Levi, I'll admit that something has changed between us, but it doesn't matter. I still can't marry you." Was that a catch he heard in her voice? Or wishful thinking on his part?

"Can't? Or won't?" Levi was more shaken by her refusal than he cared to admit. He knew his voice held the anger he felt but he couldn't help it. It was as if he were trying to draw a different response from her. To make her admit she cared. He sought to erect a wall of defense around his heart.

"I don't have a choice, Levi."

Why couldn't she see that a marriage between them would be the best solution? It dawned on him it was the solution to his problem, not hers.

Books by Rhonda Gibson

Love Inspired Historical

The Marshal's Promise
Groom by Arrangement
Taming the Texas Rancher
His Chosen Bride

RHONDA GIBSON

lives in New Mexico with her husband, James. She has two children and three beautiful grandchildren. Reading is something she has enjoyed her whole life, and writing stemmed from that love. When she isn't writing or reading, she enjoys gardening, beading and playing with her dog, Sheba. You can visit her at www.rhondagibson.net, where she enjoys chatting with readers and friends online. Rhonda hopes her writing will entertain, encourage and bring others closer to God.

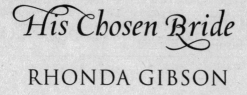

His Chosen Bride

RHONDA GIBSON

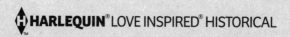

HARLEQUIN® LOVE INSPIRED® HISTORICAL

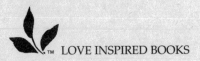

LOVE INSPIRED BOOKS

Recycling programs
for this product may
not exist in your area.

ISBN-13: 978-0-373-28264-7

HIS CHOSEN BRIDE

Copyright © 2014 by Rhonda Gibson

www.Harlequin.com

Printed in U.S.A.

For I the Lord your God will hold your right hand,
saying to you, Fear not; I will help you.
—*Isaiah* 41:13

A special thank you to all my critique partners...
I couldn't have finished this book without you.

Chapter One

Granite, Texas
Fall 1886

Millie Hamilton stood in the stagecoach doorway and looked out on the town before her. Dusty, rustic and sparse. Most certainly not like her beloved hometown of Cottonwood Springs, New Mexico, with its trees along Main Street and flower boxes in front of businesses. No, she was finally in Granite, Texas, six months past her original arrival date.

"Miss Millicent Summer?"

Millie knew without being told that the man in front of her was Levi Westland, the man who'd expected to marry her six months ago. She was to have been his mail-order bride. She recognized him from the photograph he'd sent her in his last letter, though the small picture hadn't done him justice. Surely he hadn't continued to meet the stage daily.

"Yes?" Millie allowed him to take her gloved hand and assist her from the stage.

"I'm Levi Westland."

To say Levi Westland was handsome would have been an understatement. Piercing green eyes shone from his face like gleaming porcelain, and two dimples appeared as if loving fingers had squeezed his cheeks. She was caught off guard by the sudden flutter in her heart. He was the most handsome man she'd ever met, and that meant trouble for her.

Levi Westland smiled up at her and continued to hold her gloved hand in his. He smelled of fresh-cut wood and warm earth, but his attire appeared to be that of a rancher. Leather cowboy boots, a black Stetson hat and a shiny belt buckle were not the standard dress of a woodworker, which was what he said in his letters that he did.

"It's nice to meet you, Mr. Westland." Millie removed her hand from his. "I wasn't expecting you to be waiting for me—after all, it has been over six months since I was supposed to have arrived."

The stagecoach driver tossed two bags down to the boardwalk in front of them. Millie grimaced at the thud that they made and was thankful she'd thought to put her charcoal and paints in her satchel instead of in one of the bigger bags.

Levi picked up the luggage. "I wasn't really waiting for you, Miss Summer. I just happened to be walking by when the stage arrived. When the driver called out your name, I stopped." He offered her what looked like a nervous grin. "To be painfully honest, I'd given up on your arrival months ago."

Millie nodded. "I see." She inhaled deeply and turned to face the handsome man. It was time to be honest with him, as well. "Mr. Westland, I would appreciate it if you would address me as Miss Hamilton. My full name is

Millicent Summer Hamilton. I only used my middle name to protect myself while traveling." She paused as she felt a slight heat enter her face. Millie took another breath and rushed on, "And when I was sending letters to strangers who wanted to get married."

He chuckled. "Then Miss Hamilton it is."

"Thank you." Millie knew she'd been foolish in not revealing her full name in the letters they'd exchanged. It was one of many things she'd done to prevent her parents from finding her. It had been foolish to run away from home, but something she'd felt she had to do then also.

Now that she'd spent some time away from her home, Millie wasn't ready to return.

Millie watched as he motioned for a gangly young boy to come toward them. The teenager stopped a few feet away. "Can I do something for you, Mr. Westland?" the lad asked.

"Amos, would you take Miss Hamilton's bags to the boardinghouse?"

The floppy hat that covered his blond locks bobbed agreement. "I'd be happy to, Mr. Westland." His young voice cracked and a red flush filled his neck.

Levi dug into his pocket and pulled out some change. As he handed it to Amos, he continued, "Please ask Beth to put the bags in room four."

"I will. Thank you, sir." He shoved the coins into his front pocket, took the bags from Levi and ran across the street and around a corner.

Millie's first instinct was to chase after the young man. Everything she needed was in those bags including most of her money, her only sketch pad and drawings. Now she wished she'd kept her money with her instead of hiding it within the bags. She could replace the sketch pad and drawings but not without money.

"Don't worry, he's reliable. Amos will take them straight to the boardinghouse. You've nothing to fret about." Levi tucked her hand into the crook of his arm and proceeded down the boardwalk.

Had her face shown her concern? Or had it been the wringing of her hands that had given her away? Millie realized she'd need to learn to control her expressions if she wanted to be taken seriously as both an artist and a woman.

"I've some business to take care of and then we'll head to the boardinghouse where you can see for yourself that your bags are fine."

Millie nodded and allowed him to guide her in the opposite direction of the way the lad had run. She wanted to scream, but since the only reason she'd come to Granite was to return the money Mr. Westland had sent for her travel expenses, she'd go along with him for now. After making him wait so long for her to arrive, Millie didn't feel it would have been right to explain her change of heart regarding marriage in a letter. No this had to be done in person.

As they walked, Millie struggled inwardly with her emotions. Just like her mother, Levi Westland had taken charge, not bothering to ask her what her plans were. For now, she'd give him the benefit of the doubt, but if he thought just because they were supposed to get married, that he could control her every move, well, he had another think coming.

She wasn't marrying him or any other man. Millie had come to Granite to tell him that she'd been mistaken in answering his mail-order bride advertisement.

She had thought at the time it was the only way to escape her controlling mother and to flee from the law.

But on the trip out, she'd changed her mind. Because Millie knew it wouldn't be right to keep the money he'd already spent on her passage to Granite, Millie had taken a job in Lubbock Texas.

It had taken her six long months to earn his money. She'd grown up during those months and realized she should have stood up to her mother and told the law what had happened.

Millie still wasn't sure if the U.S. marshal was after her or not. Burning down Eliza Kelly's house had been an accident, but now she understood that by running away, she appeared guilty and it wouldn't look at all like an accident to the law.

Her thoughts calmed a bit as she glanced around the small town of Granite. It looked like a nice place to settle. Millie thought about the art gallery she hoped to have someday. If all went well, she might just stay here and make that dream come true. Then she could return to Cottonwood Springs a success and with a little money to pay a good lawyer.

In his letters, Levi had described Granite and its people as warm and welcoming. As if to prove his point, a woman with a small boy in hand smiled and waved at them. Millie returned her smile and wave. If everyone was as friendly as the woman Millie felt sure she'd be happy here. But would Levi allow her to stay once she told him she didn't wish to marry after all? Or would he expect her to pack up and move on?

Levi had said he'd given up on her. That was good. She'd be able to tell him that marriage was out of the question and she had earned enough money at Miss

Hattie's Laundry, and by selling a few of her drawings in Lubbock, to pay him back for the trip to Granite.

To break the silence, Millie said, "This looks like a nice town." She noted a furniture builder's shop and inhaled deeply. Was that Levi's carpentry business?

The soothing scent of wood filled her nostrils. Millie didn't think the scent drifted out from the store; more than likely it came from the man beside her.

Her papa worked at the sawmill in Cottonwood Springs. The smell of fresh wood shavings always gave her comfort. Today the scent reminded her of Papa, and longing entered her heart to see him again.

Levi offered a stiff chuckle. "We like it."

He continued walking with her, nodding at the locals, so Millie allowed her thoughts to drift back to her father. She missed him dearly but couldn't see herself returning home just yet.

Mother was as demanding as the day was long and Papa was as meek. He allowed her mother to boss him around. She told him what to do and where to go as if he were a child. No, Millie had had enough of that in her eighteen years at home.

Reflecting on her parents' relationship, Millie knew she didn't want or need a loveless marriage, in which one person ruled the roost and the other lived life in misery. It was sad that she thought of her parents' marriage like that, but doing so had enlightened her that she didn't want such a life.

Her gaze moved back to the handsome man beside her. He seemed lost in his own thoughts so Millie tried to work through hers. How was she going to tell him they weren't getting married? Did he still expect her to marry him? For all she knew, he could already be married.

Levi suddenly stopped. "I'm sorry. I just realized you must be tired after your long trip. My business can wait until this afternoon. Why don't we go eat lunch at the boardinghouse and afterward you can rest?" He didn't give her time to answer, simply turned around and began walking back the way they'd come.

Millie frowned at him. He flashed a smile in her direction and once more she was taken aback by his good looks. Maybe Levi Westland had charm, but no matter how much he planned on using it to get her to marry him, he could just forget it. All her life she'd been coddled and pampered, but at what price? Millie sighed. Until she'd run away from home, she'd never been free. Her mother had made sure she was hardly ever alone and that she'd never made any decisions on her own.

As they continued along, Millie thought about the event that had forced her into thinking she needed to run away.

Mrs. Eliza Kelly had asked her to watch her shop while she took her friend schoolteacher Hannah Young to the train station in Durango, Colorado. It was an all-day trip so she would be gone for a day and a half. She'd told Millie that if she wanted to spend the night in Eliza's house, she could. Her mother had agreed to let her stay.

Millie had made the mistake of telling her friends that she planned to spend the night at Mrs. Kelly's and would have the house to herself. The other girls had decided it would be fun to come over and smoke a few cigars. The boys always snuck around smoking the horrible things.

Her friend Charlotte had brought a handful to the
shop and said it was time they found out what was so
wonderful about them. They'd made plans for the girls
to come over later, after the shop had closed, and try
them out.

If only she hadn't tried to smoke one of the horrible cigars before the other girls arrived. She'd just lit
it when her mother had come barging into the house.
Millie had panicked and tossed the other cigars out the
kitchen window. She'd laid the lit cigar on the window-
sill and hurried into the dining room to meet her mother.

Mother had decided she shouldn't spend the night
alone and forced her to go home. Before Millie could
sneak out and back to Mrs. Kelly's, the cigar had rolled
out the window and into the dry ground below. It had
set the grass and remaining cigars on fire. The house
and dress shop had gone up in flames and burned to
the ground.

Millie lassoed her thoughts with a snap. No use crying over spilt paint. The only thing to do was set things
right. And that, she planned to do. Millie shaded her
eyes with her hand.

Granite wasn't a bad-looking settlement and so far
she hadn't seen a saloon. That was a huge plus in her
books. However, she did miss the trees and flowers that
lined Main Street in Cottonwood Springs.

They took a side street that didn't have as many businesses. Her companion remained silent as they passed
Bob's Mercantile and the Sewing Room.

Bob's Mercantile had a window on each side of the
open door, with an old flyer advertising the newest para-
sols from New York City. The plank exterior was newly

whitewashed, and Millie could see barrels in the center aisle near the door.

But the Sewing Room grabbed her attention, and she slowed, trying to take it all in. Every frill imaginable had been showcased in the two windows; a quilt, hankies, ribbons, bonnets…even an apron. A sign hung in the window stating it would soon be closing and everything was on sale.

"We're almost there," Levi finally offered.

Millie quickened her steps and simply nodded. The smell of baking bread tickled her nose as they passed the bakery and she inhaled deeply. Her stomach rumbled.

A warm chuckle was the only indication that Levi had heard the sound. Butterflies replaced her hunger pains at the rich sound of his amusement. A dimple flashed in his cheek. She almost groaned aloud.

He truly was a handsome man. Maybe she should move on to another town once her business with Levi Westland was done. It wouldn't do for her to fall for a take-charge man and lose her newfound independence.

Levi enjoyed the soft scent of lavender that Millicent Hamilton wore. With each step they took, it filled his senses. He was still a little shocked that she'd arrived six months later than he expected. She'd been so silent in the time they'd been together that he'd had time to do some thinking.

A little over a year ago, at Christmas, his mother, Bonnie Westland, had surprised him and his brother with the news that she wanted a grandchild and that she expected them to get married and provide her with that child. She'd pitted her boys against one another by stating that the first to marry and have a child would inherit the ranch.

Levi knew Daniel wanted the ranch more than he wanted to live. So at first Levi had enjoyed playing the game, mainly just to irritate his older brother. He'd never intended to win the ranch. He shook his head at how foolish that sounded now.

Levi pushed the gate open in front of the boardinghouse and allowed Millie to slip past him. As they walked up the path, his thoughts returned to his mother and the contest she'd started. When Daniel had married Hannah in the fall, Levi had thought that would satisfy their mother. Daniel loved the ranch and so did his wife, but Levi's mother had informed him that he was still expected to compete for the ranch. Why was it so important to Mother that he marry, too? The question swirled through his mind like a wild tornado.

Bringing himself back to the present, Levi heard the lacy blue curtains flutter in the breeze. The smell of roasted meat drifted out the open window of the boardinghouse's restaurant.

He heard the soft rumble of Millicent's stomach and said, "The food here is wonderful. Beth is probably the best cook around." He placed his hand in the small of her back as she climbed the short steps to the entryway.

"Beth?" Millicent's blue eyes searched his face as he stepped around her and opened the door to the boardinghouse.

He pointed to the sign that read Beth's Boardinghouse and Restaurant. "Mrs. Beth Winters. She runs this fine establishment." He didn't mention that he owned the boardinghouse since there would be time enough for that later.

A bell sounded over their heads as they entered. Levi watched as Beth hurried toward them. She patted her dark brown hair into place and swiped at the flour upon her blue apron. A smile touched her lips and brown eyes as she realized it was him. "Levi, I wasn't expecting you to be here so early in the day."

"I decided to have an early lunch." He watched Beth's eyes dart from Millicent back to him. "Beth, I'd like you to meet Miss Millicent Hamilton. She will be staying here for a while."

"It's nice to meet you, Miss Hamilton. So the bags Amos brought in earlier were yours?"

"Yes, they were," Millicent replied. A sweet smile of relief graced her pretty heart-shaped face.

Beth smiled back and then turned to enter the restaurant portion of the boardinghouse. "Levi, your table is ready." She glanced over her shoulder. At his nod of approval, she continued. "Miss Hamilton, we put your bags in room number four. I hope it is to your liking."

She took the reserved sign off Levi's favorite table, which was in the far corner of the room. From this vantage point he could see everyone who entered and exited the dining room. Levi smiled his thanks and moved to pull out the chair that would sit to the right of him.

Millicent took the seat Levi pulled out for her. "Thank you, Mrs. Winters. I'm sure the room will be fine."

Beth handed Millie a menu once she was seated. "You can call me Beth. Everyone does."

Millicent took the menu and smiled. "Please, call me Millie."

Millie. The name had a sweet ring to it. So far everything about the woman screamed sweetness—her name, her fragrance and the way she tilted her head when she seemed to be thinking of something, like now as she studied the lunch menu.

Levi pushed the thoughts away. He would not become enamored with Millie. Having his heart broken by Lucille Lawson had hurt too much. Even before his mother's contest, he'd asked Lucille to marry him, but once she'd found out he wasn't going to take over the ranch, she'd broken off their engagement and their friendship. No, his heart couldn't take another breaking.

"Millie it is. Are you planning to stay long in Granite?" Beth asked.

"I was considering it."

Levi heard the doubt in her voice. He knew she'd come because of his invitation so what had changed? Had spending an hour with him changed her mind? Maybe she didn't want to be his mail-order bride. He hoped that was the case.

"That would be nice. Granite doesn't have a lot of young women. Another one is always welcome." Beth assured her. "What can I get you to drink, Millie?"

"Tea, if you have it."

Beth nodded. "Iced? Or hot?"

Levi got some satisfaction in seeing the amazement in Millie's face at learning that they served iced tea. He loved cold beverages and had made it a point to get ice delivered every morning. It cost a pretty penny but was worth it to him.

Millie's expression turned from surprised to pleased. "I'd love iced, if it isn't too much trouble."

"No trouble at all. Levi, coffee? Or iced tea?" Beth waited.

He pulled his gaze from Millie. "I'll have the same. Thank you, Beth."

"You're welcome. I'll be right back with your drink orders." Beth turned and hurried back to the kitchen.

Millie went back to studying the menu so Levi looked about the dining room. Only one other couple was there, and he recognized them as Mr. and Mrs. Sullivan. They were passing through Granite on their way to Austin and were staying at the hotel.

"You seem familiar with this restaurant. What would you recommend, Mr. Westland?" Millie asked, bringing his attention back to her.

Levi smiled. "I'd recommend the roast beef sandwich. The bread is always soft and buttery and the beef tender."

She laid the menu down. "Sounds wonderful, I'll order that."

For the first time, she smiled at him, and it reached her eyes. Beautiful blue eyes with thick, light-colored lashes. Her face reminded him of a doll he'd once seen sitting in a store window while visiting Austin.

Beth arrived at that moment and set down their drinks. "Did I hear you say you'd like the roast beef sandwich?" she asked Millie, as she stood and pulled out a small pad of paper and a stub of a pencil.

"Yes, please." Millie picked up her tea glass and took a small sip. "Mmm, this is very good." She smiled up at Beth.

"I'm glad you like it. What about you, Levi?"

He handed the menus back to Beth. "I'll have the same."

Beth nodded and wrote their orders down on the

small pad. "I'll have that right out." She smiled, then left to make the sandwiches.

Millie pulled the napkin from the table and smoothed it out over her lap. "Mr. Westland, I hope you don't take what I'm about to say the wrong way, but I really feel we need to settle this now." She paused, but when he didn't answer, Millie continued. "I've changed my mind. I no longer wish to marry." Before he could respond, she pressed onward. "I want to return my travel fare to you." Millie pulled the money from the handbag she carried and laid it on the table in front of him.

He admired her spunk. Levi pushed the money back to her side of the table. "I can't accept your money." He held up his hand to stop her from protesting. "I, too, have changed my mind about marriage and so it would be unfair for me to take the money back."

When he lowered his hand, she asked, "You have changed your mind also? Honestly?"

Levi offered her what he hoped was a reassuring smile. "Yes, when you didn't arrive on schedule I was relieved because I wasn't ready to get married. I should never have placed that advertisement."

She took a sip from her tea, then gently set the glass back down. "I'm glad to hear that. I was worried you wouldn't understand and I imagined you would wonder why I answered you in the first place."

He pushed forward in his chair. "It has crossed my mind. I mean, you are still here even after you've decided not to marry me. It's only natural that I wonder."

Millie looked him straight in the eyes. "I have a scheming mother. She controlled me to the point that I lost all signs of independence. I had to get away, but once I left, I realized I couldn't marry someone who would be the same way."

Levi felt his jaw drop. They'd just met. How could she have formed an opinion of him so quickly? Or was she talking about not marrying any man, not just him?

Her soft laughter surprised him. "I'm not saying you are controlling, although since our first meeting you have taken charge of my life."

He crossed his arms and leaned back in his chair. "How so?"

It was her turn to lean forward. "First, you sent my bags here, told Beth which room to put me in, and then proceeded to drag me off to some business meeting. Halfway there, you changed your mind and turned me around and now here I sit at your table ordering lunch. It never dawned on you to ask what I wanted to do."

Levi felt his ears turn red. She was right. He'd taken over the situation and not once had he stopped to hear her out or see what she wanted to do. How could he have assumed he knew what she wanted or needed? Had he turned into his mother?

He shook his head. "You're right, and I'm sorry."

She tilted her head to the side and studied him. "It's all right. You were working on the assumption I still wanted to get married." Millie lowered her gaze and, with her fingertip, traced the pattern on the tablecloth.

"Thank you for understanding."

Beth arrived at the table with two steaming plates. Levi was pleased to see she'd added fried okra to their meal.

"I hope fried okra is to your liking, Millie." She placed the dishes on the table and smiled.

Millie wrinkled her nose slightly but answered, "It's fine, thank you."

He bit his tongue to keep from speaking. The desire to tell her to send the plate back if it wasn't to her liking filled him. But, if he did say that, Millie would probably think he was being bossy again.

"Do you need anything else?" Beth asked, looking their table over and making sure their drinks were still full.

Both shook their heads. Levi was the one to answer. "I believe we are fine for now, Beth."

"All right, I'll bring the tea pitcher by in a little bit to refill your glasses." And with that, Beth turned from the table and headed back to the kitchen.

Levi said grace, and then after several long moments of silence while they ate, he asked, "Since you aren't going to marry me, what are your plans?"

Millie sat up a little straighter in her chair. "Well, if I decide to stay, I will need to find a place to live." She held up her hand as if to ward off any protest he might have. "I have enough money to spend the night here tonight and I thank you for sending my belongings here, but tomorrow I will need to find less expensive accommodations. I'm sure this lovely boardinghouse is more than I can afford."

He didn't argue with Millie, but he didn't like the idea of her staying at the hotel, and as far as he knew there wasn't a room in town for rent or a house to buy.

The hotel was a nice place, but Levi felt protective toward Millie. Maybe it was because he'd brought her here. Maybe because she'd revealed she'd never lived alone. Whatever the reason, he planned to have a chat with Benjamin Olson, the hotel owner, and make sure that Beth's Boardinghouse offered Millie the lowest rates in town. With that thought in mind, he asked, "And then what will you do?"

"I'll need to seek out employment." Her hands worked the fabric of the napkin.

Beth arrived back at the table with the promised pitcher of tea. She refilled their glasses and looked to Levi. A quick glance at Millie revealed her pushing the okra around on her plate.

If Beth hired her, she would stay on at the boardinghouse as part of her payment and he wouldn't need to talk to Mr. Olson. Levi thrust his chin upward and hoped Beth would take the hint to play along with him.

"Can I get you anything else?" Beth asked.

"No, the food is great, but we were just discussing possible employment for Miss Hamilton."

Millie's head jerked up.

Before she could comment, Levi pressed on. "You wouldn't happen to have a position open, would you, Beth?" He prayed Beth would understand what he wanted her to do.

Without missing a beat, Beth looked to Millie. "Can you cook, wash dishes and wait on tables? I could use another set of hands at the noon and evening meals."

Millie looked down at her hands. He wondered what she found so fascinating about them. "I can." Her voice came out strained.

Beth laid a hand on her shoulder. "Why don't you enjoy your lunch and we can talk about it when I show you to your room? How does that sound?"

Millie nodded, and Beth returned to the kitchen. Happy that was settled, Levi reached for his sandwich. He'd raised it to his mouth and was about to sink his teeth into the fragrant meat when he saw the angry expression on Millie's face. Now what? He lowered the sandwich.

"You didn't need to do that, Mr. Westland. I am capable of finding my own job," she ground between her teeth.

Levi offered her his most charming smile. "I'm sure you can, but now you don't have to." He expected her to argue, but instead her eyes grew wide as she stared toward the dining room door.

His gaze followed hers. His brother, Daniel, and Daniel's new bride, Hannah, waved and headed toward their table. Levi stood to welcome them.

Daniel greeted him with a broad smile and a rough slap on the back. "Haven't seen you since the wedding. We've been missing you out on the ranch."

Levi raised an eyebrow. "That right? Me? Or the fact that you lost an extra cowhand when I moved into town?" He grinned at his brother. "With a new wife and the ranch to keep you busy, I'm surprised you'd miss me at all."

"Oh, we miss you all right," Hannah added her assurance to her husband's comments.

"Miss Hamilton, I'd like you to meet my brother, Daniel Westland, and his beautiful bride, Hannah. Daniel, Hannah, this is Miss Hamilton." He paused then added, "My mail-order bride."

Hannah gasped, but Daniel laughed and shook his head. "Well, isn't this something?"

Levi hadn't seen his brother this pleased since his wedding day. When Daniel looked this happy, it usually didn't bode well for him. Levi asked suspiciously, "What's that supposed to mean?"

He searched his brother's dancing eyes and realized the answer wouldn't be coming too soon. His gaze moved to Hannah. She stood staring at Millie as if she'd seen a ghost. What was wrong? Both women simply stared at each other.

Daniel's booming voice captured his attention once more. "You aren't going to believe this, but Ma has three more mail-order brides at the house waiting for you to come out and meet." Daniel hooted and held his sides.

Hannah elbowed her husband in the ribs. He quickly straightened his face and turned to Millie. "I'm sorry, Miss Hamilton. It's nice to meet you."

"What?" Levi sank into his chair. What had his mother been up to? He noticed Millie hadn't said a word. She simply stared up at Hannah. Her face had gone pale, and she looked as if she might be sick. Levi knew how Millie felt, even if he didn't know why she felt that way.

Daniel placed his hands on the back of one of the empty chairs. "Remember those other three mail-order-brides that wrote to you a few months back?"

Levi nodded. His stomach pitched. He pushed his untouched sandwich away and grabbed the iced tea.

"Ma sent them all letters and invited them to come to the ranch to meet you. They all arrived at different times. I believe the first one arrived two weeks ago. Anyway, Ma sent Hannah and me to town today to invite you out to dinner so you can meet the ladies."

Levi felt his tongue thicken and his throat close. Just when he'd thought he'd managed to escape Bonnie Westland's plans of marriage, his mother had taken matters into her own hands again.

What must Miss Hamilton think? Three mail-order brides. All in Granite, Texas. All there to marry him. What on earth was he going to do with them all?

Chapter Two

Millie stared at Hannah Young. It had never occurred to her that she might run into someone in Granite from Cottonwood Springs. Granite was so far from Cottonwood Springs, New Mexico, she'd felt confident she was safe. What if her old schoolteacher knew that she'd burned down Mrs. Kelly's house and business? Would she tell everyone that Millie was an arsonist? What about Seth Billings the U.S. marshal? Would Hannah let him know where to find her?

"Millie Hamilton? Is that really you?" Hannah leaned toward her and brushed the hair back off Millie's forehead.

With that one action and two questions, Hannah made Millie feel as if she were a young student in Hannah's classroom once more. "Yes, ma'am, it's me."

The squeal that issued from Hannah's throat scared Millie so badly that she knocked over her tea. She watched in horror as it spilled into Levi's lap. Before she could react, Hannah grabbed her in a tight hug about the shoulders, then pulled back and held her at arm's length. "Millie, I can't believe it is really you. I'm so glad to see you. I've missed Cottonwood Springs horribly. Oh, this is wonderful. I can't wait to get caught up on all the news from home. Why don't you come out to the ranch for supper tonight, too?" Hannah took a breath, released Millie, and then grabbed her husband's arm. "Daniel, Millie is from back home."

Daniel laughed. "I got that, honey."

"Oh, Levi, I'm so sorry." Millie handed him her napkin and watched as he dabbed at the tea on his pants. She realized she'd used his first name but at the moment she didn't care. All she could think about was, how much did Hannah know?

He offered her a weak smile. "It's all right, Millie. Hannah has a way of shocking people. I blame her." Levi turned his grin on his sister-in-law.

"I'm sorry, too, Levi." Hannah returned her attention back to Millie. "I still can't believe it's you." She clapped her hands together like a kid who'd just been offered a pony ride.

Millie swallowed the lump in her throat. "It's me."

"What brought you here? Oh, don't answer that. I want to be able to sit down and catch up on everything."

"I think you are scaring her, Hannah." Daniel chuckled and wrapped his free arm around his wife's waist. "Besides, didn't you just hear Levi say Millie is his mail-order bride? Ma's going to be disappointed that Levi didn't need her help luring a mail-order bride here."

Hannah's mouth worked as if she'd just swallowed a lemon drop whole.

Beth arrived at the table with the promised tea refills. "What can I get for you, Mr. and Mrs. Westland?" She grinned at Hannah.

"Oh, nothing for us. We just stopped by to invite Levi to supper out at the ranch," Daniel answered. "And now that we've done so, we've got shopping to do before we head back out to the ranch."

Beth refilled Levi's and Millie's glasses and then left the table.

Finally, Hannah said, "You have to come out with Levi, Millie. I can't believe we're going to be sisters-in-law." Excitement rose in her voice once more.

Millie didn't have time to respond. Daniel chuckled and turned his wife toward the door. "You can talk all about it tonight. We have to get Ma's shopping done and then I need to get back to the ranch. I have work to attend to."

Millie couldn't let Hannah go without finding out what she knew. Panic threatened to choke her as she called out, "But, we just reconnected. Can't you stay for lunch?"

Daniel seemed to ignore her and continued to guide his wife away.

"We'll have dinner and catch up," Hannah answered, smiling and waving goodbye over her shoulder.

What choice did Millie have? Of course she'd go out to their ranch. Millie needed to know what Hannah knew about the events that had taken place in Cottonwood Springs. She'd know if the U.S. marshal was looking for her. Surely, if he was, Hannah would have said something. Still, her stomach quivered in fear. Millie turned toward Levi. "Can I ride out with you?" she blurted.

He nodded. "Of course. I'll have to clear up that we aren't getting married." Levi called to his brother's retreating back. "We'll be there around six."

"Good. We'll see you tonight." Daniel waved as they left the restaurant.

Levi sighed. "Those two came in here like a whirlwind. I'm sorry, Millie. I hadn't planned on letting them continue to think we're getting married."

A frown marred his handsome features, and for the first time Millie realized she wasn't the only one with a new problem. Had Daniel said there were three other mail-order brides waiting for Levi out on the ranch? How did that happen? Levi looked downright nauseated. She felt the same way.

Hannah had looked as happy as a little girl with a new puppy. Millie realized she'd also have to tell her schoolteacher that they were not going to be sisters-in-law. What a mess this was turning out to be. "What did your brother mean by more mail-order brides waiting for you?"

"Didn't you hear him?" Levi wiped at the moisture on his pant leg.

Millie tried to remember what else had been said but couldn't. "I'm sorry, I didn't. I was too surprised to see someone here from Cottonwood Springs," she admitted.

"Do you remember me mentioning in my letters to you that last winter my ma started a contest between Daniel and I?"

Millie nodded. "Yes, if I understood it right the first brother to get married and have a grandchild would inherit the family ranch. Is that correct?"

"Yes." Levi took a deep breath and then sighed. "After you didn't show up, I received three more letters to the ad I'd placed. I didn't want to answer any of them, but Ma insisted. She said that if I didn't marry she'd sell the ranch before the year was out. At first I'd planned to go along with her, but then I realized that I could buy time by letting her believe I'd answered one of the letters."

"But you didn't," Millie said.

"Well, I did, but then I changed my mind and wrote all three ladies and told them I'd decided not to get married at this time." He paused and took a deep drink from his tea glass. "I would have written to you, as well, but I thought you'd changed your mind about coming and I didn't see the need to."

Her heart lurched in her chest. Millie quietly thanked the Lord he hadn't written. If he had, her parents would know where she was now. When she'd been home it had been her job to collect the mail each day, but with her gone, Millie felt sure her mother was doing the collecting now.

She took a deep breath and pretended his last statement had had no effect on her whatsoever. "You didn't tell your mother what you'd done?" Millie studied his face. She noted his ears had slowly begun to turn pink.

The more she learned about Levi's mother, Bonnie Westland, the more she could see her own mother's personality emerging from the other woman. It was nothing for Ma to manipulate things to her way of thinking.

"No, I didn't tell her. I thought that by the time she figured it out, Daniel and Hannah would already be expecting their first child, and Ma would forget about her crazy scheme to get me married, too."

"But isn't that like lying?" Millie asked.

He set his glass down slowly. "I didn't really think of it that way. I just figured I'd tell her later and explain again that I'm not ready to marry right now."

Millie decided not to press the issue. She knew what

it was like to have a mother who tried to control your
every move. What Levi did or didn't do was between
him and his maker, not her. A smile teased her lips.

"You find my situation funny?" Levi asked. A new
growl had entered his voice but not his soft green eyes.

She tried to control her facial muscles. "Well, not
funny-ha-ha. But it does seem that your mother has
found another way to get you to marry one of those
ladies." Millie pursed her lips together in an attempt
not to laugh.

A grin began to part his mouth, and twin dimples
twinkled in her direction. "Oh, go ahead and laugh.
It wouldn't be the first time my mother's antics were
laughable."

Millie immediately sobered. Her own mother had
caused her pain and embarrassment more times than
she could count. "I'm sorry, Mr. Westland. It really
isn't funny."

He leaned forward on his forearms. "What happened
to calling me Levi?"

Millie looked down at the tablecloth. "I'm not sure
it's proper to call you by your first name."

"Good thing we aren't proper here in Granite. Please,
call me Levi." He laid his napkin on the table and stood.
"I need to get to work. If you need anything, I'll be at
the furniture store. I have a little carpentry shop set up
in the back."

She nodded. "Thank you."

As if he'd eaten persimmons, Levi said, "It will take
us a while to get out to the ranch, and then Ma will
want to introduce everyone. I'll pick you up around
three." With those instructions, Levi turned and left
the restaurant.

Millie stood also. Once more she felt as if Levi was taking matters into his own hands without waiting to see what she had to say. What if she'd changed her mind about going out to the ranch? Had he thought about that? No, he'd simply assumed he knew the best plan, told it to her and strolled away.

Beth stopped beside the table and asked, "Are you ready to see your room?"

Millie nodded and picked up her handbag. She noticed the money Levi had left on the table and scooped it up. "What do I owe for the meal?" she asked, looking to Beth.

"Nothing. When you work here, meals are free." She smiled and headed toward the exit. "I don't expect you to start work today, but we'll need to hurry. The lunch crowd will be here shortly and I need to make up a few more sandwiches before they start coming in."

Millie followed her hostess and now employer from the restaurant. "How much is the fee for the room?"

"Levi doesn't charge us for room and meals when we work for him." Beth led her up a staircase off to the right of the front door. She stopped in front of room four and looked at Millie. Beth gave her the key and then held the door open for Millie to enter.

Millie couldn't get her legs to move. "I'm confused. I thought I would be working for you."

"You are, but Levi is the owner of the boardinghouse and the restaurant so he does the paying, and I do the bossing." She smiled to take any sting out of her words.

"I see." Anger seeped through Millie. Why hadn't he told her he owned the boardinghouse? So far, he'd manipulated her into staying at the boardinghouse, given her a job and was calling her by her first name. Was there no end to the man's boldness?

Levi arrived a little before three o'clock. He'd met with his banker and then spent the rest of the afternoon in his workshop stewing over what to do about the mail-order brides out on the ranch.

Absorbed in his thoughts and the intricate carving on the chest he'd been working on, Levi was running late. Even as he walked up the sidewalk to Beth's he couldn't shake the question that had haunted him all afternoon. How had his mother known he had written to all three ladies explaining he wasn't ready to marry? Or obtained their addresses for that matter?

He stepped into the boardinghouse and found Millie sitting on a small bench in the lobby. She'd freshened up and now wore a pretty blue day dress with a matching bonnet. Levi realized he should probably change his clothes and perhaps wash his face before they left.

The grandfather clock chimed the hour with three soft bells. He knew if they were to get out to the ranch at a reasonable time, they had to leave now. His mother wouldn't take kindly to them arriving late. He'd have to forgo the cleanup and pray that he looked presentable.

She stood and wiped her hands over the front of her dress. Her skirt swished as she turned to pick up a covered pie plate. The scent of warm peaches filled the air between them. "I'm ready," Millie announced in a tight voice.

Was that anger he detected? His gaze moved to the clock once more. He wasn't late so why was she upset? Would he ever understand women? This one was turning out to be as rough as an unsanded board. "The buggy is right outside."

Levi held the door open and then followed her to the buggy he'd rented earlier. Until today he'd had no use for one, but he realized that if Millie was going to ride out to the ranch with him she probably wouldn't want to double up on his stallion, Snow. He took the pie and helped her up one-handed into the buggy.

"Thank you." She took the pie and proceeded to stare straight ahead.

As he circled around the buggy, Levi tried once more to figure out what could have made her angry. He pulled himself up. Maybe she'd had time to rethink her desire to get married and didn't like that three other women were now here to say I do.

He endured the stony silence until they were out of town and then gently pulled the team of horses to a stop. Levi set the brake and then turned to face her. "Millie, did I do or say something to anger you?"

She blew a blond curl off her forehead and sighed heavily. Without looking at him, Millie asked, "Seriously, you don't have a clue why I might be upset right now?" Then she turned and her blue eyes flashed in his direction.

"No, I don't. When I left you were fine."

Millie studied his face. Her anger seemed to dissolve and confusion laced her pretty features. "Maybe manipulation comes to you naturally. Is it really possible you don't know what you've done?" A frown marred her pretty forehead.

Levi didn't know whether to be angry or laugh. He had no idea what she was talking about. How could he?

She took a deep breath. "Do you deny that you insisted we leave at three?"

"No, I don't. We had to leave at three because it takes a couple of hours to get out to the ranch and Ma will expect us to socialize for at least thirty minutes to an hour with the other—" he paused "—guests before dinner." He didn't point out that they were wasting time discussing what time they left when they should be on their way.

"Do you own Beth's Boardinghouse?"

So that was it. He picked up the reins and released the brake. She didn't like that he owned the boardinghouse. What did it matter if he owned it?

A small ache began to seep up his neck and into his temple. The women in his life were going to drive him to madness. He realized she was still waiting for an answer. "Yes, I do." Levi slapped the reins over the horses' backs.

Millie grabbed the seat and held on as the big animals moved forward once more. "And you didn't bother to tell me." Her words came out harsh and ragged.

"Why would I tell you? We just met. I'm not in the habit of telling my business to people I've just met. I'm sorry if it makes you angry that I own the boardinghouse."

Once more she sighed heavily. "Levi, you own the boardinghouse where I now work and live. You are controlling my every action—that's what makes me angry. I don't like people manipulating my every move."

Didn't he have enough to deal with, with facing his mother and the other three brides? Maybe he should turn the buggy around and head back to town. At least there he had some control over his life. With that thought, it dawned on him that Millie was feeling the same way he felt right now.

He pulled the horses to a stop once more and turned to face her. "I really am sorry, Millie. I didn't see it that way. My reasoning was that you needed a place to stay and a job. I knew Beth could use the help, and with the job came the room and board. It never dawned on me you would take offense."

Millie stared at him with big blue eyes. Her emotions warred on her heart shaped face. He could tell she wasn't sure of his sincerity.

"Honest. And to prove it, I vow to never meddle in your life again." He gave her what he hoped was a sincere grin. "Promise," Levi added, praying she'd accept his apology.

She nodded. "All right. I'm sorry, too. I may have overreacted." Millie twisted away from him.

He turned back to the horses and the business of riding out to the ranch. "No harm done. I'm glad we got that settled."

"Me, too."

His thoughts turned to the ranch and the women who were waiting for him. He still hadn't decided what to do about them.

Her soft voice asked, "Levi, may I ask you a question?"

"You may ask whatever you want to, Millie." He focused on the backs of the horses and the dirt path in front of them. She could ask, but he didn't have to answer, he quietly thought.

"Why don't you want to get married?"

That wasn't the question he'd expected. Levi swallowed. Maybe he could distract her. "Why don't you?"

A swift answer spewed from her lips. "I don't want or need a man to boss me around."

He couldn't help but wonder what man had bossed her around in the past. Or was she thinking of her mother? She'd said the woman had been manipulative; maybe she'd been bossy, too. "It's your turn to answer the question." She grinned at him and raised a fine blond eyebrow.

Levi decided to be honest with her. "Women want love when they get married. Love is no longer in my future. I can't promise love so I don't want to marry anyone."

She sobered. "I can understand that, but what about your mother?" Millie traced the pattern on her dress with her finger. "She seems pretty insistent that you marry, and soon."

"Honestly, I'm not sure what to do about her. She's invited these women to the ranch and expects me to pick one out like you would a nice piece of furniture." Levi shook his head. "I'm not sure what to do about the mail-order brides, either."

They rode along in silence. After several miles, Millie spoke again. "Levi, why do you have to do anything with them? Your mother invited them. Why don't you let her figure out what to do with the ladies?" A mischievous gleam filled her pretty blue eyes.

Millie had a valid point. He shouldn't be held accountable for the other three ladies. The only one he'd invited to Granite was Millie. Could he tell his mother they were her responsibility? And what would she say if he did?

He silently prayed, *Lord, I mean no disrespect for Ma, but I don't feel I should have to deal with these mail-order brides. Please be with me when I tell her just that.*

Chapter Three

Levi helped Millie down from the wagon and turned just in time to face his mother. She sprang off the front porch of the family ranch house like a mountain lion after its prey. Her green eyes blazed, leaving no doubt that she'd talked to Daniel and found out about Millie.

"Hello, Mother. How are you this evening?"

His causal greeting did nothing to slow her down. She ground out between clinched teeth, "You and I have business to discuss in the barn now."

Levi handed Millie her pie and turned to his mother again. "Mother, I'd like you to meet Miss Millicent Hamilton. Millie, this is my mother."

"It's nice to meet you, Mrs. Westland." Millie held out her hand. Her fingers shook, but she held her head up high. Levi felt a moment of pride at the way she held his mother's eyes and waited for her to respond.

Bonnie Westland took Millie's hand and shook it hard. "I'd like to say it's nice to meet you, too, Miss Hamilton, but at the moment, I'd rather hold my opinion."

He watched as Millie's spine straightened. "I'm sure

when you get to know me, you will find me very likable."

His mother's mouth dropped open and her eyes widened. Then a smile graced her lips. "I like a girl with spunk. You keep talking to me like that and you might be right."

The slamming of the front door drew their attention. Hannah raced down the stairs and grabbed Millie in a tight hug. "You came!"

Millie hugged her back. "Of course I came. You invited me."

He couldn't see her face but knew Millie was smiling. Hannah turned her toward the house, and they started clucking like a couple of hens. A smile touched his lips as he realized neither woman would like that analogy.

"Come on, son." Bonnie led the way to the barn. Levi followed, dread filling him. He knew his mother wasn't happy and was determined to tell him about it.

She stopped in the open barn door and watched as he unhitched the rented buggy from the horses. Levi had learned a long time ago to wait her out. She'd have her say in her own time.

"Daniel tells me that Miss Hamilton is yet another mail-order bride. What are you going to do about all these mail-order brides?" She finally snapped.

Levi led the first mare into the second stall on the right of the barn. He heard her boots shift through the hay as she followed. "Miss Millie and I have an understanding at the moment, so I'm not going to do anything about her. As for the other three..." He stood to his full height of five feet, ten inches, locked eyes with his mother and then continued. "You invited them, not me. I'd say they are your responsibility so I'm not going to do anything about them."

For the second time today, Levi had the satisfaction of finding his mother stumped. At least for the moment. He tossed fresh hay into the stall and then walked past her to get the other horse. When Levi returned, his mother stood in the same spot. Her arms were crossed over her chest and her green eyes studied him. He led the other mare into the stall beside the first one and tossed her hay also.

"Levi Matthew Westland."

Here it comes, he thought. He stood before her. "Yes, Mother?"

"We had a deal. You get married before the year is out or I sell the ranch." She stared him straight in the eyes and dared him to argue.

"No, you made that declaration and I didn't say anything," he countered.

"You led me to believe you'd written to the Rodgers girl," she accused.

He nodded. "That is true and I did. I just didn't write to her what you thought I did. By the way, Ma, how did you find out I'd changed my mind?"

She took a deep breath. "I did what any mother would do and I opened your letters and read them."

Levi laughed, but no merriment filled the hollow sound. "I doubt that other mothers would do such a thing, Ma. Most mothers leave their adult children alone and let them find their own mates."

Bonnie nodded. "Yes, and most sons get married before they are thirty," she countered.

He shook his head. "Daniel is married now. You'll have your grandchild and he can have the ranch. And I can live my life the way I want to." Levi started to walk away. He'd never just walked away from his mother before, but today Levi didn't see any other alternative.

She didn't speak loudly or harshly, but the command in her voice stopped him in his tracks. "Levi, we aren't finished here."

Levi turned to face her. "Mother, on this subject we are. Like you pointed out, I'm thirty years old and I am in no rush to get married."

Bonnie squared her shoulders, walked up to Levi and looked him in the eyes. "Now look here, I promised those women a husband. That if you didn't marry them, there were other eligible bachelors in the area and I'd help them settle down in Granite, Texas. You *will* choose one and I'll see that the others find husbands, as well. Levi, you have one year from today to get married or I will sell the ranch and everything that goes with it to the highest bidder. I don't care which girl you marry and I don't care if your brother and Hannah have two children. There are four women in that house—pick one." With that she walked from the barn.

Had he seen tenderness in her eyes before she'd hardened them and made her demand? What drove his mother to insist that he and his brother marry? Every time he'd asked her in the past she'd simply said she wanted grandchildren. Today, it didn't matter if Daniel had children; she wanted them both to be married.

Levi sighed and followed her out of the barn. His mother was already going through the front door of the ranch house. He leaned against the face of the barn, not wanting to go inside but knowing he'd have to eventually.

"She's a stubborn woman, our Ma." Daniel eased around the corner of the barn.

Had he been there the whole time? "What do you make of that? I always thought she wanted grandchildren and that you and Hannah would be giving her what she wants. But now that doesn't matter." Confusion laced his soul.

"Yeah, I heard. It sounds like she doesn't want them from me, little brother. She wants them from you." Daniel's eyes held the hurt that Levi heard in his voice.

"I don't think that's it. She didn't say anything about me giving her grandchildren. She just said I had to be married before the year is up." Levi knew his words sounded empty to his brother. Did Daniel think their mother loved him more? She'd always favored Levi, but he didn't believe for a moment that she loved him more.

Daniel clapped Levi on the shoulder. "Well, it doesn't matter. She's in for a surprise tonight."

Levi looked to his big brother. Unbridled pride now showed in Daniel's face and eyes. "Does that mean you are going to announce you're soon to be a papa?"

"Sure does. But don't tell Hannah I told you. She wanted to surprise the family with the news."

The two brothers hugged. Levi was happy for Daniel and Hannah. Plus, a baby in the family might just soften their mother up and she might forget all about him getting a wife.

Daniel released Levi and looked at him. "I know what you're thinking and you might as well forget it. Ma's not going to forget her threat. Either you marry or we both lose the ranch."

The renewed worry and sorrow in Daniel's voice sobered Levi up. He kicked a rock across the yard. Daniel needed the ranch. Especially now that he had a family to raise. It had been wishful thinking on Levi's part.

"Aw come on, it isn't that bad." He gave Levi a gentle shove toward the house. "I enjoy married life. Didn't think it would be possible, but believe me, it is."

They stopped at the washroom where they both scrubbed their faces, hands and arms. Levi wet down his hair and combed it into place. "I'm glad married life agrees with you, Daniel. Hannah is a wonderful woman."

Daniel nodded. "She sure is." His grin turned roguish and he said, "There are four women in there waiting to see who will be the next Mrs. Westland. One of them is bound to be a wonderful woman, too."

Millie entered the sitting room with Hannah. She felt rather than saw the three pairs of eyes that swiveled in her direction as they stepped into the room.

"Oh, good, you're all here." Hannah pulled Millie toward an overstuffed short couch to sit beside her. "I'd like you all to meet Millie Hamilton. She grew up in Cottonwood Springs and attended my school when I taught there."

Millie offered what she hoped looked like a friendly smile, instead of a nervous grimace. "Hello."

Hannah turned to the woman who sat on the left-hand side of the room. "Millie, this is Anna Mae Leland. She's a schoolteacher. I'm hoping she'll agree to teach out here on the ranch, but so far she assures me she'd rather teach in town. Isn't that right, Anna Mae?"

Anna Mae's soft brown eyes met hers. "That's right." She offered a soft smile. "It's nice to meet you, Miss Hamilton."

"Please, call me, Millie." Millie looked at the other two women, as well. "All of you."

"Thank you, we will. I'm Susanna Marsh." She played with a blond curl that fell across her left shoulder. Susanna held herself ramrod straight. Her voice sounded a bit frosty.

Millie looked into Susanna's light blue eyes and smiled. There was a challenge within the other woman's that almost caused Millie to laugh. Had the other women already heard she was Levi's first pick in a mail-order bride? If Susanna's sulky look was any indication, they had.

Hannah took over the conversation once more. "Millie, I'd like you to meet Emily Rodgers."

A dimple in Emily's right cheek flashed as she offered a shy grin. "I've heard a lot about you, Millie. I'm glad you decided to join us for supper."

"Really, Emily. We don't even know her. How can you sit there and pretend to like her?" Susanna snapped. She stood and walked to the window.

Emily offered Millie another grin. "I don't have to pretend, Susanna. Some folks you just know you're going to enjoy being around the moment you meet them. I think Millie is one of those people."

Millie decided to speak up before Susanna could respond. "Thank you, Emily. I'm sure you are right."

Susanna huffed. She turned and eyed all the women in the room. "Don't you all find this a little strange? It was bad enough when three of us showed up and now to have a fourth bride." She pointed at Millie.

Hannah cleared her throat and became the schoolteacher Millie remembered. "That will be enough, Susanna. God only knows what the outcome of this will

be, but until He reveals His plan, you will all get along."
Her eyes snapped to each face.

Anna Mae and Emily immediately nodded their
agreement. Millie watched through lowered lashes as
Susanna crossed her arms and proceeded to try to stare
Hannah down. A grin threatened to break through Millie's lips as the two women faced off. Susanna would
soon learn Hannah could stare all day and she would
win.

Susanna dropped her eyes and lowered her arms.
"How long should this go on?" she asked in a soft voice.

"Until my son chooses a bride." Bonnie Westland
swept into the room and smiled at everyone. She stood
in front of the fireplace looking much like a queen in a
picture Millie had once seen in one of her schoolbooks.
"You will all remain my guests until he decides." Her
green gaze landed on Millie and said, "Except Miss
Hamilton. She will be returning to town after supper."

Millie acknowledged the command with the slight
bowing of her head. She had no intention of staying
under this woman's roof any longer than she had to.
Bonnie Westland reminded Millie so much of her own
mother she felt like weeping. The sad thing was she
wasn't sure if they were tears of joy or sadness that she
felt stinging the backs of her eyes.

"Hannah, since Levi has already met Miss Hamilton, would you be so kind as to take her to the library?
My son will be here shortly and I'd like him to meet
the other three ladies."

It really wasn't a request, and both Millie and Hannah knew it. Hannah stood and smiled at the other ladies. "Ladies, we'll see you in a little while."

Millie followed but not before she saw Anna Mae's

face pale and Susanna flash a look of triumph. Emily closed her eyes as if in prayer. She could only imagine what each woman thought. Well, if truth be told, Millie knew Susanna saw her as competition. She wondered if she should tell the other woman she had no interest in marrying Levi or any other man.

Hannah led her into a big room with wall-to-wall bookshelves. Large comfy chairs sat about with end tables between them. She grabbed Millie's hands and declared, "You must tell me everything you know about Cottonwood Springs. Have I missed much since I've been gone?"

Where did she begin? Millie allowed Hannah to lead her to one of the chairs, where she released her hands and took the chair opposite her. "Haven't you received any news from Mrs. Kelly or Mrs. Billings?" she asked, stalling for time and praying Hannah's two best friends hadn't figured out that she'd burned down Mrs. Kelly's house.

"Oh, well, both have written, but I'd hoped you'd have newer news." Hannah leaned forward in her chair as if Millie's next words would be golden.

Millie straightened in the chair. "Let's start with their letters. What did they tell you? I'll be able to fill in anything else I might know."

"Eliza wrote that her house was burned down and that they think it was a group of boys that might have caused the fire, but she refuses to press charges against anyone. She's married now to the new blacksmith, Jackson Hart, and they have adopted a little boy." Hannah smiled across at Millie. "What she didn't tell me was what kind of man her new husband is. All I know is that he brought Eliza home from Durango the day after I got on the train to come out here. What do you think of him? Is he a God-fearing man? What does he look like?"

A smile crept over Millie's face. So Hannah didn't know she'd burned down Eliza's house and she basically wanted more information on the new blacksmith. "I didn't know they got married, but she did seem sweet on him. And, yes, I have to say he's as handsome as they come." But not as handsome as Levi. She pushed the troublesome thought away and continued, "As for him being a God-fearing man, I have no idea. I left shortly after they arrived back from Durango."

"Why?" She waved her hand as if to stop whatever answer Millie was about to give. "Oh, I know you came to be Levi's wife, but why did you decide to be a mail-order bride?"

The time had come. Millie knew she had to be as honest as she could with Hannah. "I ran away from home. Since Rebecca came to Cottonwood Springs as a mail-order bride, and she and Seth are so happy together, I thought that doing the same would get me out of Ma's house and far away from her bossiness."

Hannah raised her hand to her mouth. "You didn't," she whispered.

"Yes, I did. I left home shortly after you did." Millie leaned back into the soft cushion of the chair. She prayed Hannah wouldn't mention Eliza's house again, so that she wouldn't have to confess her part in its destruction.

Horror now filled Hannah's face as she shot off her questions. "But I left over six months ago. Where have you been all this time? I bet your mother is worried sick. Have you contacted your parents? Told them where you are?"

Millie leaned forward and grabbed Hannah's hands between hers. "I'll answer your questions, Hannah, but you have to promise me that you won't write and tell anyone from home where I am. I'm not ready to face my parents yet."

Hannah gently removed her hands. "Millie, I can't force you to contact your parents, but you have to let them know you are safe. You can come out here and live with me and Daniel, tell them that and they will at least know you are all right."

"Thank you for the kind offer of letting me stay with you, but I have a job and place to live in town. I will tell them I'm here." Millie felt the air rush from her lungs as panic seeped through her blood. "Just not yet."

"But why?"

Millie tried to control her emotions. "You know how Ma is. I just need more time to prove myself as an artist. She will never let me do that if I go home now. And if I contact her and tell her where I am, she and Papa will be on the next stage out here. They will insist I'm too young to be on my own."

Confusion covered Hannah's face. "But I thought you were going to marry Levi."

Millie knew she was botching this conversation. She took a deep breath and tried again. "I was, but when I arrived in Lubbock, I realized I'm not ready for marriage. I worked for about six months and sold a couple of my drawings so that I could give Levi back the money he sent for my passage here. Then I took the next stage and came on out to tell him I'd changed my mind. I arrived today."

"Have you told him yet?" Hannah's eyes were the size of summer apples.

Millie grinned. "Yes, I did, and he was just as re-lieved as I was. He'd changed his mind, too."

Hannah shook her head. "And here Bonnie has been collecting other mail-order brides for him." Her eyes twinkled with merriment. "Speaking of which—" she pushed up out of her chair "—maybe we should head back to the sitting room and try to rescue my brother-in-law from the other ladies."

Millie fought her way out of the cushions. "Han-nah, are you going to contact Ma and Pa?" She had to know before they left the room. As much as she liked Granite, if Hannah planned on contacting her family, Millie knew she'd move on to another town and prob-ably in another state.

"No, you should do that." Hannah turned and faced her. She rested one hand on her stomach and the other on the doorknob. "But I know if a child of mine ever ran away, I'd be going out of my mind with worry. Promise you'll let them know soon?"

How soon was soon? Millie knew she had to make her own way before she told her parents where she was or before she returned to Cottonwood Springs. Plus, she wanted to make enough money to rebuild Eliza's home and business. How long would that take? Honestly, Mil-lie didn't know, but she didn't think it would be soon enough for Hannah. "I can't promise soon, Hannah. I need time, but when I can, I will."

Hannah nodded. "I won't say anything, but I really hope you will pray about it and let them know. They are your parents, Millie. They love you."

Millie nodded. Although she knew they loved her, she also knew she couldn't go home and live under their roof again. She had to prove to them she was an adult now and could make her own way. *It is not good that man should be alone,* whispered through her mind. Millie tried to ignore it even as she wondered if that applied to women, too.

Levi had never been so happy to see an evening end as he had this one. He helped Millie into the buggy and then hurried to join her. Though the mail-order brides weren't that bad, the continued questioning from his mother had been horrible. He knew she was only trying to help the ladies get to know him better, but, confound it, he didn't want to get to know them better.

Hannah stood beside the wagon. She appeared both happy and worried. "We are having a birthday party for Daniel in a couple of weeks. Be sure and come out for it. All right, Millie?"

Millie took the empty pie plate Hannah was handing up to her. "I will."

"Good." Hannah allowed Daniel to wrap his arms around her waist. She smiled up at him, and love shone from her eyes.

Why couldn't Lucille have loved him like that? Bitterness touched his soul for a brief moment as he watched the happy couple. Love had shown in Lucille's eyes but it had not been for him. It had been for the ranch. He pushed the unpleasantness aside and decided to be happy for his brother and Hannah. Levi tore his eyes from them.

His mother had been thrilled with their baby announcement, and the brides had all looked at him expectantly—all but Millie, who was too busy congratulating her friend to pay attention to him.

He clicked his tongue, and the horses moved forward.

Millie waved at Hannah and called, "I'll see you in a couple of weeks." Then she turned and placed her hands in her lap.

Levi wasn't sure what to say so he didn't say anything. More than once this evening, he'd felt Millie watching him, but Levi didn't think she was looking at him as husband material. During dinner, she'd seemed entertained by his situation with the brides.

His mother had complimented Millie on the pie she had brought and then promptly began praising Emily Rodgers's baking skills. According to his mother, Emily's cinnamon buns would melt in his mouth. Since he favored the buns over most desserts, he assumed his mother had been trying to make Emily more appealing in his eyes.

He'd smiled at the redhead only to have Susanna Marsh state that she could sew better than anyone back home and then that if he'd like, she'd make him a new Sunday shirt. Levi had almost spewed his coffee all over the dinner table at the offer. That had been when he'd caught Millie's grin. It hadn't been the first one of the night, but it had been the brightest.

She broke the silence in the wagon. "So did you speak to your mother about the brides?" Humor laced her voice.

"I listened more than I spoke. She was more than happy to tell me she'd read my letters and rewrote them."

Millie frowned. "How did she get your letters?"

Levi sighed. "I placed them in the box beside the front door, to be mailed by the next person who went to town. That was foolishness on my part. I should have taken them to town myself."

"What did she write? Surely she knew you couldn't marry all three of them." Confusion laced her pretty face.

"I don't know the exact words, but Ma said she promised them that if her son didn't marry them that there were other eligible bachelors in the area and that she would help them settle down in Granite, Texas." Misery wrapped itself around Levi's shoulder like a winter's fog.

"I see."

"No, you don't. No one does. She is determined that I marry and has given me a year to do so." He didn't wait for Millie to comment. "If I don't, she's going to sell the ranch." Levi realized he was pouring his heart out to a virtual stranger, but Millie made it easy to talk to her.

The wheels of the wagon crunched loudly in the silent night. "That's not much of a threat. You live in town."

Levi sighed. "That's true, but Daniel lives on the ranch. It's his home."

"Couldn't he find a new home? People move all the time."

She meant well, Levi was sure of it. Millie just didn't understand because she didn't know the Westlands or their history. "It's not that simple. Daniel promised Pa he'd make sure the ranch continued to run before he died. In the process of doing that, Daniel fell in love with the land and he would do anything to hang on to it, including placing a mail-order bride ad and falling in love with Hannah." He thought the last part of his explanation would be enough for Millie.

"Then why doesn't Daniel tell his mother how he

feels? I'm sure she'll relent and let him keep it whether you marry or not."

It all sounded so simple when Millie put it like that but again, she didn't know Bonnie Westland. The woman had thrown down the ultimatum, and now they would all pay if he didn't do as she said.

"It's not that simple, Millie. Daniel would never disrespect our mother. The land isn't his to fight with her over, and once Ma makes up her mind, there is no changing it."

Silence hung between them once more. After about half an hour, Millie spoke again. "So you will cow down to your mother's bossiness." It was a statement that sounded full of disappointment to him.

"No, I will marry because I love Daniel and I want him to be happy. After Pa died, Daniel became a second father to me. He's stood in front of charging bulls to keep me safe. This is the least I can do for him." Once the words were out of his mouth, Levi knew he'd marry before the year was up.

What other choice did he really have?

Chapter Four

Millie felt sorry for him. She'd thought her ma was bossy, but Ma would have had a hard time keeping up with Bonnie Westland tonight. At dinner, Bonnie had positioned herself at one end of the table and Levi at the other. She'd made sure everyone could see and hear her handsome son. She'd told each of them where to sit and then the questions began. Fortunately for Millie, Bonnie had paid very little attention to her.

The mail-order brides had answered Bonnie's questions, and Millie had learned a lot about each of them.

Susanna Marsh had worn her widowhood like a badge of honor. She'd boasted of being an excellent wife and housekeeper, and claimed she specialized in making clothes for herself, her husband and the needy.

Anna Mae Leland had spoken quietly. She'd confessed she loved to teach and really would like to live in town.

At that point, Hannah had leaned over and whispered in Millie's ear, "That's why I'm having such a hard time getting her to take over the ranch school." Millie realized quickly that nothing passed Anna Mae's attention.

Anna Mae raised a fine brown eyebrow in their direction as if to tell them whispering in public was rude.

Emily Rodgers had explained that she was the oldest of twelve and loved to cook and bake. She'd grown up on a small farm in Kansas, enjoyed gardening and hoped to find a job in town.

Millie had expected to be questioned in the same manner, but instead, Bonnie had complimented her on the pie she'd brought and then proceeded to tell Levi that Emily's cinnamon buns were much better. Millie's only consolation had been that Beth had baked the pie, not her. Of course, she didn't say that. Millie was wise enough to simply smile and let the conversation flow right over her.

When Bonnie had directed her clear green eyes straight at Levi, Millie, who had been seated the farthest away from him, had leaned forward slightly in her chair. She'd wondered what his mother would expect to happen next. It hadn't taken Bonnie long to demand Levi tell the ladies a little about himself.

The mail-order brides had sat up straighter in their chairs. Daniel had scoffed and Hannah had grinned. Looking back on it now, she could understand why Levi's ears had turned bright pink.

Levi had laid his fork down, cleared his throat twice, and then proceeded to tell them that he placed God above all else.

From the corner of her eye, Millie had seen the frown that Susanna had hurried to mask. Millie wondered if it was because Susanna expected to be first in her husband's life or did she have something against God or Christians? Having been raised in church, Millie figured the other woman simply wanted to come first in her future husband's life.

He'd then told them that he owned several businesses in town that were run by other people. Levi's face had relaxed and a smile had touched his lips as he'd told them about the furniture business that he ran. He'd leaned forward and shared that right now he was the only builder but someday, he might take on a partner because business was so good. As if he'd realized everyone was staring at him, Levi had concluded with saying that should he choose a bride, then she'd have to be willing to live in town. Both Anna Mae and Emily seemed to breathe a sigh of relief.

Hannah had saved Levi from having to answer any further questions by saying she had an announcement to make. She and Daniel had stood up and turned to face Bonnie. "Daniel and I are going to have a baby, probably around the last of September or the first of October." Her brilliant smile warmed Millie's heart.

Everyone had congratulated the happy couple, and Millie hadn't missed the subtle glances the brides had given to Levi. It was no wonder that soon afterward Levi had announced it was time to return to town.

Millie had agreed and covered a yawn proving she was tired from her long day. Now, sitting in silence beside him, she wanted to offer some form of comfort, but what?

Levi stopped the wagon in front of the boarding-house and came around to help her down. His hands felt warm and strong around her waist. "Thank you for taking me with you this evening," she offered as her feet touched the ground.

He looked down at her, and a gentle smile covered his lips. "I noticed you didn't say, 'I enjoyed myself.'"

She liked the way a teasing light lit his eyes. "No, I can't say I enjoyed most of it. Although, it was kind of fun watching you skitter around those brides like they were hot coals popping out of the fireplace."

Levi's dimples flashed as he laughed. "My favorite part of the evening was when you told my mother that once she gets to know you, she will like you. I've never seen her stumped like that before in my life."

Millie stepped out of his hands. "Yeah, it was kind of rude of me to be that forward, and I noticed she didn't have much to say to me after that. Maybe I should apologize."

"Don't you dare. I think she might have met her match in you." He continued to stare at her and his face sobered. "If you change your mind about getting married, let me know. I'm in the market for a wife, ya know?"

Had he just proposed to her? Millie took a step away from him and clasped the gate handle. "I know, and that's about the saddest proposal I have ever heard. Nonetheless, I'm afraid I'll have to pass it up. I'm going to continue with my plans of opening an art gallery in Granite someday." Millie hoped to lighten the mood and winked at him. "Ya know—" she paused for effect "—you have three prospective brides waiting for you out on the Westland ranch."

He groaned. "Yeah, I know. But seeing as you're already in town, it will be easier to court you." Levi pulled himself back up onto the wagon and winked down at her before turning the wagon around and heading back along the street.

Millie realized her jaw hung open and she snapped it shut. Had he insinuated he planned to court her? The gate creaked as she opened it. A yawn escaped as she made her way into the house and up to her room. No, surely he was simply teasing her.

She used the key to open her room. It was a nice space with tan walls. The window faced out over the front porch. She pushed back lavender-colored curtains and cracked it open. Crickets and locus sang on the soft evening air.

Tiredness enveloped her like an old friend. Millie changed out of her dress and into her nightgown. She pulled the quilt back on her bed and then blew out the lamp. The cool sheets welcomed her like dew on a crisp autumn morning.

And yet, sleep eluded Millie. She turned over and punched the pillow. Levi Westland was not going to try and court her, was he? Once more, she told herself they'd only been casting about playful banter.

Still, with three beautiful women at the ranch ready to marry him, why had Levi suggested she marry him? So what if she was already in town? That was no reason to focus on her. Especially since she'd already told him that she'd changed her mind about marriage.

Millie grew irritated from both lack of sleep and her wayward thoughts. If he thought he could woo or bully her into a marriage with him, Levi Westland had another think coming.

The next morning dawned bright and early. Millie hadn't slept well and felt as prickly as a hedgehog. She dressed in her Sunday best and fixed her hair before heading downstairs to meet the rest of the boarders and to have breakfast. Beth had shown her around the day before so she knew exactly where to go in the big house.

Millie entered the dining room with a smile plastered on her face that she prayed looked believable. Beth looked up from cutting a young boy's sausage. Levi had mentioned the evening before that Beth had a six-year-old son named Mark.

Mark smiled up at her, and she saw that he'd lost his front tooth. The boy seemed big for his age. Her papa would say the lad was built like a lumberman. She genuinely smiled at the thought of her papa.

"Good morning, Millie. I pray you slept well last night."

She didn't want to lie to her hostess so simply said, "Good morning, how are you today?" Millie averted her eyes from the two curious people who sat at the table.

The scents of bacon, eggs and hot biscuits filled the room.

A buffet had been set up against the far wall. It hadn't been there the day before, and Millie wondered if it was something that Beth did every Sunday morning. She'd check, and if so, Millie decided to get up earlier to help her next Sunday.

"Very well. Go ahead and help yourself to breakfast. We aren't formal here." Beth waved toward the table lined with food.

Millie did as she was asked. The food looked and smelled wonderful. Once more, she thanked the Lord for the new job and the benefits it had to offer. She chose a little of everything on the table. Last night, she'd picked at her food; this morning, she intended to enjoy it. A genuine smile touched her lips; maybe today she wouldn't have to deal with any of the Westlands and could just take pleasure in her first Sunday in Granite.

Millie poured herself a cup of coffee before picking up her plate and turning back to face the table. The rich aroma of the hot beverage soothed some of the prickles she'd been feeling.

There were four people present: Beth, Mark, an older woman who looked to be about seventy and a man with brown hair and soft brown eyes. Thanks to the coffee and their welcoming faces, Millie felt as if she could relax.

"Please, sit by me. I am so anxious to get to know you," the gray-haired woman invited. Her steely blue eyes twinkled up at Millie.

How could she refuse such a kind offer? "Thank you." Millie pulled out the chair beside the woman and sat.

"My name is Mrs. Englebright. I believe your room is right next to mine." She picked up her cup and took a sip. When she set it back down, Millie noted that the older woman had added either cream or milk to the coffee.

"I'm Millie Hamilton." She reached for the butter. Millie thought the woman already knew who she was, but she didn't know what else to say.

Beth smiled about the table. She nodded to the gentleman, who sat up a little taller in his seat.

He cleared his throat and then announced, "Miss Hamilton, my name is Gerald Lupin. I work for the newspaper office. We will be printing our first issue one day next week." He returned to his eggs.

As Millie buttered her biscuit, she replied, "It's nice to meet you all. I didn't know Granite had a newspaper office, Mr. Lupin." She picked up a napkin and placed it in her lap.

He laid his fork down and then wiped his mouth before speaking. "We've been here about a month, but until recently didn't have all the equipment we needed to print our paper." Mr. Lupin tore his biscuit in half and reached for a small jar of honey.

Millie wondered who "we" and "our" were but didn't ask. She was afraid she might disturb Mr. Lupin with further questions. He seemed a little preoccupied with his meal. She looked down the table at Beth, who simply shrugged.

"Sorry I'm late," Levi Westland said as he entered the room. His hair was damp and he wore a crisp white shirt with dark trousers and black boots. "I wanted to finish Mrs. Lewis's table before we went to church. You know she will be asking me about it this morning after services. It'll be nice to tell her it's done." Levi continued on to the buffet and began filling his plate up with food.

Millie thought she was going to choke on her bread. What was he doing here? Was he stalking her? Or did he normally eat his meals at Beth's Boardinghouse? But Beth had told her the day before that the house wasn't open to customers on Sunday, only residents.

"You are fine," Beth said as she wiped jelly off Mark's mouth.

Levi scooted into the spot across from Millie, between Mark and Mr. Lupin. "I take it introductions have been made."

It was Mark who answered around a mouthful of eggs. "Yep, they been talkin' and talkin'. Miss Millie hasn't even had her first bite of Ma's wonderful biscuits yet." The six-year-old grinned up at Levi.

"Thank you, Mark, for that nice compliment but don't talk with your mouth full." Beth beamed.

The little boy swallowed. "Yes, Ma."

Levi looked across at her. "You have to try them, Millie. They are very good."

Her hackles rose. There he went, telling her what to do again. Millie offered him a sweet smile and said, "All right, but do you think Beth's rolls will be as tasty as Emily's cinnamon buns?" She was rewarded with Levi's sudden choking cough.

Levi sloshed coffee down his throat to wash down the suddenly dry biscuit. Millie took a dainty bite of hers, looking as innocent as the day she was born. Why did she have to bring up the mail-order bride?

Mark asked, "Who's Emily?"

"She's one of the mail-order brides we met last night." Millie smiled sweetly at Gerald Lupin.

Did she hope Gerald would think he had a front-page story and start asking questions? Wouldn't that set the little town of Granite into a tizzy? He could see the headlines now: Mail-Order Brides Descend On Granite, Texas, Thanks to the Westland Family. Levi wiped his mouth off and proceeded to eat his breakfast.

Mark asked, "What's a mail-order bride?"

Levi wanted to groan and crawl away at the same time.

He was shocked when Gerald answered, "Mark, a mail-order bride is a woman who answers an advertisement in a newspaper, magazine or catalog. The ad is usually placed by a man who is looking for a wife or

a bride. It's a fairly common practice in some places."
As if speaking to himself he added, "I wonder if we
should consider offering that kind of ad in our paper."

"Oh." The little boy sounded as if he had more questions.

Gerald placed his napkin on the table and stood.
"If everyone will excuse me, I need to get ready for
church."

Beth picked up her plate and Mark's. "We need to
finish getting ready, too, son."

Thankfully, Mark hurried after his mother with no
further mention of mail-order brides. Levi sighed and
tucked into his eggs.

Mrs. Englebright pushed her almost-empty plate
back. "How many brides were there?" She directed
her gaze to Millie.

Millie lowered her roll. "There were three."

"And they all came to marry our Levi?"

Levi felt her gaze upon him but decided to ignore
both Mrs. Englebright and the heat he felt burning in
his ears.

He heard the laughter in Millie's voice. "They sure
did. I think they are smitten with him." She was really
enjoying his discomfort. What could he do to stop her?

The question filled his mind as Mrs. Englebright
continued with questions of her own. "And what did
you think of the young ladies, Millie?"

Millie picked up her coffee and blew on it. "They
seemed nice enough. I'm sure whichever one Levi
chooses he'll be happy with."

"You're probably right. After the war, women from
my hometown were answering those ads. I just couldn't
bring myself to do it. When Harvey didn't come home

and I heard he'd died in battle, I thought about it, but, well, I wasn't ready." She paused as if deep in thought and then turned a brilliant smile on the both of them. "But most of them gals that did get new husbands were happier than seasoned punch. I asked them to write me after they were married and they did. It was nice hearing about the lives they'd begun."

Levi decided to speak up and maybe turn the teasing card around to Millie. "They were all very nice, but I think I've set my cap on marrying Miss Millie. After all, she was the first mail-order bride to answer my advertisement. Isn't that right, Millie?" He sat back and crossed his arms, daring her to deny it.

"Yes, but as I've already told you, I've changed my mind." Millie's cheeks turned pink and her eyes studied the plate full of food in front of her.

Mrs. Englebright chuckled as she pushed out of her chair. "I think I'll go freshen up some before church, too."

Levi watched her leave. She was a sweet woman, and he was glad her kids had set her up here at the boardinghouse. He turned his gaze to Millie.

She'd quietly left the table and taken her plate and Mrs. Englebright's with her to the washtub.

He stuffed the rest of his biscuit into his mouth and grabbed up the remaining dirty dishes on the table. It surprised him when she rolled up her sleeves to do the dishes.

"You don't have to do those. Beth usually gets to them when she does the lunch dishes." Levi set the plates into the hot water.

Millie offered him a smile that didn't quite reach her eyes. "Why does Beth always have to do them?"

She had a point. Levi rolled his sleeves up, too, and moved to the washtub. He could tell he'd pushed too far with his teasing. Millie released pent-up air that drifted across the hairs of his arms.

"If you insist on helping, please let me wash and you dry. I have no idea where these go." She handed him a tea towel.

Levi scooted to the side, and she moved into his spot in front of the dishpan. He took the first plate that she'd washed and dried it. "I'm sorry if I embarrassed you with Mrs. Englebright."

"Are you?" There was a slight twinge of doubt in her voice.

Was he? Levi didn't like the fact that he'd upset her. He'd simply been trying to take the attention off himself and she had been the most convenient person in the room to direct it to. "Yes."

She bobbed her head once. "Then thank you for that."

Levi took the dishes as she passed them to him. When they finished, they had a nice stack piled on the sideboard and he felt a sense of accomplishment. How many Sundays had Beth come home to dirty dishes? Too many. He decided to change the way things were done on Sundays, and he had Millie to thank for that.

Millie kept quiet as they worked. Was she still angry with him? Levi decided to find out. "As soon as I toss out this water and put away the dishes, how would you like to sit with me on the front porch while we wait for the others?"

Her pretty blue eyes searched his. He could see questions within their depths and couldn't help but wonder what she was thinking. She pushed a stray curl off her forehead and nodded. "All right. I'll even help you put the food away, but when we get out there, I have a few questions for you, Mr. Westland."

She scooped up two platters and headed toward the kitchen. Dread filled Levi. She'd called him Mr. Westland in the same tone that his mother used when she said his full name. What new questions did she have for him now? Dread crept up his spine and into his hairline.

Chapter Five

Millie hurried as she put away the leftover food. She was tired of playing games with Levi Westland. He'd mentioned again his interest in marrying her. She needed to nip that line of thinking in the bud. He had no business even considering her as a future wife.

When the kitchen was straightened and all the food had been stored, Levi asked, "Ready?" He rolled his white sleeves back down.

Her gaze ran over the cleared buffet. "I believe so." She led the way out to the front porch.

Levi held the door open for her. Again, Millie inhaled the sweet scent of fresh-cut wood. One of the reasons she'd answered Levi's mail-order bride letters was because he'd written that he was a carpenter and enjoyed working with wood. Millie grinned at her own silliness, just because her father worked in a sawmill and worked in wood, she'd thought at the time her husband should, too.

He indicated for her to sit on the new hanging swing. Had he put it up this morning? She didn't recall it being there yesterday. It swayed slightly as he sat also.

"Is this new?" Millie asked, feeling the smoothness of the arm of the swing.

His green eyes sparkled with pride. "It is. I'm hoping that our neighbors will see it and want one. Do you like it?"

Millie nodded. "It's very comfortable." She sat back and enjoyed the gentle rocking motion.

After several moments of comfortable silence, Levi cleared his throat. "I understand you have some questions for me? The others will be out soon." He gently reminded her.

She turned on the seat so that she could look him in the eyes. "I do. Why do you keep insinuating you'd like to marry me when you know perfectly well I've changed my mind about marriage?"

He chuckled and cleared his throat. "Last night, I was teasing you. This morning, well, I'll be honest, I was in an embarrassing position and wanted to get the attention off me with a little playful banter with you. It worked, too. Mrs. Englebright left the dining area without any more talk about mail-order brides." He beamed a dimple-filled smile at her.

Frustration filled her. "Yes, she did, but did it ever occur to you that she might have taken you seriously and even now is plotting some form of matchmaking?"

He stared back at her with a blank expression.

Millie felt lost in the sea of green that was his eyes. They flashed with specks of yellow and hints of little-boy mischief and grown-man joy. Levi always seemed to be smiling or at least his eyes were.

She shook her head and turned her gaze from his. Eyes didn't smile. What was wrong with her? If she didn't watch it, next thing she knew she'd be fantasizing about his mouth and finding different meanings for his words. Like some silly girl whose head was full of romantic nonsense.

"No, but would that be so bad?"

She quickly cut her gaze back to him in disbelief. Was the man deaf? Hadn't she just told him she didn't want to get married?

He held up both hands in a show of surrender. "I'm not saying we have to get married. As long as Ma and everyone else assume we're courting, they won't be after me to choose one of the other brides." Levi tilted his head as if saying, *Think about it*.

Millie stared at him. Did she understand him correctly? He wanted everyone to believe they were courting just so he wouldn't have to deal with his mother and the other brides. Was that fair to the prospective brides? Was it fair to his mother? Could she seriously go along with his plan?

Levi turned on the bench and faced forward. "I'm not ready to get married, either, Millie. But I feel like I'm being forced to make decisions for my future that I don't feel comfortable with. All I'm asking is that we be friends. If others read more than friendship into that, that is their business. I need time to figure out which bride I'm going to marry." His voice sounded tired. She recognized the cause. She'd lived with it all her life: the inability to chart your own course in life because of an overbearing parent. She considered the pros and cons of his suggestion.

Being friends with Levi would be nice, and she could move around freely in the town under the umbrella of his protection. The bad part was, his mother seemed to be even more assertive than hers and Millie would have to endure even more contact with her. But who better than herself to deal with an aggressive mother, since she had vast years of experience?

She took a deep breath and offered, "I'm willing to be friends, Levi, but I don't want to deliberately mislead others into thinking it is more than friendship. Agreed?"

His shoulders relaxed, and he turned his head back around to look at her. His eyes studied her with curious intensity. Finally, he let out a long and audible breath and said, "Agreed, and thank you."

Millie offered him a gentle smile. "You're welcome." She smoothed the folds of her dress over her lap. "Can I ask you a personal question?"

He regarded her with open amusement. "I'd say we've passed the need to ask before we speak of personal matters, but sure, ask anything you want."

"Do you spend a lot of time here at the boardinghouse?" She picked at imaginary lint on her dress.

Was he secretly in love with Beth? Is that why he seemed to spend a lot of time there? Though she felt comfortable with him, she didn't dare ask those questions.

He seemed to take a long time answering so she switched her gaze back to his face. Amusement danced in his eyes once more, and he said, "Since I live here and take my meals here, I suppose I do."

"You live here?" Millie couldn't have been more shocked. She'd thought he had a small house somewhere else in town. But now that she thought about it, Levi would have been foolish to live anywhere else. He owned the building and had a built-in maid and cook. It was no wonder he didn't need or want a wife.

He pointed toward the roof. "Top floor. I converted

it into my own private quarters when I purchased the building."

"I see. When did you make it into a boardinghouse?" She turned to face him more fully. Levi was just the person she needed to talk to if she intended to start her own business.

"A little over a year ago, Beth and Mark entered my life. Beth was a godsend. She needed a job and place to stay and I needed someone to turn this place into a real business." He grinned at her. "It was Beth's idea to add the restaurant. We've agreed that if she should ever want to buy it, she can."

So why didn't Levi marry Beth? They seemed to get along well and were good business partners, according to him. "Why not ask Beth to marry you?" The question popped out of her mouth before she could stop it.

Levi laughed. "Beth is still in love with her late husband and she's also about ten years older than me."

Millie lowered her voice. Disbelief filled her voice. "She's ten years older than you?"

His laughter filled the porch. "You just turned nineteen, didn't you?"

Millie nodded.

"Then Beth must seem really old to you."

She shook her head. "Twenty-one years isn't that much older. It's just that she just looks so young." Millie prayed she'd look as young as Beth did now when she turned forty years old.

Levi leaned back against the seat. "That's what comes from living a God-filled life. Sin ages a person, but clean living keeps us looking young." He grinned across at her.

"One more question," Millie said.

"All right."

"If you live here, where were you going last night?" She studied his face.

Levi seemed to release pent-up air. "To the livery. I had to return the horses and buggy."

Mark ran through the front door. "Are you ready to go, Mr. Levi?" he asked, coming to a stop in front of Levi.

He pushed his way up. "Sure am."

Millie walked along with Beth and Mrs. Englebright as the men led the way to the church. It was a nice walk, and she enjoyed the women's company. Millie's gaze moved to Levi's back. He walked between Mr. Lupin and Mark. The little boy kicked at stones along the way.

"We'd love for you to join our quilting bee, Millie. Some of us ladies meet on Thursday afternoon," Mrs. Englebright offered as she readjusted her handbag.

"I wish I could, Mrs. Englebright, but I'll be helping Beth in the restaurant starting tomorrow." Millie hadn't worked on a quilt since she'd left home. She and her mother had been active members of the quilting bee in Cottonwood Springs.

Millie wondered briefly if the ladies had finished the wedding ring quilt that Mrs. Miller had planned to give her husband's niece. Millie pushed the thought aside. She didn't want to become homesick today.

"That's too bad. Maybe Beth would let you have a couple of hours off so you could come for a short visit."

Beth answered, "I'm sure we can arrange something."

Millie smiled at her boss. "Thank you."

"Which quilt are you working on now?" Beth asked. She hadn't missed the longing in Beth's voice. Millie

realized that with the boardinghouse, the restaurant and
Mark, Beth probably didn't get to socialize very often.

"Right now we're working on a log cabin Christmas
quilt. We plan to raffle it off at the county fair this fall.
The money will go to Dr. Bryant. During the winter, he
doesn't receive much in the way of payments." Mrs. Englebright smiled at the two ladies. "Doesn't that sound
like a nice, Christian thing to do?"

"It sure does," both women chimed and then laughed.

Millie watched a resigned look cross Beth's features,
and her sense of fairness kicked in. If the woman wanted
to quilt then there had to be a way to make it happen.
An idea came to her and she blurted it out. "You know,
maybe you and I could take turns going to the quilting bee, Beth." She didn't give Beth time to respond.
"Would that be all right with you, Mrs. Englebright?"

"What a wonderful idea, Millie. It's fine by me and
I'm sure it will be all right with the other ladies, too."
Mrs. Englebright beamed her pleasure.

Millie felt Beth's hand squeeze hers. "That's very
kind of you to offer, Millie."

It felt good to be accepted by others. Millie hadn't
realized how much she'd missed having friends. In Cottonwood Springs, she'd been a girl dealing with other
girls. Here, Millie felt as if she were a grown woman
being accepted by other women.

Would all of that change once her family found out
where she was? Would she once more be thought of and
treated as a child? A young girl who needed constant
supervision and guidance? A shiver ran down her spine.
She could not let that happen.

Levi followed Millie into the pew. He sat beside her
but felt as if she were unaware of his existence. "Are
you feeling all right?" he whispered in her ear.

Millie jumped. "I'm fine. I was just deep in thought." She looked about the small church as if she wasn't sure how she'd gotten there.

For a moment, he'd seen fear in her eyes. What did she have to fear? Protectiveness swelled inside his heart. He looked about the church for danger.

She clutched a small Bible in her hands. Her fingers trembled on its black cover.

Levi reached down and covered her hands with his. "You're among friends here. You've nothing to fear." He didn't know if she would accept his comfort or not.

Millie offered him a soft smile. "Thank you." She pulled her hands out from under his. "I'm fine now, really."

Everyone stood for the first hymn. Levi joined her in song. Her voice sounded sweet and wholesome. She seemed more at ease, but he couldn't shake the feeling that Millie had been battling some inner turmoil.

He'd enjoyed their visit on the porch. In time, Levi was sure that he and Millie could become close friends. He cut his eyes in her direction as they sang. She grinned at him.

If he had to get married, he'd rather marry a friend than a stranger. Levi knew he could never give her his heart like a true husband. But maybe she'd consider a marriage of convenience.

For the rest of the service Levi tried to focus on the singing and the sermon. The soft scent of lavender teased at him every time Millie moved. She listened to the preacher and nodded in all the same places as he.

When the final amen was spoken, she turned to him and smiled, her eyes alight with pleasure. "I enjoyed my first church meeting in Granite."

"I'm glad." He looked over her head and saw two ladies elbowing each other. Levi couldn't resist the urge to look at them and wink.

His grin faded as he saw his mother and the brides headed his way. Levi knew a lunch invitation was forthcoming even before she reached his side. He felt more than saw Millie move to leave. Acting on instinct, he grabbed her wrist and held fast.

Thankfully, Millie didn't pull away. He slowly released her hand. Then he watched in wonder and disbelief as Millie stepped around him.

"Hello, Mrs. Westland. How are you doing, ladies?" she asked.

His mother titled her head and narrowed her eyes. "Miss Hamilton. It is good to see you in church this morning."

"Thank you. I enjoyed the service. Did you ladies enjoy it, as well?"

Levi noted that Millie wasn't giving his mother any quarter. Millie directed her gaze at the three mail-order brides. He felt a moment of pride in her actions. Not many men stood up to his mother, and yet here this slip of a girl was doing just that. Levi didn't know why she did so, but he knew he liked it.

The three ladies agreed that the service was nice. Levi placed his hand in the small of Millie's back and applied a gentle pressure. She moved forward as he'd anticipated.

Millie nodded to the ladies. "It was nice seeing you all again and I hate to rush off, but we are headed to the boardinghouse for lunch. Beth has made a wonderful stew and I'd hate for it to overcook. You are welcome to join us," she invited even as she took a step away from them.

Bonnie Westland answered in a strained voice. "Thank you, but we prepared a picnic and I was hoping my son could join us."

Levi opened his mouth to answer but was interrupted by a familiar voice. "Excuse me, Levi. I was wondering if you've finished my table. If so, Mr. Lewis and I would like to take it home with us."

He had never been so happy to see Mrs. Lewis. He'd known she'd want her table today but hadn't expected her to save him from lunching with his mother and the ladies. He gave her a large smile. "I finished it this morning. Give me a moment and then I'll ride over with you and Mr. Lewis to the shop."

"Bless you, Levi. I can't tell you how happy you've made me. I'll just go get Mr. Lewis and we'll meet you at our wagon." She turned to retrieve her husband.

Relief filled Levi, as if he were a little boy who'd just been saved from a trip to the woodshed. He turned to his mother. "I'm sorry, Ma. I did promise to give them the table today." He smiled at the brides. "Ladies, I'll try to come out one day next week and have dinner with you all."

A pleased smile crossed Millie's sweet face. "Good day, ladies." She headed up the aisle.

Levi quickly followed her. They stopped long enough to shake the preacher's hand and then both hurried from the church. Millie looked as if she was going to continue toward the boardinghouse. He stopped her by laying a hand on her arm.

She turned, her sparkling blue eyes flashing up at him. He noted they looked like flowers with specks of white within their depths. The dark pupil made a beautiful center. "Thank you, for back there." He hooked a thumb over his shoulder pointing toward the church. When she'd turned at his touch they stood so close his breath fanned the hair that had escaped her clasp.

"I should have minded my own business," Millie said as a pink flush filled her cheeks, but he'd seen the teasing look in her eyes.

He laughed and laid his forehead against hers. "I'm glad you didn't." Levi inhaled the sweet scent of lavender and heard the sound of gravel crunching behind him.

Millie pulled away first. Her gaze moved over his shoulder.

"I believe Mr. and Mrs. Lewis are waiting for you."

Levi looked over his shoulder and saw the Lewises sitting in their wagon. Behind their wagon sat the Lawsons' wagon. Lucille sat beside her mother.

Seeing his old girlfriend was like a splash of cold water in his face. The warmth he'd been feeling for Millie melted. What was he doing? Lucille had broken his heart. Neither Millie nor any other woman would have the chance to break it again.

Millie whipped around and started walking again. Her heart pounded in her chest. Levi had run to the Lewises' wagon as if his britches were on fire. She didn't blame him. What had gotten into her? Had she looked at him like a lovesick cow? All she'd wanted to do was help him get away from his mother and the brides, but she'd ended up looking like she wanted him all for herself.

She sighed as the boardinghouse came into view.

The new porch swing gave the place a homey look. As matters stood right now, it was her home. Millie entered the door and inhaled. Beth's warm stew soothed her rugged nerves. What was it about the smell of hot food that made a body feel better?

Millie laid her Bible and handbag on the little table by the stairs with the other boarders' things and then continued to the dining room. As she entered, she heard Beth ask, "Mrs. Englebright? Are you the one who cleaned up in here?"

The older lady chuckled. "Nope. Not me."

Millie answered. "Levi and I cleaned up for you. I hope you don't mind."

"Mind? Of course I don't mind. I think that's the nicest thing anyone's done for me all week. Thank you." Beth set the stew in the center of the table and began dishing up bowls while Millie and the others took their seats.

Mark came into the room carrying a large basket of bread.

"Give the bread to Mr. Lupin, son." Beth placed a bowl in front of Millie. "What did you think of our little church, Millie?"

She grinned up at her host. "I liked it. Everyone was so nice and the preacher's sermon was very good." She took the bread basket from Mrs. Englebright. "Thank you."

"You're welcome, dear. I'm glad you enjoyed our little congregation." Mrs. Englebright laid a napkin in her lap while Beth took her seat at the head of the table.

Everyone bowed their heads as Mr. Lupin said grace. When he finished, everyone began eating. Millie wondered why they didn't ask about Levi but didn't want to be the one to bring him up so she began to eat, too.

"I noticed Mrs. Westland and those brides you mentioned this morning were in service." Mr. Lupin tore a chuck of bread from the roll he'd picked up.

Millie couldn't help herself; she asked, "Doesn't Mrs. Westland come every Sunday?"

Beth answered. "Yes, but this is the first time all three of the brides have come, too. It looks like Bonnie Westland is trying to get Levi to hurry up and make a decision." Mrs. Englebright and Beth shared a knowing grin.

"Oh, I see." Millie ate as fast as she could without looking as though she were in a pie-eating contest.

Had Mrs. Englebright already shared what Levi had said this morning with Beth? Were they thinking she might become the next Mrs. Westland? Millie felt her head begin a steady pounding. All she wanted now was to go up to her room and forget about Levi, Mrs. Westland and the brides.

"Tim said his papa said that Mrs. Westland is demanding Levi up and marries one of them." Mark stuffed bread into his mouth. "That's why they was in church this morning." He spooned stew into his already full mouth, unaware of the adults' surprised looks.

"Well, it's not our place to gossip and spread rumors so I'll have no more talk about Levi getting married to any of the mail-order brides, Mark." Beth shook her spoon at the little boy.

The little boy swallowed. "But, Ma. You all said they were mail-order brides so isn't that the point of getting one? So's you can marry up with them?" He grabbed his milk glass and drank deeply. Before it even hit the

table again, he asked another question. "How is talkin'
about it gossip and spreadin' rumors?"

Beth sighed. "It just is, son, and I'll hear no more
talk from you on the subject."

"Yes, mum. But I heard lots of folks whisperin' about
it this morning."

Mrs. Englebright laughed. "I'm sure you did."

He nodded happily, but one look from his mother and
Mark focused on his food again. The little boy sneaked
a look at Millie.

Had he heard whispers about her, too? Was that why
Beth wanted him to hush up? Well, what should she
have expected? She'd shown up shortly after the mail-
order brides, and Levi had chosen to sit next to her in
church.

From the looks on Mrs. Englebright's and Beth's
faces, Levi's plan was working. Folks were assum-
ing they were courting. The pounding in her head increased.

Would she be able to keep a friendship with Levi?
Or would the good people of Granite make so much of
it that she'd eventually have to move on?

Chapter Six

Levi jumped down from the supply wagon and was greeted by Mark. "Can I help you unload the supplies this morning, Mr. Levi?"

"You sure can. Your ma ordered extra this week."

Mark grabbed a box and pulled it from the wagon bed. "Why didn't you bring them yesterday morning?"

Levi's gaze moved up to Millie's bedroom window. Had the curtains just fluttered? He hadn't seen her in two days. "I was kind of busy yesterday and to be honest, they slipped my mind." After seeing Lucille on Sunday, Levi had decided to put a little distance between himself and Millie.

He pulled a large barrel of flour from the wagon and followed Mark around the building to the kitchen door.

The boy dropped his small box inside the door and turned for another load.

Levi set the flour barrel down and grinned at Beth. "Good morning, Beth. How is our latest guest doing this morning?" He hadn't meant to ask about Millie and wanted to bite his tongue off for doing so.

She turned from the stove and grinned back. "I don't

know, haven't seen her this morning." Her gaze moved to the provisions. "I see you finally decided to bring my supplies. We missed you yesterday. You must be busy over at the furniture store."

Mark dumped another armload of supplies inside the door. "I'm beating you, Mr. Levi." A competitive grin filled the little boy's face.

Levi chuckled. "He has a point. I better get back to it."

He followed the six-year-old back to the wagon. He'd avoided Beth's comment because he didn't want to tell her it wasn't the store that had kept him away.

The boy climbed inside and pushed a basket of apples toward Levi. "Where did you find apples this time of year, Mr. Levi?" he asked as he jumped down and pulled a smaller, lighter box from the bed with a grunt.

"Mr. Moore sold them to me. I'm not sure how he got them. Didn't want to ask too many questions." He winked at the boy. "But when I saw them I bought all he had. I could just taste your ma's hot apple pie. She makes the best around."

Levi grabbed the apples and fell into step beside Mark.

"Yeah, Pa used to say she could sweeten a cranky ol' mule with her cookin'. I suppose he was right." He cut teasing eyes at Levi.

"Are you calling me a cranky ol' mule?" Levi laughed.

"You said it, Mr. Levi, not me." Mark giggled at his own joke.

"Now why would you think such ill thoughts of me?" Levi grinned.

Mark stopped under the big oak tree and set his box

down. "I heard Mr. Lupin and Mrs. Englebright talkin' about you last night, Mr. Levi. They seem to think you are sweet on Miss Millie and thought maybe you were stayin' away from the house because of her. Mrs. Englebright said you were as stubborn as a mule when it came to women." The boy took a deep breath. "So, I guess I should have called you stubborn instead of cranky." He laughed again, unaware of the thoughts running through Levi's head.

Levi set his apples down, too. "That right? What else did they say?" He didn't like being talked about and really didn't like Millie being talked about, as well.

The boy shrugged and picked up his box. "Not much. Just that you might as well set your mind to marrying one of those gals because your ma is hankerin' to get you married." He left Levi standing under the tree.

"Out of the mouths of babes," he muttered. So Millie had been right. Mrs. Englebright had started the gossip mill running. In all fairness, he had started it. Levi sighed, then hefted the apples up and continued on to the kitchen.

"You better hurry up with those apples. Ma is wantin' to make apple pies." Mark ran past him for another load.

He laughed at the boy's antics and shook his head at the dropping of the letter *g* on every "ing" word the kid spoke. It drove Beth crazy, but she'd decided a couple of months ago to pick her battles. It seemed Mark had won the *g*-dropping battle.

As soon as the wagon was unloaded, Levi drove it back to the livery stable, where he housed it along with his stallion, Snow. The horse called out to him when he entered the barn. "Time for a good ride?" Levi asked the big stallion.

Snow nickered an answer and pushed against the stall door.

Levi laughed. "All right, hold your reins. We have to get you saddled first."

One of the stable boys ran out and took over the grooming of the mare that had pulled the supply wagon. Levi thanked him and then continued to Snow.

The stallion pranced out of the stall and then waited patiently while Levi saddled him. It was a beautiful morning and Levi decided he needed to get out of town and into some fresh air.

After a brisk run, he headed the horse toward the wooded area behind the boardinghouse. It was a beautiful spot where Levi went when he wanted a few minutes of peaceful silence. Snow enjoyed the greener grass there, as well.

He swung from the saddle and tied Snow to a nearby tree. A large rock sat on the edge of the woods and offered comfort from the sun. It would be lunchtime soon, and Levi knew it was time to face Millie again.

If only he hadn't seen Lucille on Sunday. She'd brought back the memories of rejection and loss. Levi had pondered his feelings all day Monday. He realized he didn't love Lucille but still had feelings for her. When she'd rejected his proposal, it had been like losing an old friend. What he'd thought was love had been more like comfortable acceptance. Still, it had hurt to be rejected, and Levi couldn't allow anyone that close to him again, especially Millie Hamilton.

Instead of sitting on the rock like he'd first thought to do, Levi ventured a little farther into the cool woods.

A small bird sang in the tree branches above his head. The sound of a lizard or other ground creature rustling through the grass added music to the birdsong. He continued walking and enjoying the sweet sounds of nature.

Just when he'd thought to turn around, he saw something light purple within the green and brown foliage. Curiosity had him making his way toward the color. His boots made a crunching sound as he pushed through the undergrowth.

"There's a small path toward your left. It would be easier to get over here, if you take it."

Levi groaned. He knew that voice. "Thanks, Millie. I'll be right there."

"Why are you here?" she asked. Her head was bent over a pad of paper, and she held a piece of charcoal, suspended above the paper ready to draw.

Levi walked the rest of the way toward her. "I come out here all the time. Usually after I take Snow, my horse, out for a ride. What brings you out here?"

She sat on a log with her back to the town. Millie wore a light purple dress, and her hair was pulled back in a ponytail. A pencil stuck out of her hair where the rubber band held it up. "I'm sketching." She looked up at the tree in front of her and sighed.

He walked around behind her and leaned over her shoulder to look at her drawing. The lines were soft, but he could see the beginnings of a picture. The outline of a branch with a butterfly clinging to it was positioned off to the right of the paper.

Millie closed the sketch pad and stood. "I should be getting back. Beth will be expecting me at the restaurant in a little while."

Levi realized he'd missed her and would have liked

to have stayed there and visited for a little while, but he had to get back to town, too. He followed Millie along the narrow animal-made path. It seemed to take longer for them to walk out of the woods than it had for him to enter.

When they came to the clearing, Snow greeted them with a snort. "Millie, you probably shouldn't go that deep into the woods again. We have mountain lions here and they aren't friendly."

She straightened her back, and her gaze moved to the woods. "Have you seen any lately?" Seriousness and something else filled her pretty blue eyes.

"No, but…"

Venom dripped from her voice. "Thank you for your advice, Mr. Westland." Millie turned on her heels and stomped away.

What was that about? Levi decided not to follow her and find out. As soon as he'd told her about the mountain lions, fire had entered her pretty blue eyes. How was it that he could extract anger from her so swiftly?

The ground hurt her feet as she marched toward town. How dare he boss her around! She had every right to go into the woods. Mountain lions indeed! He only wanted to prevent her from going to the woods and sketching.

He hadn't said he liked her drawing. Levi probably disapproved her of art, just like Ma. Well, she didn't care what he thought. She'd go into the woods if she wanted to and she'd sketch, paint and create any other form of art she wanted to do, as well. He wasn't the boss of her.

To prove her point, Millie headed to the general store.

She hadn't been there yet and wanted to see what kind of art supplies they carried. The bell over the door jingled as she entered.

Carolyn Moore, the owner of the store, stood behind the counter. She offered Millie a big smile. "Hello, Millie. What can I help you find today?"

Millie remembered Carolyn from church and returned her smile. "I wanted to see if you carried any art supplies." She felt foolish for asking as she looked about the small building.

"I'm afraid not, but there is a chance I can order them from a supplier in Austin." Carolyn came around the counter, and Millie saw that she was heavy with child. Why hadn't she noticed that in church? Probably because all she'd been able to concentrate on was Levi.

"You can do that?" Millie asked, jerking her gaze from Carolyn's stomach.

Carolyn picked up a dust rag and began to wipe off the shelves to her right. "Oh, yes, we order all kinds of individual things from Austin. The schoolteacher is forever ordering books. Levi Westland has all his special lumbers brought in from there, and just the other day we received an excellent order of fresh fruit, which I'm sad to say has all sold."

"Fresh fruit—that is pretty amazing this time of year." Millie wondered what kinds of special lumbers Levi ordered. She knew he was a carpenter, but so far hadn't seen anything he'd made except the porch swing.

A sigh filled the room. "Isn't it, though? This baby is craving hot apple pie. I should have told Wilson, my husband, to hold a few apples out for me." Carolyn rubbed her tummy with a dreamy look on her face.

Millie wasn't sure if she should interrupt the woman's daydream or not. She walked over to the fabric table and looked at a pretty green material with little white flowers on it.

"Anyway, do you know what kind of art supplies you'd like for me to try to get you?" Carolyn asked, having returned to her dusting.

The material slipped through her fingers. She didn't have extra funds for fabric or art supplies right now. "No, I wanted to see what you had before deciding what to get." Millie turned from the table. "I'll think on it and bring a list in later."

"All right. Is there anything else I can get for you now?"

She shouldn't have come into the store. "Not today." Millie walked to the door.

Carolyn called after her. "Come again soon."

Millie hurried out onto the sidewalk. It was just as well that the general store didn't have any art supplies. Now that she'd allowed her anger to cool, Millie realized coming to the store had been an act of rebellion. She'd only come because she thought Levi didn't want her to.

As she walked back toward the boardinghouse, Millie realized how silly she was being. Levi hadn't bossed her around, not really. He'd simply warned her to be careful around the woods. She shuddered at the thought that there were mountain lions in the area.

Now that she thought about it, Millie knew she wasn't angry at him but was hurt that he hadn't complimented her drawing. She'd assumed he thought her art was a waste of time because her mother thought it a waste of time. Why did she still allow those old hurts to sneak up on her? It wasn't Levi's fault she had issues with her mother.

Millie pushed through the boardinghouse door and hurried up to her room to change clothes for work and to put away her sketch pad. She knew she'd have to apologize to Levi for her rudeness. As she pulled on a white apron that Beth had supplied earlier, Millie prayed she wouldn't see him until later in the evening. She needed time to get her thoughts together and figure out the best way to explain her behavior.

Beth was waiting for her in the kitchen when she arrived. "Oh, good, right on time." She pointed at a basket of apples. "Look what Levi brought with the supplies this morning."

"Carolyn's apples," Millie answered with a smile. "She said she's craving an apple pie."

"She's not the only one. I think I'll bake a few tonight after we close the restaurant." Beth handed Millie a menu.

Millie looked down at it. "I was thinking that I might take a pie over to Carolyn in the morning, too. If that's all right?" She quickly added, "I'll pay for it."

Beth laughed. "No, you won't. I was thinking of baking one for her and asking you to take it to her."

"Really?" Millie studied Beth's face. She wanted to make sure that the other woman wasn't just being kind.

"Yes, really. Now I want you to sit down in that chair and learn that menu. It hardly ever changes. The nightly special does, but that menu is what we serve every day." Beth picked up a tray of glasses filled with tea and pushed through the door that connected the kitchen with the restaurant.

Millie spent the first half of her second working day memorizing the menu, learning how to prepare salads and, as Beth called it, familiarizing herself with the kitchen.

She'd quickly learned the day before that tea and water glasses were something Beth needed lots of so she steadily kept those filled. As dirty dishes came in, Millie took it upon herself to wash and dry them so they could be rapidly refilled.

Around one-thirty, Beth came into the kitchen and sank into the closest chair. "I don't know if I could have kept up today, Millie, if you hadn't been here. I think that has been our busiest lunchtime yet."

"I'm glad I could help. I felt bad staying in the kitchen while you rushed around like that." She dried her hands on the semidry tea towel and picked up a fresh iced tea.

Beth took the glass from Millie. "Oh, no, you were a big help in here. I couldn't have gotten done nearly as quick if you hadn't been filling glasses and plates for me." She took a big drink from the tea. "And look at this kitchen. I don't have to wash dishes all afternoon."

The smile on her face was reward enough for Millie. "I had no idea how much went into running a restaurant," she confessed, taking a seat across from Beth.

"Most people don't. But, I've wanted to own a restaurant all my life." Beth set the glass down and stood to take off her apron.

Cooking and cleaning up after people weren't things Millie wanted to invest her life in. She stood also and picked up the broom. Common sense told her that the kitchen needed to be spotless before this evening's crowd began to trickle in.

Beth continued, "Levi says when I'm ready he'll sell

this one to me. Can you imagine owning your own business?"

Millie nodded because she could imagine it. She wanted to own an art gallery but probably not for the same reasons that Beth wanted to own a restaurant. She knew what her motivation was, but what was Beth's? "Why do you want to own a business so badly, Beth?"

"I love helping others. Owning the restaurant means I am giving businessmen a place to eat when they can't go home for a good meal. It is also helping wives and mothers have a night off from cooking. And my favorite part is watching children eat a dessert that they normally wouldn't get at home. For me it's all about serving others."

The excitement on Beth's face humbled Millie. She'd never done anything for others for the pure pleasure of helping them. What did that say about her? Was she as self-centered as she felt?

"You go rest for a couple of hours. I'll finish this up and then I think I'll do the same." Beth took the broom from Millie's hands.

Millie nodded and left the room, thankful that the lunch hours were from 11:00 a.m. until 1:00 p.m. She thought about what Beth had just told her.

Her motivation for wanting an art gallery was nowhere near as noble as Beth's desire to own a restaurant. Millie mainly wanted to prove to her mother that drawing wasn't a waste of time, that there was value in having a talent for art.

Was that a selfish motivation? How could her talent serve others? Millie frowned. She'd never considered helping others. *Oh, Lord, am I truly a spoiled child? Everything we do should be to glorify You. Should I*

give up this dream and return to Cottonwood Springs?
Or is there a way I can be of service to others and still
keep the dream?

Chapter Seven

Millie was still pondering her prayer when she returned four hours later to work. The dining room had a couple of people in it, but no one sat at Levi's table. She heaved a sigh of relief. Millie knew she'd have to face him eventually, but right now, she just didn't feel up to apologizing.

Beth smiled at her as she hurried from the kitchen. "Did you rest well?" she asked as she passed. The scents of cinnamon and sugar moved with her, and Millie knew her boss hadn't taken the break as planned.

"Not really. Did you?" Millie shot back before dashing into the kitchen to make sure everything was in order.

The smells of baking apples, cinnamon and sugar caused her mouth to water. Full tea glasses sat on a tray and several tea pitchers lined the counter. A hot bucket of soapy water sat in the sink, and from the looks of everything, Beth had been working for at least an hour, if not all afternoon.

Millie turned back around and headed to the front, where new customers stood waiting to be seated. She took the first group to their table and then hurried back to get the second group. The thought came to her that they could easily seat themselves, but she remembered that Beth felt it was a special privilege to show them to their tables.

As soon as she had three groups seated, Millie began to take their drink orders. The evening continued with people coming in and eating, and as soon as that crowd was done, another took its place. It was all she and Beth could do to keep up.

Just when things started to settle down, Millie felt as if someone was watching her. She looked toward Levi's table and saw that he, his mother and his brother, Daniel, had all entered the restaurant. She'd been so busy with the other customers she hadn't noticed Beth seating them.

Millie hurried to the kitchen, where Beth stood dishing up a bowl of ham with beans and potatoes. She twisted her apron in her hands; she wasn't ready to face Levi yet.

"Levi and his family just arrived. Would you mind taking out that tray of tea glasses to them?" Beth asked as she added two biscuits to the tray of food she was preparing.

Her heart rate jumped. She couldn't talk to him yet. It was one thing to know she needed to apologize but quite another to actually do it in a place filled with people. And especially in front of his mother.

"Millie?" Concern filled Beth's voice. "Are you all right?"

The desire to lie and say she was sick threatened to spill from Millie's lips, but she knew better than to lie. "Yes, but, well, Levi and I had words this morning and I'm not ready to face him just yet, especially since his mother is with him." She scrunched her apron even more and still her palms felt sweaty. "Would you mind taking care of them this time?"

Beth handed her the tray she'd just filled with food. "That goes to table number one. I'll do it for you this time, but you are going to have to face him sometime. He does live here, ya know?"

Millie nodded. "I know." And then she hurried to deliver the bowls to table number one.

She didn't look in Levi's direction, just hurried to do her job and then rushed back into the kitchen. Even the sweet scent of apple pies baking did nothing to calm her nerves. Frantic for something to do, Millie looked about the kitchen.

A large pan of dirty dishes beckoned her to wash them. Millie grabbed the dishcloth and began scrubbing. Beth was right. She would have to face him and probably later tonight in the sitting room. How would she apologize?

Millie tried to imagine their conversation, but no matter how she foresaw it, she came off sounding like a crazy person. Why had she allowed hurt feelings from her past to make her behave so badly with Levi this morning? She didn't know, but she did know it was time for a change. A change for the better.

Levi watched Millie dart back into the kitchen. He felt sure she was trying to hide from him and that added to the acid already churning in his stomach. Whatever he'd said to upset her, Levi wanted to make it right.

All day he'd been trying to figure out what he'd said or done that had set her off. He still didn't know, but he'd seen the hurt in her eyes right before her anger had flared. If he lived to be a hundred, Levi knew he never wanted to cause Millie pain.

He pushed his chair back and laid his napkin down. "If you will excuse me, I need to take care of something in the kitchen. I'll be right back."

Beth looked up from the table she was serving and smiled at him. Did she know what was wrong with Millie? Had Millie confided in her new friend?

Millie turned as he entered the kitchen. Her eyes grew large, and she stared at him like a newborn fawn. A telling shade of pink filled her checks, confirming what he'd suspected. Millie Hamilton had been trying to avoid him.

Levi moved into the room and rested a hip against the table. "Millie, I feel really bad about this morning and came to apologize. It isn't my place to tell you where you can and can't go. I'm sorry if I came off as bossy." There, he'd said it. The words were out, but he didn't feel any better.

She turned away from him. "You aren't the one who should be apologizing, Levi. I should." Millie picked up the clean tea towel and dried her hands.

Her blue eyes drank in his face. She offered a soft smile. Sadness filled her features and he wanted to offer comfort, but something deep down told him that Millie wouldn't want that right now.

He pushed away from the table. "I don't understand."

Millie took a step back. "I overreacted this morning." A deep sigh forced itself from her lungs. "All I have done since we've met is snap at you, and for that I truly am sorry, Levi. I promise I'll try to behave better in the future." Millie folded her hands in front of the white apron she wore over a light green dress and lowered her eyes.

Levi wasn't sure if he liked this submissive stance. Had she apologized to someone else before and been instructed to behave in this manner? He didn't know what to think of her behavior, but wanted to make her feel more at ease with him. "No harm done. Thank you for the apology and I hope you have accepted mine, as well."

Millie nodded but still did not raise her head to meet his gaze. Levi couldn't seem to stop himself. He closed the distance between them and lifted her chin. Liquid blue met his gaze. He brushed the hair from her cheek and smiled. "I'm glad we are friends again." Not trusting himself, Levi dropped his hands and left the kitchen.

What had gotten into him? Levi tried to act causal as he walked back to his table. His hands shook and he really felt like going back and hugging Millie. She'd looked so vulnerable and he wanted to offer her comfort. Of course he'd feel that way toward any woman who looked as downtrodden as she had. And he had a thousand cattle on the hillside in Granite, too, he mocked sarcastically.

"Is everything all right in the kitchen?" his mother asked as he sat back down.

"Yes."

"Good." She folded her hands on the table and got right to business. "One of the reasons I came into town today was to talk to you about Anna Mae, Emily and Susanna. As you are well aware, those ladies came to town Sunday to have lunch with you."

Levi glanced at his older brother. Daniel tried to

hide his grin behind his tea glass. He was doing a poor job of it.

"Yes, and as you saw, I had other business to attend to and couldn't make it." Levi watched as Beth carried a tray with their meals toward them. He knew his mother would wait before continuing with whatever it was that she found so important to come to town for on a Wednesday.

Beth placed their food in front of them. "Can I get you anything else?" she asked politely.

Levi looked from his mother to Daniel. Both shook their heads so he answered for all of them. "No, this looks wonderful. Thank you."

She smiled and turned to leave.

Daniel said a quick prayer over their meal before their mother picked up where she'd left off. "Well, I know you were busy Sunday, but you can't continue to ignore them."

"Mother, I'm not ignoring them. They are staying with you out on the ranch. I only come out on weekends, and not every weekend at that, and special occasions, you know that." Levi dipped his spoon into the bowl of red beans. Spices teased his taste buds.

"Yes, but now that they are here maybe you could make the effort to come out more often." She was giving no quarter.

Daniel grinned across at him. "You might as well agree. You know she's not going to let up until you do."

Levi laid his spoon down and wiped his mouth. "I have a full year to choose a bride. Mother, nothing you can say will make me decide any sooner on which lady I will choose."

"I see." She laid her utensils down and focused her

green eyes on him. "So when do you plan on getting to know these women?"

Daniel leaned back in his chair and crossed his arms. He seemed overly pleased at the confrontation playing out in front of him. Levi decided to ignore his older brother.

"My next trip out to the ranch will be on Daniel's birthday. I can talk to the ladies then." He took a long swig of his tea and prayed that would satisfy her.

Bonnie smiled at him. "Then I'll make sure all three are there."

He'd expected her to argue more since Daniel's birthday wasn't for another week and a half.

Then he realized what she'd said. Where else would they be? They were living with her at the ranch. Levi didn't much care for the new gleam in his mother's eyes. She was up to something, but what? He looked to his brother.

Daniel shrugged and went back to his meal. His mother also picked up her spoon and dipped it into the warm ham and bean dinner. Levi sighed. Why fight it? Whatever Bonnie Westland was up to would be revealed in her time. Until then, Levi chose to breathe freely and have a pleasant meal with his family.

It was later in the evening when he finally made his way to the sitting room. The other boarders were already there and having a lively discussion.

Mrs. Englebright sat in an overstuffed chair beside the fireplace, and Millie sat across from her on the couch. He noted that Millie's cheeks were a faint pink, as if she'd somehow embarrassed herself before his arrival.

Mrs. Englebright smiled at him as he entered the room. "I'm sure Levi will side with me."

"Side with you on what?" he asked, pulling up the footstool and sitting down beside the widow. His gaze drank in the fresh blue dress that Millie wore. Her eyes matched the color of the dress to perfection.

"Our Millie says peach pie is the best. I disagree and think that apple is much tastier."

Levi laughed with relief. He was thankful the topic wasn't something more serious than pie.

"I contend you are both wrong." Mr. Lupin spoke up. He stood beside the piano holding what looked like a cup of coffee. "Pecan will always be the best of the pies."

"Nuh-uh, my ma's apple pie is the best," Mark insisted.

Mrs. Englebright winked at the boy and nodded. He smiled at her and then returned to the plywood puzzle he'd been trying to put together.

Beth entered the room carrying a covered dish. The scent of hot apple pie preceded her. A long table rested against the far wall. She carried it to the sideboard and smiled at them all. "Who would like a slice of fresh apple pie for dessert?"

"Me!" Mark jumped up from the small table and raced to his mother's side.

"I would." Levi grinned at Millie and Mrs. Englebright. "I think I'm going to say that my favorite pie at the moment is the one Beth just brought in."

Laughter filled the room as everyone stood and made their way to Beth. She'd already brought in dessert plates and forks for everyone. A pot of coffee and several cups were also present.

This was the time of day that Levi favored most. All the boarders coming together each evening had been another one of Beth's ideas. She'd pointed out that if they all lived under the same roof they should try to spend time together at least once a day. Evening was the most reasonable because everyone's work was done for the day and they could all relax.

Beth served Mrs. Englebright first. The elder woman inhaled the fragrance of the pie. "Beth, I do believe you have outdone yourself with this."

"You best taste it first before you start throwing compliments about," Beth teased.

Next, Beth handed a slice to Mark, then Millie and lastly to the two men. "I hope these pies turned out nice. I made two for the restaurant and one for Carolyn Moore. You are still going to take it to her in the morning, aren't you, Millie?"

Millie smiled. "Yes, I will. Thank you for baking one for her."

"It was my pleasure."

Levi used his fork to cut into the pastry. Juicy apples and flaky crust coated his fork. He savored that first bite and then grinned like a cat with a bowl of cream. "It is better than nice—it is…"

"Magnificent," Mr. Lupin filled in for him.

"Yes, it is," Millie agreed. She nibbled at the crust and then dipped her fork into the syrup that the apples, cinnamon and sugar had created. "I wish I could bake like this."

"As do I," confessed Mrs. Englebright after she'd swallowed her first bite.

A pretty blush filled Beth's face. "Oh, stop. It's only

apple pie. I'm sure both of you have talents you haven't shared yet."

Mrs. Englebright waved her comment away. "The only thing I'm good at is quilting and most women can do that."

"Most women can cook, too," Beth replied.

Mark used his finger to wipe up the extra apple on his plate. "Ma, may I have more, please?"

Beth looked down on her young man. Pride shone in her eyes. "Yes, but only a small piece and then off to bed with you."

Levi watched as the boy scooped out a nice size slice of pie and began devouring it like a hound dog pup. Depending on when he married, Levi realized he could have a child by this time next year. His gaze moved to Millie. He still hadn't approached her about a marriage of convenience.

The comforting sound of silverware scraping plates filled the otherwise quiet room. Everyone seemed content to savor the pie without speaking. They also didn't seem to notice that he was admiring Millie.

Millie looked up at him and blushed, then diverted her eyes back to the dessert in her hands. She finished the pie and took her plate to the sideboard. He admired the gentle swaying of her dress as she moved to the table where Mark had been playing. Millie studied the pieces of the puzzle. Her brow scrunched up as if she were in deep thought.

"What hidden talents do you possess, Millie?" Mrs. Englebright brought everyone's attention back to the subject at hand.

She looked up with a start. "Oh, I don't know."

Levi walked back to the stool and sat down. "Sure you do." He winked at her. "Millie is a fair artist."

"Is that right?" Mr. Lupin seemed to take an interest in that bit of information. He and Beth joined the group, each taking a seat at one end of the couch.

"What kind of art?" Mark asked around a mouthful of pie.

Millie graced him with a grin. "Mainly, I draw and paint."

Mark set his empty plate down and asked, "Can we see something you've done?"

"I'm afraid I don't have anything finished right now to show you." She folded her hands in her lap and turned the question on Mark. "What hidden talents do you have, young man?"

"Aw, I don't have any that I know of." He picked up a piece of the puzzle and placed it with its match. "Will you teach me how to draw, Miss Millie?"

She mussed his hair with her long fingers. "Sure I will."

Beth stood. "Come along, Mark. It's time good little boys went to bed."

"I don't want to be good," Mark protested, taking his mother's hand.

Beth chuckled. "Too late. You were born good. Now tell everyone good-night."

"'Night, Mr. Levi. 'Night, Mrs. Englebright, 'night, Mr. Lupin, 'night, Miss Millie." He sighed dramatically and allowed his mother to pull him from the room.

"He really is a cute little tyke, isn't he?" Mrs. Englebright pushed herself up from her chair and went to put away her dessert plate.

Millie picked up one of the puzzle pieces. "Levi, do you have boards like this in your shop?"

He glanced at the puzzle. "Some, why?"

"I'd like to borrow a piece. I want to see if I can draw on it."

"Let me get a closer look at that." Levi stood up and walked to where she sat. He didn't really need to look at the wood but felt compelled to get closer to Millie. She held the wood up for his inspection. "That's a piece of plywood. I'm pretty sure I have a couple of pieces lying around the shop."

Mrs. Englebright sat down at the piano. "I wish I had learned to play one of these." She sighed and pressed a couple of the keys.

Levi handed the wood back to Millie. "I'll get it for you tomorrow."

She put the puzzle down and said, "Thank you." Millie walked to where Mrs. Englebright sat looking at a page of sheet music. "If you really want to learn, I could teach you," she offered, sitting down beside her on the bench.

The older woman's eyes lit up. "I'd love to learn."

"If you will all excuse me, I think I'll head on up to my room," Mr. Lupin said and then drained the remainder of his coffee.

As soon as he was gone, Mrs. Englebright whispered, "Do you think he thought the lessons were going to begin tonight?"

Millie's sweet laughter joined the older woman's. "I don't know." She placed her hands on the keys and began to play "What a Friend We Have in Jesus."

Mrs. Englebright began to sing, and Millie's soft voice blended in with hers. Levi found himself joining in. They sang the whole song. When Millie stopped playing, they turned at the sound of clapping. Beth stood in the doorway. "That was beautiful."

"Join us," Mrs. Englebright invited.

They sang several more songs and were about to call it a night when someone knocked on the front door. Beth looked to Levi, and he nodded.

"I'll go with you. I'm sure it's safe, but at this time of night there is no telling who might be standing on the other side of the door." He followed Beth to the front door, aware that both Mrs. Englebright and Millie were following them.

Beth reached for the doorknob.

"No, I'll open it," Levi ordered. He didn't like that three women might be standing in harm's way.

"Thank you." Beth smiled at him and stepped back. She motioned for the other two women to stand off to the side.

Levi opened the door. He couldn't believe his eyes. Susanna Marsh stood on the other side. She held a small suitcase in her hands and a big smile graced her pretty face.

"Good evening, Mr. Westland."

Realizing he was staring, Levi pulled the door farther open and allowed her inside. The strong smell of roses entered the room with her. "Mrs. Marsh, what are you doing in town?" he asked, realizing as the words were spoken that they didn't sound inviting.

She batted her eyelashes at him. "I decided I'm not cut out for ranch life, Mr. Westland, so I asked Mr. Tucker to escort me into town. I'm looking for a room."

Levi looked to Beth. He wondered if she or the other ladies could see the panic he felt in his eyes. His mother had set this up. She'd been so smug at dinner, he should have known that if he didn't go to the ranch, then she would send the women to him.

He felt a groan grow in his chest and suppressed the desire to release it. What was he going to do if all three mail-order brides moved into town?

Chapter Eight

Millie had moved to the stairs and was about to go up when Levi opened the door. She now stood watching him to see what his reaction was to one of the mail-order brides arriving on his doorstep. Apprehension flashed through his eyes and his breathing accelerated.

"You don't have to look so distressed, Mr. Westland. Your mother has offered to continue to pay my expenses while I'm living here. She really is a generous woman," Susanna pressed.

Beth took over the situation. "I'm sorry, Mrs. Marsh, but I don't have any available rooms at this time." She gently moved between Levi and Susanna. "But I'm sure the hotel has a room you can stay in tonight."

A frown marred Susanna's pretty features. "I see. I'd hoped to stay at your lovely boardinghouse, Mrs. Winters. I've heard so many wonderful things about it. Are you sure you are full?"

"Thank you, and yes, I'm afraid I am," Beth answered more firmly.

Millie watched Levi visibly relax. It looked as if he'd been holding his breath.

His voice came out steady as he said, "I'm sure Mr. Tucker won't mind escorting you to the hotel, Mrs. Marsh." Levi started to walk to the stairs toward Millie.

"But I sent him back to the ranch."

Millie watched frustration, anger and the fight to calm himself war for first place on Levi's handsome face. He took a deep breath. Again, she felt sorry for him. She knew what it was like to be manipulated by another.

She moved past him and offered, "I'll walk you to the hotel, Mrs. Marsh. It isn't that far from here and I could use the fresh air." Millie noticed Susanna wore a lightweight traveling jacket. "If you will excuse me, I'll go get my cloak and be ready to go in a minute."

Susanna's voice stopped her on the stairs. "That really isn't necessary. Besides, you'll have to walk home alone if you go with me."

"I'll grab my coat and will walk with you both," Levi responded.

Susanna pursed her lips but didn't protest further. Millie continued up the stairs. She heard Levi's boots as he followed her.

When they got to her floor, Levi reached out and stopped her. "You don't have to go, Millie. I can walk her to the hotel," he offered.

Millie studied him for several moments. "Would you like to be alone with her?" She didn't think that was his intention, but then again, with his mother pressuring him to make a decision, maybe he did want to spend time alone with the young widow.

"Of course not, but I don't want you to feel you have to go, either." He dropped his hand from her arm. "She is my responsibility."

Levi Westland really was a good man. He didn't want to be alone with Susanna but he also didn't want Millie to feel she had to go. For the first time since she met him, Millie thought she was seeing the true kindness that made up Levi. "I'll get my cloak and be right down."

A relieved look crossed his handsome features. He nodded and continued up the stairs to his own rooms and coat.

Her cloak hung just inside the door on a small hook. She pulled it on and then relocked her door. Millie tried to remember what she'd learned about Susanna when she'd been out at the ranch. The only thing that came to mind was that she enjoyed sewing and thought of herself as an excellent wife.

Everyone was waiting at the foot of the stairs when she arrived. Levi looked handsome in his light brown coat. Beige patches covered each elbow, and his hands were tucked deeply into his pockets.

Susanna smiled sweetly up at her as she descended the stairs. "You really don't have to come with us, Millie."

Millie stepped off the last step and linked her arm within Susanna's. "Oh, but I want to. I would love to hear more about your sewing abilities." She opened the door and practically pulled Susanna through it.

Levi followed behind them as Millie made their way down the walkway. She thought she heard him chuckle but wasn't sure until Susanna twisted around to see him better.

"There really isn't much to tell, Millie." She tugged at her arm.

Millie refused to let her go. "That's where you are

wrong. I've never been very good with a needle and thread. Did your mother teach you?" She offered what she hoped was her sweetest smile.

"Mr. Westland, you are welcome to join us up here," Susanna called over her shoulder, once more trying to see Levi behind them.

"I'm perfectly fine back here, ladies. You go on. I'll catch up."

"Levi's been cooped up in the house with us women all evening. I'm sure he's just enjoying this fresh air." Millie tugged on Susanna's arm to get her attention once more.

The widow frowned at Millie. "No, I am self-taught when it comes to sewing."

"That's how I learned to draw," Millie confessed. She pressed on. "Mother didn't approve of me learning any type of art, so what I learned, I learned from books that Papa sneaked to me."

"So your father didn't mind you drawing?" Susanna asked. She seemed resigned to the fact that Levi wouldn't be joining them.

"Not at all. He said I had real talent, but Papa also didn't want Mother to know that I was secretly learning." They walked in silence for several moments while Millie thought about what she'd just revealed.

Papa had kept her drawings to himself. When she was younger, she'd given him several of her favorites. Now Millie wondered what he'd done with them.

She smiled at Susanna again. "I'm planning on opening an art gallery here in Granite. Maybe you could open a dress shop. I noticed we have a sewing store, I bet you could buy all kinds of supplies from there."

Millie saw the idea she'd just planted take root in Susanna's mind. She slowly released the other woman's arm and chanced a glance back at Levi. He was still about ten paces behind them, but his gait was slow and steady. She knew that if they needed him, he'd make up the space in a heartbeat.

"I do like that idea. Do you really think I could do that, Millie?" Susanna patted her lips with the ring finger of her right hand.

"Why not?" Millie asked, pulling her gaze from Levi and focusing again on Susanna.

Susanna dropped her hand. "Because I don't have the money to start." She sighed. Her gaze moved back to Levi. She lowered her voice so only Millie would hear. "That's why I need a husband."

They stood in front of the hotel. Susanna looked up at it with a nervous grin.

Millie linked arms with her again. "Come on, let's get you settled." She lowered her voice and said, "Let's think on that dress shop. Maybe we'll find a solution to your money problems that doesn't involve a husband."

Half an hour later, Millie and Levi headed back to the boardinghouse. She was tired and more than ready to fall into her nice warm bed.

She pulled her cloak tighter about her body. Now that she wasn't walking fast or pulling someone else along, Millie could feel the chill in the air. The moon hung low in the night sky, casting a white glow over them as they walked.

"Thank you for what you did tonight." Levi buried his hands deeper into his pockets.

Millie grinned. "I didn't do that much."

"I think you did more than you know," Levi said, staring up into the night sky.

Her gaze moved upward, but unlike him, Millie felt she had to watch where she was walking and quickly brought her focus back to earth. "You're making too much of it, Levi. All I did was accompany you and Susanna to the hotel."

He stopped and turned to face her. "It was more than that, Millie. Mother set it up. If I had walked her to the hotel alone, both she and Mother would have made a bigger deal out of the walk than what it was and to save Mrs. Marsh's reputation, my choice in a bride would have been made for me."

Millie looked at him in disbelief. "You really think your ma would use that situation to force you to marry Mrs. Marsh?"

Sadness entered his eyes. "I believe so, yes."

"Why would she do such a thing?" Millie felt his hurt. She couldn't explain how she felt it, but she did.

Levi turned from her and began walking once more. "This afternoon she came to try to talk me into visiting the ranch more often so that I could get to know the ladies. I refused. I know my ma well and saw in her eyes that she was up to something. Mrs. Marsh's arrival tonight was just the beginning of Mother's plans."

"I see." Millie had thought it odd that Susanna had only brought an overnight bag with her. Thinking out loud, she asked, "Do you think someone from the ranch will bring the rest of her things to town tomorrow?"

He shook his head. "No, I think she'll ask me to drive her out there tomorrow to get them."

"So that she can spend more time with you. Very clever." The sound of their feet on the boardwalk was the only sound in the still night. "But why Susanna?

Why not one of the other ladies? And I wonder how Emily and Anna Mae feel about this new development."

"Mother would have picked Mrs. Marsh because she's twenty-five years old and the oldest. If I remember correctly, Emily is twenty-three and Anna Mae is twenty." He stopped in front of the gate and held it open for her.

Millie thought about Bonnie Westland. If she considered Anna Mae and Emily too young for Levi, she would have been terribly unhappy if Millie had gone ahead and married him. There were eleven years between their ages.

"As for how the other ladies feel, I have no idea. They may not even be aware that Mrs. Marsh has left the ranch. I'm sure she left after supper. Ma would have hurried home and then sent Tucker and Mrs. Marsh to town as quick as possible."

As she passed him, the scent of pine and warmth flooded Millie's senses. "But wouldn't they miss her when she didn't come to bed?"

Once more Levi shook his head. "No, Ma gave them all their own rooms. With Daniel and me out of the house, she has three empty bedrooms." His voice sounded defeated. "Maybe with some sleep, I'll figure out what to do about Mrs. Marsh tomorrow." He held the front door open for her.

Millie walked past him and to the stairs. "I'll pray that God will help you through this time, Levi."

His eyes searched hers. For a brief moment, his smile slipped. Then he brought it back into place, but within the depths of his eyes she saw that he really would like that prayer answered.

"My papa always says, 'God's plans don't always feel

right, but if they are His plans they will always work out to our good.'" She paused and considered the rest of the saying before speaking it. "'And, if they aren't His plans, He will take what was meant for evil and turn it around for good.'" Millie didn't know why she was telling Levi what her Papa said, but at this moment it felt like the right thing to say.

Levi studied her, and the look of hurt and confusion slowly melted from his eyes. The dimples came back in full force, and he chuckled. "Thank you, Millie. I keep forgetting that God is in control. And when you see your papa next time, thank him for me."

Millie nodded. "Good night, Levi." She turned to go to her room. This evening had turned out different from how she'd planned. Her plans had been to go to bed early and get a good night's sleep. But now she wasn't sure if she could sleep at all.

Levi wasn't the only one who kept forgetting God was in control. When would she learn to lean on Him? Why did her fears of being controlled continue to haunt her? Why couldn't she trust God to make sure that if she married it would be a marriage of love and not control? And why did she think that it could all happen overnight?

The next morning Levi came downstairs feeling refreshed and carefree. After his talk with Millie, he'd gone to his room and prayed. He'd poured his heart out to the Lord and asked Him to take control of this situation and then he'd fallen asleep so fast, he'd forgotten to turn down his light.

He carried a book with him that covered the local

wildlife and plants around the area. It had colorful drawings that Levi thought Millie might enjoy.

There were also a few chapters about mountain lions and other dangerous wildlife that he prayed she'd pay attention to. Levi wondered if he should mention that chapter or let her discover it on her own. Probably the latter would be best; he just prayed she'd heed his warning and stay out of the deeper part of the woods.

Millie looked up as he entered the room. He was surprised to see she had circles under her eyes as though she hadn't slept all night. Had she stayed awake praying for him? A wobbly smile greeted him.

Beth welcomed him from her place at the table. "Good morning, Levi. Pancakes are on the sideboard."

He noted that neither Mrs. Englebright nor Mr. Lupin had come down yet. "I hope you don't mind if I grab something and run. I'm supposed to meet with a customer this morning and don't have time to sit down." He walked over to the table and laid the book beside Millie's plate before heading to the sideboard. "I thought you might enjoy the drawings in this book, Millie. It also has some great information about this area."

Millie picked up the book and flipped through the pages. "Thank you."

Her voice sounded tired and bland to his ears.

"Can I look at your book after Miss Millie is done with it?" Mark asked.

"You sure can." He scooped up a pancake and stuffed it with sausages. Then he asked, "Are you feeling all right, Millie?" Levi rolled the pancake up much like a burrito and then headed back to the table to hear her answer.

"I am feeling fine, just a little headache," Millie

answered, setting the book down and picking up her coffee.

"Millie, I have some powders that will ease your head. I'll go get them for you." Beth stood and laid down her napkin on the table.

"You don't have to get them right now, Beth," Millie protested.

Beth waved her words away. "Nonsense, it won't take a moment. Mark, you behave yourself while I'm gone." She gave her son a stern look and then left the room.

"I hope you get to feeling better, Millie," Levi offered as he walked to the door. He really hated to leave but had no real reason to stay. Millie was in good hands with Beth.

"Thank you, I'm sure I will."

Levi left the house. What was it about Millicent Hamilton that made him feel so protective around her? He'd wanted to tell her to go back to bed after she took the powders Beth offered but didn't want her to think he was bossing her around again.

He chewed his breakfast and wished he'd taken the time to fill a coffee mug before leaving. His thoughts turned to Millie. What would she do after taking the powders? Go back to her room and rest? Or would she head to the woods to sketch?

Millie took the medicine that Beth brought her for her headache and then carried Levi's book up to her room to look at later. She put on her cape before picking up her sketch pad and the apple pie.

"Are you sure you feel like taking the pie to Carolyn this morning?" Beth asked as she cleared the table.

It was nice having someone care about her, and Millie was glad she and Beth were becoming fast friends. "I'm sure. It's just a headache, I expect it will be gone by the time I get back." She smiled at Mark. "Want to go to the general store with me before you head off to school?"

"Can I, Ma?"

Beth smiled. "Only if you promise to be good."

"I promise. I'll go get my stuff, Miss Millie." He ran from the room with a happy smile on his face.

Millie looked to Mrs. Englebright. "Do you need anything from the store?"

"Would you mind picking up a spool of the blue thread?"

Mrs. Englebright had been making quilt squares using mainly blues and greens. Millie enjoyed watching her sew in the evenings. "Not at all. Do you want me to take a string so I'll get the right shade of blue?"

"No, just tell Carolyn it's for me. She'll know which one to give you. Tell her to put it on my account."

Mark ran back into the room. He slid across the floor and stopped right in front of Millie. "I'm ready."

Beth placed both hands on her hips and demanded, "Mark Winters! What have I told you about running in the house?"

He bowed his head. "Not to."

"That's right. If you want a puppy this summer, you better mind your p's and q's around here."

At the mention of a puppy, Mark's head came up. "I will remember, I promise. No more running in the house."

"Good." Beth came over and gave him a hug. "You have fun at school today."

He placed his hands on the sides of her face. "I will."

Beth pulled his hands down and kissed the backs of them. Then she stood and handed him his lunch pail. "Thanks again, Millie."

Millie nodded. She followed Mark out the door and wondered what it would be like to have such a sweet little boy. Since she'd decided to become a spinster, Millie knew she'd never know. Sadness shrouded her much like her cloak.

Mark skipped ahead for a few minutes, leaving her with her sorrow-filled thoughts. When he returned, he asked, "Miss Millie, are you going to marry Mr. Levi?"

"No."

He twisted his face and said, "Why not?"

How did you explain life to a six-year-old? Mark's mother was nothing like hers. He wouldn't understand her desire to be free from bossiness and manipulation. "It's hard to explain."

"Oh." He skipped off again.

She could tell he was thinking about her answer. Millie didn't think Mark would grow up to be bossy or manipulative. He wasn't being raised that way, but Levi—well, Levi's mother was proving that she was both.

"Ya know what, Miss Millie?"

"What?"

"Well, I've been thinking and I think you should marry Mr. Levi. He's real nice and he likes you. I can tell." Mark's young voice carried, and two women sharing the sidewalk with them smiled in her direction.

Millie bent down in front of Mark. "I tell you what, Mark. If you stop talking about marrying me off to Levi, I'll buy you a lemon drop."

His little head bobbed, and the gap in his teeth shone.

"All right, but you really should think more about it." With that, he opened the door to the general store and hurried inside.

The two ladies laughed. Just as the door closed behind Millie, she heard one of them say, "Out of the mouths of babes."

Millie gave Carolyn the pie and bought Mark's candy and Mrs. Englebright's thread. She was about to leave when Carolyn said, "Oh, I ordered a couple of sketch pads and some watercolors. I'm pretty sure they are in one of those boxes in the back. If you want to come in tomorrow morning, I'll show them to you and return Beth's pie plate."

Millie's heart skipped a beat. She'd wanted to play with watercolors for some time but never had the chance. "Do you think about mid-morning would be a good time to stop in?"

"That will be perfect. Maybe we could have a cup of tea, too."

"I'd like that. Thank you, Carolyn." Millie waved and then closed the door behind her.

Mark had seen a toy windup car in the store he'd like to have for his birthday and chattered nonstop about it until they reached the school. She waved goodbye to him and then returned to the boardinghouse.

After giving Mrs. Englebright her thread, Millie excused herself. She went to her room and sat down beside the open window. With her trip to the store and school, she really didn't have time to go to the woods to sketch. The light breeze helped to soothe her head.

Mark's words drifted through her mind. *He's real nice and he likes you.* Yes, Levi seemed very nice and he did like her, but as a friend. She rubbed her temples. And friendship was all they would have, Millie told herself.

Especially now that Susanna was in town, Millie expected Levi to spend more time with the mail-order bride. Susanna had made it very plain that she wanted to be more than friends with Levi. Susanna wanted to be his wife.

Millie laid her head down on the table and closed her eyes. After several long minutes, a vision of a little boy with brown hair and green eyes entered her mind. She could see him holding both her and Levi's hands. He swung between them and looked up with at her with laughter in his eyes. Eyes that were grass-green and looked just like Levi's.

She awoke with a jerk. Had the headache powders put her to sleep? And what about the dream? Was she secretly harboring dreams of life with Levi and having a family with him?

Millie continued to plague Levi's thoughts even after Mr. Monroe came to the shop, ordered a porch swing like the one at the boardinghouse and left. Levi looked about his shop. He had lots of work to do today but decided he would rather check on Millie.

At nine-thirty, he turned the open sign to closed, and left another sign, handwritten, under it that said, Be Back At Ten. Levi realized as he headed to the boardinghouse that if Millie was in her room, he couldn't just knock on her door and ask how she was feeling. He might wake her. He slowed his footsteps.

Maybe she'd gone to the woods to draw. Levi turned and headed to the spot where he'd found her the day before. If she wasn't there, he'd assume she'd stayed home.

Home. The word stuck in his mind. What would it be like once he married? He wouldn't be able to stay at the boardinghouse. His new bride would more than likely want her own house. Levi frowned. Why hadn't he thought of that before? As far as he knew, there weren't any houses in Granite for sale. He'd have to build one.

He arrived at the big boulder but didn't see Millie on the edge of the woods. Levi walked within the canopy of trees, thinking she might have decided to ignore his warning and gone to the log where he'd found her before.

Levi was both disappointed and relieved when he saw that she wasn't there. He'd wanted to talk to her about his house situation. As crazy as it sounded, he realized he was beginning to depend on Millie.

When she wasn't as prickly as a cactus, Millie was easy to talk to and smart when it came to dealing with the other brides and his mother, and he liked the way she reasoned things out in her mind. Levi knew he could never fall in love with her, but he already felt a bond growing between them.

Did she feel the same way toward him? What would Millie have thought if he had found her this morning and asked what kind of house he should build? Once more the thought came to him that he should offer her a marriage of convenience, but would she accept?

Chapter Nine

By the time Levi arrived back at the boardinghouse it was late in the evening. He had gotten so busy at the shop that he'd missed lunch and ended up having dinner at The Eating House with another customer. It irritated him that his thoughts were never far from Millie and how she might be feeling.

He heard muffled voices on the front porch as he approached. The sun was fading in the sky and shadows covered the two people sitting on the swing. As Levi got closer, he recognized Mark's young voice.

"What do you think of my dog?" the little boy asked.

Millie answered, "I think he is coming along well. You still need to work on making your marks just a little lighter so you can correct anything about him that you don't like."

Levi quietly stepped up onto the porch. Millie and Mark's heads were together as they studied the paper in Mark's lap.

"It's getting hard to see out here," Mark commented. When he looked up, Mark said, "Oh, hi, Mr. Levi."

"Good evening, Mark, Millie." Levi walked across

the porch and sat down beside the little boy. He leaned forward and studied Mark's picture. "Hey, that's pretty good."

Mark's face lit up. "Thanks. Miss Millie's been teaching me." He looked down at the picture once more. "I hope Ma will like it."

Levi wondered where Beth was, but didn't ask. "I'm sure she will."

The screen door creaked. "Mark, time to get ready for bed." Beth motioned for the little boy to join her inside.

"Ma. Look what Miss Millie taught me." Mark jumped off the swing and waved the paper up at her.

Beth took his drawing and studied it. "That's very good, Mark. I like it." She handed it back to him. "Go put your night clothes on. I'll be there in a minute."

Dejection filled his young voice. "Can't I stay up just a little longer and work on my dog?" He held the paper up for her to see again.

Beth looked down on him like only a mother could and answered in a firm voice. "No. Now off to bed with you."

"All right. 'Night, Miss Millie. 'Night, Mr. Levi." Mark walked around his mother with his head down.

As soon as he was in the house, all three adults chuckled. "He sure is growing," Levi said.

"He sure is." Beth smiled at Levi and said, "You must have had a busy day at the shop. I don't think I've seen you since breakfast."

He leaned back on the swing. "Very busy. I didn't know there for a while if I was coming or going. Things should slow down a little now, though. I hired Amos to help out around the store and to do the odd jobs that I have been doing, like delivering your supplies on Tuesday mornings."

"That is an excellent idea. His ma and sisters could use the extra money." Beth wiped her hands on her apron and then asked, "Have you had supper?"

"I ate at The Eating House."

She nodded. "I better get in there. There is no telling what that boy is doing." Beth returned inside.

The swing swayed gently as Millie stood. "I need to be going, too."

"That's too bad. I'd hoped I could talk to you about something."

Her skirts brushed the top of his boots. "Oh?" She stood in front of him, waiting. "Does it have anything to do with Mrs. Marsh? Did she ask you to take her back to the ranch?"

Levi liked the fact that she was interested in what Susanna Marsh was up to. "No, I didn't see her all day."

"Don't you think that is odd?" Millie asked.

Now that she mentioned it, it did seem strange that the mail-order bride hadn't searched him out all day. "Maybe she was busy doing something else," he offered.

"Maybe." Millie looked out across the front yard. After several minutes, she turned back to him. "If you didn't want to talk about Susanna, what did you want to talk to me about?" she asked.

He'd meant to ask her about the house, but then felt strange about it so he said instead, "Daniel's birthday is in less than two weeks and I have something in mind that I want to give him, but I need your help."

She tilted her head sideways and studied his face. "If I can help, I will."

Levi sat up straight. "Please sit back down. I promise I won't keep you long." He patted the seat of the bench.

Millie moved back to her spot and sat down. He noted that she'd moved as close to the opposite arm of the swing as possible. Surely, she wasn't afraid of him. So why sit so far away?

There was an edge to her voice when she spoke that caused him to think that she might have perceived his request as bossing her around. "All right, I'm sitting. What do you need me to do?"

He pressed on before she changed her mind. "I want to do an art piece for him using wood."

Millie seemed to have forgotten her anger and leaned toward him. Her eyes sparkled in the lingering light as she asked, "What kind of art piece?"

"When we were kids, Daniel and I were in Austin once and a gentleman traveling through was selling goods out of the back of his wagon. He had a horse head in a nice wooden picture frame. Daniel loved it but the man wanted way more money than either of us could afford at the time. I've always wanted to duplicate it for Daniel."

Horror filled Millie's face. She pulled back and rested a hand on her chest. "A real horse head? Levi, that's disgusting."

Levi chuckled. "No, silly. Not a real horse head. It was a wooden one, only flat like a drawing."

Her hand dropped, and a smile crept across her face. "Oh, well, thank goodness it wasn't real. So what do you want me to do?"

"Well, I thought if you could sketch a horse's head, maybe I could use it as a template and recreate what we saw all those years ago." He laid his arm across the back of the swing and leaned toward her and whispered, "Of course, I'd have to swear you to secrecy until after his birthday."

She leaned forward and whispered back, "I think I can keep your secret." A giggle slipped from her, and he laughed.

"Good." Levi stared into her pretty blue eyes. Her face was mere inches from his. His gaze moved to her lips.

Millie pulled back. "Levi, I have to admit I'm not sure I can make a good horse's head, but I'll try." She pushed up from the swing once more. "I really should be getting back inside."

He didn't know why, but Levi wasn't ready to let her go. Levi stood and grabbed her hand, stopping her from walking away. "I hope I wasn't too forward in asking you to sit earlier. I only did so because my neck is sore from bending it most of the day."

She turned and looked down at their clasped hands. "It's all right. I'm trying to learn that not everything you say is meant to control me." Millie pulled her hand from his and opened the door. "I'll try to get the sketch to you in a couple of days. Good night, Levi."

And then she was gone. He sat back down on the swing. What had gotten into him? He'd almost kissed her.

Millie couldn't sleep. She tossed the covers back and lit the lamp. Her emotions were running too high tonight.

Spending time with Levi on the porch, she'd discovered that she really liked him, even considered him a friend. Until they'd been nose to nose. It was at that point her emotions had begun to act crazy. She felt sure he'd intended to kiss her and that both excited and scared her.

Grabbing her sketch pad, Millie decided to try drawing the horse head Levi had asked for. She reached for her charcoal. If she could get the picture like she wanted, Millie would redo the drawing in pencil.

Although sketching usually soothed her, tonight it didn't. She managed to create a fair-looking horse head, but not because her concentration was on the drawing. No, she was still focused on Levi.

Levi was like no other man Millie knew. When he entered a room, Levi didn't come in talking or whistling like her father had. He seemed to take in what was going on before speaking. His eyes seemed to dance with some hidden joy every time she looked at him. Tonight he'd smelled strongly of fresh-cut wood. Millie laid the charcoal down and leaned back in her chair.

She closed her eyes and inhaled. He must have spent a lot of time in his workshop today to carry the scent for so long.

It was true that she didn't have a lot of men to compare Levi to. Millie's sheltered life, until she'd started on this adventure, had kept her from most men. But, on the trip to Lubbock she'd met several men and they'd smelled of light mint or very bad body odor. She'd also met a few businessmen who had put some type of toilet water on that blended with their body odors, which was almost as bad as the foul-smelling men.

The only other man she'd been as close to as she'd been to Levi tonight had been her father. He, too, carried a light sawdust smell and the scent that was unique to him, nothing like the earthy scent that attracted her to Levi.

A yawn slipped from her lips. Millie stood and stretched—maybe now she could sleep. Comparing Levi to her father had taken some of the attraction she'd felt for Levi from her. She giggled at the thought, doused the light and returned to her bed.

As she lay in the dark, loneliness enveloped her. The desire to return home and see her parents hit with a suddenness that almost made her cry. She missed the warmth of her mother's hug, if not her bossiness. Millie would love to see her papa again and snuggle in one of his fierce hugs. Millie drifted to sleep with the thought that maybe she should return to Cottonwood Springs.

Birds singing and the sound of hammering pulled Millie from a deep sleep. She lay in bed for several minutes as she came awake. When she'd lived at home she often woke to the sound of hammering because their house was close to the sawmill where her father worked.

A smile touched her lips. Papa was forever fixing or building something for Mother. She pushed the covers back.

Millie splashed cold water on her face and quickly finished her morning routine. She wore a soft green dress and pulled her hair up into a ponytail, securing it with a bit of green ribbon. Millie looped her room key through another green ribbon and tied it around her neck. She tucked it into the front of her dress and then picked up her mirror.

As she looked into the hand mirror, Millie wondered what Levi saw when he looked at her. Did he see someone he could spend the rest of his life with?

Levi would be a kind husband, she thought. Millie saw the dreamy expression on her face and in her eyes.

But what if he was bossy like her mother? What if he changed from the nice guy she knew now to the demanding person her mother had become?

Millie marched over to the washbasin; it was time to snap out of those thoughts. She filled both hands with cold water and tossed it into her own face. No! She would not fall in love with Levi Westland or any man. The danger in it was too great, and she would not be ruled by another. Ever!

Had her mother always been bossy? And if so, had her papa known it when he married her, or was it something she'd revealed after the marriage? Did it really matter?

Millie spun on her booted heels and scooped up her sketch pad and other art supplies before dashing down the stairs. She hurried out the front door and down the short steps. The cool morning air felt crisp against her face as she pressed onward toward the woods. There she would be able to focus on her art and not on the man.

She pressed deeper into the woods, looking for the log where she'd sat the first morning she'd come here. Millie felt the peace of the trees and sighed. She flipped to the picture of the horse head and then gently pulled it out.

As she redrew the horse head, Millie began to think of other ways Levi could frame the picture. What if she made it look like a puzzle?

First, she worked on the flat drawing, and then she redrew it and gave it more dimensions. A smile grew on her face as the horse's head began to look as if it stood off the page.

She was so consumed with the art piece, the morning sped by. Millie looked up into the sky and saw that she needed to hurry if she was going to make her appointment this morning and then get back to the boardinghouse to work.

The drawing wasn't perfect. It still, to her way of thinking, needed a lot of work, but it was a good start. She quickly organized her supplies, tucked them under her arm and started back toward the road.

A twig snapped somewhere off to her left, reminding her of Levi's advice about mountain lions. Had she been foolish to ignore his warning? Millie scooped up her skirts and hurried from the woods.

At the road she felt breathless and silly. A nervous giggle filled her. Nothing had followed her out of the woods. She began walking to the boardinghouse. Her stomach growled, reminding her she'd skipped breakfast.

That, too, felt foolish now. She should have gone on in with the others. It wasn't Levi's fault she'd had a restless night. She'd just have to be careful around him. He was a nice man and made a wonderful friend.

Still, she wouldn't give him or any man control over her life. At that moment, Millie began to build a wall around her heart to keep love and dreams of a future with Levi out. She didn't need a bossy man as a husband, but she might not mind having Levi for a friend.

The smell of roses entered the furniture shop, announcing the arrival of Susanna Marsh. He'd known she would be coming around sooner or later—Levi had been praying it would be later. He laid his hammer down and stood to greet her.

"Good morning, Mrs. Marsh. How are you today?" Levi picked up a damp rag and wiped the dust from his hands.

She looked about the store before answering him. "I'm well, Levi." Susanna batted her eyelashes at him. "I thought we agreed you'd call me by my given name."

He ignored her and asked, "What can I do for you today?" Levi put the cloth back down before looking at her again.

A smile graced her face. She attempted to turn the smile into a pout. "I'm glad you asked. Mrs. Moore over at the general store refuses to advance me a line of credit without your approval." She resumed batting her eyelashes again and asked in a sticky-sweet voice, "Would you mind walking over to the store with me?"

So that was the excuse she'd found to spend time with him. "I'll be happy to, but didn't my mother set up an account for you when you came to town?"

"No, we were instructed to come straight to the ranch. This is the first time I've been in your fine town since I arrived over two weeks ago. Well, except last Sunday and then I didn't get to explore the businesses." Her blue eyes roved over the various pieces of furniture before returning to him. "Can we go now? I'd really like to take care of my purchases."

Levi walked to the door that connected his workshop and the store. He called into the other room, "Amos, I need you up front."

The teenager arrived carrying a broom. His gaze ran over Susanna. "What do you need? I'm almost done back there."

He'd discovered Amos was a hard worker who enjoyed feeling responsible. So he'd taken to speaking to him like a man instead of a sixteen-year-old boy. "Mrs. Marsh and I have an errand to run. Please keep an eye on the store."

"Be happy to. I was going to sweep up here next anyway."

"Good. I won't be gone long." He took Susanna's arm and gently steered her toward the exit. "I'll be over at the general store if you need me." He released her and opened the door.

Susanna latched on to his arm as soon as they were out of the store. She looked up at him and did the eyelash thing again.

Levi didn't want to be unkind, but he didn't care for her behavior. "Mrs. Marsh, please stop doing that with your eyes. It's a little unnerving." He slipped his arm from hers. "I know you are trying to convince me that you want me to marry you, but I'll be honest. The easiest way to do that is to be yourself." The pout returned to her lips, and he sighed. "I'm sorry if that hurt your feelings."

She stopped walking and moved to the shade of one of the buildings. Levi had no choice but to follow. What game was she going to play now? He'd not had a lot of experience with women. Lucille had been his first crush and he'd never taken the time to court anyone else. He really didn't know what to expect.

"I'm sorry, too. Other than my husband, I've never tried to get close to another man. When I was sixteen, batting my eyes and smiling a lot worked. I guess I'm getting too old to play those kinds of games." She laid a hand on his forearm. "Can we start over?"

He nodded. "That sounds like a fine idea." Levi extended his arm to her and began walking down the boardwalk again. "I'm curious—what did you do yesterday?"

"Mainly, I walked around town, relaxed and thought about what I'd do if you chose Emily or Anna Mae." She stared off in the opposite direction from him as if her confession had embarrassed her.

"I see. And what are you going to do if I choose one of them?" he asked, also feeling the embarrassment of the conversation.

She looked at him and grinned. "Well, I'm not real sure, but Millie and I discussed the possibility of me opening a dress shop. Mr. and Mrs. Duffey, they own the Sewing Room—oh, you probably already know that. Anyway, they are willing to sell it to me. Mrs. Duffey's mother is ill and they plan on moving back to—" she paused and waved her hand "—oh, wherever it is she lives."

"Millie talked to you about this?" Why hadn't Millie told him that she'd talked to Susanna about opening a dress shop?

"Uh-huh. The other night when we were walking to the hotel. I think I have enough money to put a down payment on the Sewing Room, but I will need to ask the bank for a loan for the rest of the money." She looked straight ahead, deep in thought.

Levi stopped in front of the general store. He held the door open for her and then followed Susanna into the store. His gaze moved about the establishment until it landed on Carolyn Moore sitting at a small table with Millie. A pot of tea sat between them.

"Carolyn! I've brought Levi back with me," Susanna called, looking behind the counter and not at the back of the store, where the women sat.

Levi grinned and gently turned Susanna in the direction of the two women.

"Oh, I didn't see you back here." She walked toward the women.

He followed. "I see you have taken over the checker table."

"Yes, Pa and Wilson drove to Austin today so I took over Pa's table." Carolyn pushed herself up from her chair. "Do you have everything you need, Susanna?"

Carolyn and Susanna walked back to the front counter. Levi turned to look at Millie. She hadn't said anything since he'd arrived. He'd seen the surprised expression on her face when they'd entered, but now she looked relaxed and unconcerned.

"I believe so." Susanna turned to Millie. "Did you see all the material and supplies I am getting?"

Millie stood. "No, I didn't know you'd been in this morning," she confessed, joining the other ladies at the counter.

As he watched the two women discuss Susanna's purchases, Levi found himself comparing them. Susanna's hair was blond like Millie's, but it didn't have the same shine. Her blue eyes were paler than Millie's and missed a certain sparkle. They were about the same height and build, but there was something about Millie that drew him like a logger to a favored tree.

Susanna chose that moment to look over her shoulder and smile at him. She was very pretty, but compared to Millie she didn't appeal to him.

"Thanks for the tea, Carolyn. I need to get over to the boardinghouse. Beth is waiting for me." Millie waved bye and then left.

Levi knew without thinking about it that if he

couldn't marry Millie, he wouldn't be marrying Susanna, either. Susanna was nice, but she wasn't the bride for him.

Levi stood behind the bakery eating a slice of lemon pound cake and sipping on a cup of coffee. His view was the woods where he'd first seen Millie's sketch of the butterfly. He missed Millie and their quiet talks.

It had been three days since he'd run into her at the general store. They had morning and evening meals together at the boardinghouse, but other than that, Millie didn't spend much time with him or the other boarders. She seemed to have buried herself in her art.

He didn't know if she was avoiding him or simply preoccupied with the drawing he'd requested. Either way, Levi knew he missed her. He'd hoped to develop their friendship so that he could approach her about a marriage of convenience.

As he stared at the trees, Levi thought he saw movement. He lowered his coffee cup, not sure what would emerge from the woods. He'd warned Millie of mountain lions and wondered if one had come closer to town than normal.

Relief flooded him as he saw Millie emerge from the tree line. He could tell by the sketch pad in her hands that she'd been there drawing. Had she gone back to the log deep in the woods? Or had she heeded his warning and stayed within the edge of the trees and not ventured too far?

When she looked up and smiled in his direction, all his questions vanished. Maybe she wasn't avoiding him after all. Levi raised his hand and waved, almost dropping the cake.

She returned his wave and her smile grew. When Millie got close enough, she said, "I was just coming to your shop to show you the drawing."

"So it's finished then?"

A giggle escaped her. "I think so. But you can be the judge." Millie began to open the sketch pad, but she had too much stuff in her hands.

"Let's go inside the bakery and sit down." Levi shoved the rest of his cake in his mouth and took her arm. He swallowed the sweet bread and then said, "I can't wait to see what you've come up with."

They walked around the shop and entered the bakery. Levi inhaled the sugary fragrance of pastries and fresh coffee. He never tired of coming here and thankfully, since he owned it as well as a couple of other stores in town, no one protested when he dropped by to grab a goodie or two. Once more, Levi was thankful his father had left both him and Daniel a nice size trust fund. The ranch belonged to their mother, but thanks to the trust funds, he and his brother didn't need the ranch to survive.

There wasn't a lot of seating in the small building, but since it was midmorning, they were able to get a table by the window. "Can I order you anything?" Levi asked after he made sure Millie was seated.

She looked to the counter where cakes, cookies and various breads were displayed. Her stomach growled and her cheeks turned pink. "I wouldn't mind trying one of those sticky buns and a glass of milk," Millie admitted.

"Coming right up."

Levi hurried to the counter and gave Violet Millie's order. He set his empty coffee mug down while he waited.

Violet Atwood was an older woman whose husband had passed away ten years earlier. Levi had bought the building for her to open the bakery so she'd have some income. When Levi had begun buying buildings in Granite, he'd never dreamed he'd be helping both Violet and Beth when they needed assistance most.

"How did you enjoy the lemon cake?" she asked, placing a rather large sticky bun on a small plate.

"Like all your desserts, it was delicious."

"Good, I'm glad you enjoyed it. Would you like for me to freshen up your coffee?" Violet asked as she poured Millie's glass of milk.

"Thank you. I'll take this to the table and be right back for it."

A frown marred Millie's face when he returned to the table. He noted she was staring down at the drawing. Levi set the plate and glass of milk in front of her. She seemed so deep in thought that she didn't notice him.

Levi returned for the steaming cup of coffee. He called to the older woman, who was bent over a hot oven. "Thanks, Violet."

"You're welcome, Levi. Holler if you need anything else."

He returned to Millie and sat across from her.

She still focused on the picture. "Maybe I shouldn't show this to you after all. I'm not sure I have it just right."

Levi laughed and reached for the sketch pad. "Ready or not, I'm looking," he said, pulling the paper to him.

Her sketches were amazing. She'd drawn a line down the center of the page to separate the two drawings. One was a flat drawing that looked just like a real horse's head. The second stood out on the page, looking much like one of Mark's puzzles.

Millie's voice shook. "Well? What do you think?"

"These are wonderful, Millie." He couldn't pull his eyes from the paper. "How did you make this one stand out like that?"

"It's hard to explain. I was thinking about Mark's puzzles and thought it would be really nice if I could make a horse head that you could piece together." She still sounded unsure of her work.

Levi looked up at her. "I think I can duplicate it in wood. You'll have to tell me what you think when it's complete."

Millie nodded happily. "I've been thinking that if you can do this with wood, wouldn't it be nice if we could make these a little smaller and give each one of the children at church a puzzle similar to this at Christmas?"

"What a thoughtful idea. We have several families in the area whose children would benefit from puzzles." Levi looked down at the horse head. "Can you make other animals?"

Excitement filled her voice. "I'm going to try. I was thinking cats, dogs and maybe horses on a smaller scale for the kid's puzzles. Not just their heads but their whole bodies."

The joy in her voice made him smile. "Let's see if I can do the horse head and then we'll move on to those things. I think it's wonderful that you are thinking about the children's Christmas, Millie."

She picked up her sticky bun and grinned. "Well, I have to give my mother and Beth credit for my thinking about them." Millie took a big bite from the pastry and chewed.

As far as he knew, Millie hadn't contacted her family so how had her mother influenced her? "Why give your mother the credit?" he finally asked after it became obvious she wasn't going to volunteer the information.

Millie laid the sticky bun down and took a sip of her milk. "Mother always said that drawing was a waste of time, but I love it. I thought that if I do something nice, like give the children puzzles or something else related to art, that maybe she would see that it holds value for me and those around me. So it is because of her that I hope I've found a way to give joy to others."

Levi leaned back in his chair and studied her pretty face. He could see that Millie held respect and love for her mother. But he also saw her resentment due to her mother's desire to control her.

Would Millie ever overcome those feelings of needing to protect herself from others? Would she ever be able to trust him? Or anyone else for that matter?

Chapter Ten

It was almost time for Daniel's birthday party and Levi was excited about his gift. He'd spent the past week working on it and just hoped that Millie would like what he'd done with her drawing.

Levi covered Millie's eyes with his hands.

He heard the joy in her voice as she asked, "Is this really necessary?"

"It is if I want to surprise you, and I do, so yes, it is necessary." He gently walked behind her into the sitting room where the other boarders waited.

He'd hung the horse's head above the fireplace and hung a cloth over it, obscuring it from everyone's view. Levi turned Millie so that she faced the fireplace.

"About time you two got here," Mrs. Englebright complained. "I've been tempted to peek."

Levi ignored her outburst, but grinned. "Keep your eyes tightly shut," he ordered Millie. Then, when he had her positioned in front of the painting, he pulled his hands away and said, "You may open your eyes."

Millie gasped. Not sure if it was a good gasp or a bad gasp, Levi stepped around her so he could see her face.

Her hands were now covering her mouth and her eyes had grown as wide as one of his saw blades.

Unable to wait, Levi blurted out, "Well? What do you think?"

She lowered her hands slowly and said, "Oh, Levi. It's beautiful."

He looked up at the framed picture. Was it beautiful? He wasn't sure he'd call it a work of beauty. To him, it looked rustic and bold. The pine varnish he'd rubbed over the surface did give it a nice shine.

"I have to agree. That is the most beautiful picture I've ever seen," Mrs. Englebright stated, staring up at it.

Mr. Lupin stepped up to the frame and touched the smooth edge. "It's all made out of wood, too."

Levi looked to Beth. She stood staring at the picture as if she'd never seen anything like it. Which, now that he thought about it, she probably hadn't. "You are going to have to make something like that for the main entry, Levi. It's wonderful."

A laugh of pure joy burst from his chest. He clapped his hands once. "Millie gets most of the credit. It's her drawing. I simply put it to wood."

Her wide eyes turned to stare at him. In a small voice, Millie asked, "Can you teach me how to make pictures like that? It's a real work of art." She clasped her hands in front of the brown dress she wore.

"If you want to learn, I'm sure I can." Her blue eyes lit up and she turned them back to the picture. "But Millie, it took me almost two weeks to make that one."

She continued to look up at the picture. "I know. But you'll get faster as you make more and I'll work hard to learn."

His heart leaped in his chest. If he was going to teach

Millie how to make wooden pictures, then they'd be spending lots of time together. Over the past month, the two of them had spent time together, but they'd been surrounded by people. It would be only him and her for the lessons.

That meant he might be able to get her to trust him enough to marry him. Levi reminded himself it would be a marriage of convenience so that his mother would let Daniel keep the ranch. He refused to fall in love or give any woman his heart.

Levi's gaze moved to Millie once more. She was laughing with Beth about something, and both spoke to each other in low tones. Soft blue eyes sought him out, and she smiled. He basked in the shared moment. Silently, he prayed. *Lord, don't let me fall in love with this woman. Help me to harden my heart because I fear she could easily shatter it into a million pieces and I can't go through that hurt again.*

The next morning, Millie dressed in one of her prettiest dress. It was a dark green with lace about the neck and cuffs on the sleeves. She wore her cream-colored shawl over it.

Daniel Westland's birthday party was going to be an all-day event. Levi instructed Beth to close the restaurant and take the day off. He'd invited her and Mark to come with them to the ranch, but Beth had declined. Though she did agree to close the restaurant, as she wanted to take Mark on a picnic down by the river.

As Millie pulled her hair up into a ponytail, she wondered if it was time to take on a more fashionable hairstyle. She stared at her reflection for several long minutes. Unlike the three brides on the ranch, she was no beauty. Her blond hair didn't shine like Susanna's, her eyes didn't hold a mysterious look within their depths like Emily's, and she wasn't as tall or graceful as Anna Mae.

Millie knew the other brides would outshine her no matter what she did with her hair. Not that she was competing with them. She tied the matching green ribbon around the band that held her hair in place. Lastly, Millie splashed a small amount of her favorite scented water on her neck. The aroma of lavender soothed her nerves.

She reached for the bag Beth had given her for her art supplies. She slid her sketch pad inside and then left the room. Millie didn't want to go to Daniel's party. She wanted to go sketch in silence in the woods, but she'd promised Hannah she'd be there.

"About ready?" Levi asked as she stepped off the last stair.

Millie nodded. He held Daniel's present wrapped in brown paper. The words Happy Birthday, Big Brother were scrawled across the top. He'd tied the paper down with a piece of twine. She also noticed that he had a book in his other hand.

Beth and Mark stood off to the side.

"Are you sure you don't want to go?" Millie asked, wishing with all her might that Beth would change her mind.

Mark wrapped his small arms around his mother's waist. "We're going on a picnic, and I get to skip rocks on the water," he said, hugging her tight.

Beth laughed and hugged him back. "I'm sure. Today is a day for just Mark and me to spend together." She released the little boy and grinned. "You two have fun."

Millie followed Levi out to the wagon, where he put

the present and book behind the seat. She ignored Beth's teasing look. Beth and Mrs. Englebright still held hopes of her and Levi getting married, even though Millie had told them both numerous times that she and Levi were just friends.

When Levi held out his hand to help her up, Millie placed hers within it. His strong fingers closed around hers, and for a brief moment Millie allowed herself to enjoy his touch. Once seated, she placed her bag at her feet and straightened her skirt.

Levi was quiet as he guided the team out of town and down the dirt road that would lead to the Westland ranch. Did he regret her coming? Was he dreading seeing the brides? Or looking forward to it?

She cut her eyes and tried to see his face. He seemed focused on driving. Was he as uncomfortable around her this morning as she was around him? Did he regret saying last night that he'd teach her to make wooden wall art?

To calm herself, Millie pulled her sketch pad and a piece of charcoal from her bag. She looked about for something to draw. Everything was still bare from winter—only small shoots of green filled the landscape, so she decided to use her imagination and work on an Iris flower. They were her favorite and she wondered if they grew here in Texas.

The wagon seemed to hit every rock and pothole, but Millie decided to make the best of the situation. She focused all her attention on the revealing of the flower. Soon an image was beginning to spring from the paper.

Levi spoke beside her. "Your drawings are really very good. I can almost smell that flower." He offered her a grin, and his dimples flashed before he turned his attention back to the road.

"Thank you." Millie continued working on the petals. After several minutes of silence she asked, "Are you all right today?"

He sighed. "Yes, I'm just dreading being on the ranch again."

"Why?" Millie felt sure she knew but wanted to hear him talk. The sound of his voice reminded her of satin paints, strong and yet soothing as they spread across a page. What a silly thought. She grinned at her own musings.

"I believe you know why," he countered without looking from the back of the horse.

"The brides and your mother?"

"The brides. Mother isn't going to be pressuring today—she'll let the brides do that for her."

"Well, Susanna has settled down. I think she's more interested in her dress shop than you," Millie teased as she added shadowing to the edges of one petal.

"I believe you are right. When I asked if she'd like to ride out with us, she declined, but there are still two other brides. And if she does decide to come out later without her cloth and needle to distract her, who knows how Susanna will act today." Levi's voice had lost all hints of amusement.

"You could just choose one and get it over with," she commented.

"I can't. They want a real husband, a family and love. I can't give them love." He pulled the wagon to a stop.

Levi set the brake and tied the reins to it. Then he turned to her. He took the charcoal and paper from her hands and lap and set them to the side.

Her mouth went dry and her palms suddenly felt sweaty. "What are you doing?" *Please don't let him say what I think he's about to say,* she silently prayed.

Taking both her hands in his, Levi inhaled and then asked, "Millie, will you marry me? I know you don't want a real husband or family. Like me, you don't want or need love. It could be a marriage of convenience. I can never love you like a husband does a wife, but if you will have me, I'll spend the rest of my life trying to make you happy. We'd be perfect for each other."

It was tempting. But she didn't want to be controlled even if they had a marriage in name only. And what if Levi found out that she was an arsonist? He'd hate her and yet be tied to her. What would the town think of him if they found out she'd burned down Eliza Kelly's house and then ran away from taking the responsibility of doing so? The words *I can't* forced their way out of her throat.

Why did this have to be so hard? She liked Levi but Millie knew she couldn't marry him. Not now, not ever. She was an arsonist on the run and the fear of anyone ever controlling her again was too risky to say yes. Still, a part of Millie wanted to.

He released her hands. "I promise. I'll never boss you around like your mother did. Does that make any difference?" Levi's green eyes searched hers. He seemed to want this so badly.

Millie shook her head. She knew Levi meant what he said, but she didn't trust that he could keep his word. There had been times late at night when she'd heard her mother apologize to her papa for the way she'd behaved, but then in a couple of days she'd gone right back to being her old controlling self.

Disappointment filled her as the words left her lips. "Levi, choose one of the other ladies. They all seem very nice and they all seem to like you." She didn't know why, but she hated the idea of him marrying one of the mail-order brides.

It was his turn to shake his head. "I can't right now." He picked up the reins and started the horse moving forward again. "I suppose I'll have to get to know them better."

She heard the disappointment in his voice. Levi said he couldn't offer love. Would one of the other ladies be able to accept that? He was right in the fact that most women wanted love and a family. Millie knew deep down she wanted that, too, but there was too much that held her back: fear and the knowledge that she had burned down Eliza's house and then been a coward and ran.

Bitterness ate at her. Could she really go back and face the people of Cottonwood Springs? Millie swallowed, knowing she'd have to do so eventually. As for trusting Levi, she couldn't.

Levi pulled in front of the house. It had been too soon to ask Millie to marry him. The rest of their trip to the ranch had been quiet and tense. She'd seemed sad, but it could have just been his wishful thinking.

The sound of laughter floated to them from the back of the house. He jumped from the wagon, walked around it and then helped her down. He held her around the waist a little longer than he should have but Levi enjoyed the feel of her warmth in his arms.

Once Millie's feet were on the ground, Levi released

her. He handed her the bag she'd brought and watched as she slipped it over her shoulder.

"Would you mind taking Daniel's birthday present and the book while I take care of the horse and wagon?" he asked, needing to put a little space between them.

Millie did as he asked and took the package and book but didn't make eye contact. She kept her gaze down and turned toward the sound of the party.

Ol' Jeb stepped forward. "I'll take care of your horse and wagon, Levi."

Levi looked from Millie to Jeb. Jeb had been on the ranch as long as Levi could remember. He was a nice old man who had been a good friend of his father's.

He was a man of few words, but Jeb pressed, "Your ma put us men to work, watching for guests." The sound of another wagon coming up the road and Cole, the ranch foreman, strolling from the barn confirmed Jeb's words.

"Thanks, Jeb. Appreciate it."

Jeb tipped his hat once and then pulled the horse and wagon toward the barn. For a moment, Levi watched the activity taking place in the front yard. It seemed each of the ranch men were taking turns, pulling horses and wagons into the barn and corrals.

Levi turned to walk with Millie, but she'd already gone without him. He tucked his hands into his pockets and kicked a rock. She was several feet away but didn't look back.

Before she could round the corner, Levi ran and caught up with her. He grabbed her arm and pulled her to a stop. "I just need to talk to you for a minute before we face the rest of them."

Millie looked down at his hand on her arm.

He released her. "Sorry, I just didn't want to call out and draw unwanted attention."

Her eyes softened, and she offered him a wobbly grin. "It's all right. What did you want to talk about?"

Levi took her hand and pulled her away from the main walkway and to the side of the house, where he felt sure they wouldn't be disturbed. When they were in the shade, Levi released her hand. "I'm sorry if my proposal made you uncomfortable. I'd like to pretend it didn't happen and just be friends. Is that possible?" He searched her heart-shaped face.

Millie smiled up at him. "I'd like that."

He turned to go, but her soft hand fell on his forearm. "Levi?"

There was something in her voice that made him hope she'd changed her mind about marrying him. Levi turned back around. "Yes?"

"I really am sorry I can't marry you. I'm sure you will make a wonderful husband for one of the mail-order brides." She played with the cord on the present.

He took the book and present from her and set them on the ground at their feet. Levi then reached forward and lifted her chin so that she could look at his face. Tears rimmed her pretty blue eyes. His hands moved to cup her cheeks.

Whatever he'd meant to say flew from his mind as he leaned forward and captured her lips with his. Levi didn't question his actions, just knew that if she wouldn't marry him, he at least wanted to kiss her one time.

She didn't pull back or struggle. He gently lowered his hands and pulled her into his arms. The kiss deepened and yet neither of them pulled away. It was like nothing he'd ever experienced before, like coming off the range on a cold winter's day to the warmth of home.

Levi knew he had to stop kissing her. He lifted his hands back to her cheeks and then moved back slowly. His mouth released hers. He missed her closeness immediately.

Wide eyes searched his face. "Why did you do that?" she asked.

It was time to hide his feelings. Feelings he didn't understand. Levi grinned at her. "Doesn't everyone seal their friendship with a kiss?" He rubbed her cheeks with his thumbs, then released her face.

When she didn't answer, he forced a chuckle. "Come on, we don't want to keep everyone waiting." He picked up the book and present.

She didn't move, just continued staring at him as if she was in shock. Had that been her first kiss? Or had it affected her the way it had him?

Levi handed her the present and then moved to her side. He placed his hand in the small of her back and gently steered her toward the party. Levi took them back the way they'd come, and as soon as they rounded the corner, Hannah hurried to Millie.

"I'm so glad you could make it." Hannah turned her smile on him. "Hello, Levi. I believe your mother and the ladies are waiting for you over there." A teasing twinkle filled her eyes.

He looked to where she pointed and saw his mother with the three brides. They didn't rush to his side so he turned his attention back to Hannah.

Hiding the book behind his back, Levi said, "I wanted to ask you if you've read Robert Louis Stevenson's book, *The Strange Case of Dr. Jekyll and Mr. Hyde?*"

Hannah laughed. "That book just came out last year. It will probably be another year or two before it gets out this far."

He rocked back on his boot heels. "I wouldn't say that."

An excited gleam filled her face and eyes. "You have it?"

Levi laughed. "I do, but if you want to read it you have to help me juggle these brides today." He hooked a thumb over his shoulder.

Millie stood quietly looking at the ground. He wondered what she was thinking, but didn't have time to ask. She still seemed a little dazed by the kiss they'd shared.

Hannah squealed like a newborn pig. "Seriously, you have it? I've wanted to read it ever since I read about it in the papers. Of course, I'll help you." She turned to Millie and asked, "Have you ever read Mr. Stevenson's book *Treasure Island?*"

Millie shook her head no.

"I have a copy. I'll loan it to you, but I want it back. He's one of my favorite authors." A laugh bubbled up in her throat. "My favorite author changes from day to day, but he really is good. I loved *Treasure Island.*"

Levi enjoyed reading Stevenson, too, and was just lucky that someone had come through Austin last month with a copy to sell. Carolyn Moore, at the general store, had nabbed it up for the schoolteacher, Mr. Richards, but when Levi had seen it, he'd talked her into selling it to him.

"I hope you don't mind if I join you, but I heard you talking about books and, well, I thought I might join in."

Levi looked to his left and saw that it was Anna Mae Leland who had joined them. Of the three mail-order brides, she was the quietest. He smiled at her. "Not at all, we were just discussing the works of Robert Louis Stevenson."

"Have any of you read *Prince Otto?*" she asked, smiling at Hannah and Millie.

Hannah was the first to answer. "I have. I borrowed a copy from a friend. It was good, but I preferred the action of *Treasure Island.*"

"I have to agree with Hannah. The action in *Treasure Island* was more interesting than the romance in *Prince Otto.*" Levi smiled at the ladies.

"What about you, Millie?" Anna Mae asked.

Millie shook her head no, once more. "I haven't read a lot of fiction."

Hannah laughed. "That's okay. Do you still study art books?"

Levi listened to the ladies as they talked. His gaze scanned the crowds of people, and he realized his mother had invited almost the whole town.

He scooted closer to Millie and eased the book into her bag. No one seemed to notice as he stepped back into his spot. Millie's puzzled look captured his attention. She looked from him to the bag as if to ask what he was doing. Levi simply winked at her. He'd loan Hannah the book but wanted to ensure she'd help him with the ladies.

Millie jerked her gaze from his face and seemed to focus on Hannah and Anna Mae's conversation. He wondered what the trip home would be like. Levi didn't have long to worry about it because Susanna Marsh and Emily Rodgers joined them.

For a brief moment he wondered what Susanna Marsh was doing at the ranch. He'd thought she wouldn't be there. Levi felt sure his mother had something to do with Susanna's sudden arrival. He decided not to worry about it and just try to get through the evening.

He nodded in all the right places and answered their questions about his favorite authors and books he'd read. He was very aware that Millie watched him and grinned as each mail-order bride tried to gain his attention by asking a new question or making a comment about how they had so much in common. It seemed that she'd forgotten about the kiss and now enjoyed being there.

He loved books, but at the moment he'd rather be alone with Millie, talking about her art and planning the next project they would do together. What was wrong with him? He had three women who had come to Granite to marry him, and here he was mooning over a woman who came to Granite to tell him she didn't want him at all.

"If you will excuse us, Millie and I are going to go put this gift away so that she doesn't have to continue holding it." Hannah grinned at him and turned Millie toward the gift table that stood on the other side of the lawn.

If the mail-order brides saw the grin, none of them acted like it. He heard Hannah's giggle and thought to himself, if that woman didn't hurry back soon and rescue him from the brides, she wasn't getting her hands on his copy of *The Strange Case of Dr. Jekyll and Mr. Hyde*.

Chapter Eleven

Millie couldn't get Levi's kiss out of her mind. She tried to focus on what Hannah said, but couldn't. Her gaze kept returning to him. She made a quick involuntary appraisal of his features. An undeniable bond was building between them. Every time she wrenched herself away from the ridiculous preoccupation of his face, something pulled her attention back to him.

As she studied Levi across the yard, Millie relived the kiss. She could almost smell the sweet scent of wood and earth that made up the essence of Levi. Her heart began to hammer in her chest. Her fingers reached up to touch her lips. She could still feel the warmth of his mouth against hers. His strong arms had held her tight but comfortably so.

Millie mentally shook herself. She tried to reason out why she felt charmed by Levi. The kiss had taken her by surprise. That had to be the reason she continued to dwell on it. And it had been her first kiss. Did kissing always leave one feeling breathless and dazed?

Hannah's urgent voice pulled her from her musings. "Millie? Millie."

She jerked her gaze from Levi and the three brides who surrounded him to Hannah. "I'm sorry, I was distracted. What did you say?"

"I asked if you wanted to go inside and get the book now or wait until you and Levi are about to leave? But it occurs to me that you might be more interested in staying out here and guarding him." Hannah arched her eyebrows and looked in Levi's direction.

Millie felt like a schoolgirl who'd just gotten caught passing a note. Heat filled her face, and she lowered her eyes.

"You like him," Hannah accused in a soft whisper.

Millie raised her head. "Not in the way you are suggesting." She looked to where the women circled about Levi like buzzards around a fresh kill. Millie realized how unkind that thought sounded toward the brides. "I just feel sorry for him, that's all."

Hannah picked up a cookie from the dessert table that they stood beside. "Why would you feel sorry for Levi? He's successful and has three women who want to marry him. What more could a man want?"

"His freedom and a mother who isn't a meddler." Millie realized she'd spoken her thought out loud and clasped a hand over her mouth. "I shouldn't have said that since it really is none of my business." She looked about, praying no one else had heard her, especially Levi's mother or brother.

Hannah smiled at her and placed her arm around Millie's waist. Her whispered voice filled Millie's ears. "I know from your perspective that it looks like Bonnie is a cold woman who is trying to force Levi into marriage. But I know her, Millie, and she really just wants what's best for her boys." She hugged Millie and then released her to reach for another cookie.

Millie wanted to argue, but she really didn't know Bonnie. For that matter, she really didn't know Levi, either. Her gaze moved back to where he stood with the three brides. No, she didn't really know him, but she did know that she'd enjoyed his kiss, and that was dangerous.

It was time he chose a wife and stopped kissing her. She looked to Hannah, who was studying her as if she were a student who needed directions. "What kind of cookies are you are gobbling down?"

Startled, Hannah looked at the half-eaten cookie in her hand. "This one is oatmeal raisin."

"Well, scoot over. I want to try one and then I want to go get that book you are so keen on." Millie smiled to let Hannah know she was teasing. Outside of being her teacher, Hannah really didn't know Millie, either. And yet, they felt like old friends.

Hannah laughed and moved to the side so Millie could grab a couple of cookies. "I think you will like this book, Millie."

Millie nodded her agreement. "I'm sure I will, too." She felt as if someone was watching them and turned around to look.

Bonnie Westland stood with a group of women. She lifted a hand and waved to Millie. Maybe Hannah was right. Maybe she was letting her feelings for her own mother cloud her judgment of Levi's mother.

Millie waved back and then looped her arm in Hannah's. "Are you going to show me that book or not?" It was time to put Levi, his mother and the mail-order brides from her mind and get to know Hannah better.

As they walked toward the house, Millie glanced over her shoulder and discovered Levi watching her. Warmth filled her lips once more as if he had kissed her from where he stood. Millie turned back around and silently prayed that whatever emotions she was feeling about Levi and his kisses would go away.

Levi had never been so ready for one man to open his birthday presents as he was right now. The brides had talked to him about everything from armadillos to zippers. They had a topic for everything under the sun and he was tired of giving his opinion on all of them.

Everyone sat about the yard on blankets and quilts while Daniel stood beside a table opening gifts. Hannah sat at his right with a pad of paper and a pencil jotting down gifts and putting the name of the giver beside it. He was sure she'd be handing out thank-you notes next Sunday morning at church.

Daniel handed Hannah a light blue shirt that he'd just opened. "Thank you, Mrs. Marsh." He looked toward their blanket and nodded.

"You're welcome." She called back and then in a lower voice said to Levi, "It took me a couple of days, but I managed to get it finished before today."

Susanna sat on Levi's right and Anna Mae on his left. "It's very nice," he offered. Thankfully, Susanna hadn't been insistent on his attention. She'd simply joined in the conversation where she could.

Next, Daniel opened a book of poetry. He thanked Miss Leland and Miss Rodgers for the book. Both ladies told him he was welcome, and Daniel moved on to the next gifts.

Levi looked for Emily in the direction he'd heard her

voice come from. He found her sitting on a quilt a little away from them with Millie. The two ladies seemed to be in deep conversation.

Millie's light blond hair and Emily's brown were so close together that they almost looked like one person. He knew Emily enjoyed cooking and was the oldest of twelve and that Millie hadn't shown an interest in cooking and was an only child. So what had they found in common?

Did it matter? Not really. Still, they seemed so different and yet of the three brides, Emily was the one he'd choose, if it came down to it. She loved to cook, seemed humble in her dealings with others and had a sense of humor. He'd noticed several times throughout the day, various children had spent time with her and enjoyed her company.

His gaze moved to Millie. If she would marry him, he'd forget all about the other brides, including Emily. Millie seemed to bring sunshine with her when she entered a room. He loved her creative side and when he'd kissed her, it had been a wonderful feeling of warmth and… Levi stopped his thoughts there. No, it wasn't love. It wasn't a special attachment. He wouldn't allow it to be.

He returned his attention to Daniel and the opening of gifts. Daniel thanked each person as he made his way through the massive pile. Levi knew his brother was embarrassed with all the attention he was receiving and wondered, not for the first time, why his mother had insisted on giving him a birthday party. After all, he was thirty-four years old; if he had been turning thirty-five or forty it would have made sense.

Thinking of his mother, Levi scanned the crowd for

her. She sat between her friends, Bertha and Opal. A smile brightened her face as she looked in his direction. He saw the love of a mother in her eyes.

A gasp sounded throughout the crowd, and Levi looked back to see what Daniel had just opened. His brother held the picture he and Millie had created. "Levi and Millie, this is great."

Levi knew the moment Daniel remembered seeing something like it when they were in Austin several years ago. Daniel stared at the picture with a wide grin on his face.

Levi turned to look at Millie once more and saw the scowl on her face. What was it that had upset her?

Daniel recaptured his attention when he said, "Thank you both."

He nodded and Millie offered a soft "you're welcome." Levi glanced once more at Millie. The look on her face said she wasn't happy with him. But what could she be unhappy about? That he'd put her name on the card, too?

"Millie helped you make that?" Anna Mae's soft voice asked. She seemed to be looking between him and Millie.

Levi nodded. "Yes, she drew the horse head and showed me how to make it stand out on the board."

A soft smile graced Anna Mae's lips. "I like it. Do you think she could draw a hummingbird?" she asked.

"I'm sure she can. Millie is very talented." Levi realized he might have been too quick to praise Millie. "But you'll have to ask her to be sure."

"Thank you, I believe I will. That really is beautiful."

Before he could respond further, Daniel opened the last gift and then announced that cake and punch were being served. He indicated everyone should go to the tables and help themselves.

Levi pushed up from the blanket. He wanted to talk to Millie, but saw that others were already headed her way. Anna Mae stood also and was walking toward Millie.

A gentle throat-clearing drew his attention to Susanna. She held up her hand, silently asking for assistance to stand. Once Susanna was standing beside him she asked in a quiet voice, "Levi, is there something between you and Millie that the rest of us should know about?"

Her question took him by surprise. "I don't think so. Why do you ask?"

For a brief moment, Levi realized he was seeing the true Susanna Marsh. Her clear blue eyes looked into his. "Because I came here to get married, but if your heart is already spoken for…"

Levi interrupted her. "No, my heart is still my own." He smiled to take the sting out of the words.

Another soft clearing of the throat snagged his attention. He turned to find Millie, Emily, Anna Mae and half the town of Granite standing behind him. From the looks on most of their faces, they'd overheard his conversation with Susanna.

Millie spoke first. "Levi, it seems we have a lot of people who want pictures similar to our gift to Daniel."

He looked at the crowd that stood in front of them and felt Susanna slip her hand into the crook of his arm.

"I will be happy to take orders for whatever you'd like us to make," he said, "but Millie has to agree to sketch it first. I'm no artist and she is."

Martin Crow stood behind his wife. "What would

such a thing cost a man?" he asked, looking unhappy at the possibility of a new expense.

Levi gently untangled his arm from Susanna's. "Tell Millie what you'd like, see if she can draw it and I'll figure out the expense."

He had to do some fast calculations but came up with an affordable price that would pay for the supplies and Millie's time. Millie grinned across at him. Levi assumed she was no longer angry with him for putting her name on the card.

For the rest of the afternoon, Millie talked to various families and friends about the pictures they'd like for her to sketch and give to Levi so that he could make the wooden pictures for their homes. Hannah supplied Millie with a piece of paper and a pencil to list who wanted what. So far she had orders for a hummingbird, four dogs, three cats, a tulip, a rose, and an eagle. She'd promised to look at the family's dogs and cats to capture their images.

Millie still wasn't pleased that Levi had put her name on the birthday card with his. Levi had made them look like a couple. But thanks to Susanna's question, they now resembled business partners.

"Looks like you have your work cut out for you," Susanna said as she sat down beside Millie.

"I agree," Millie answered, looking over the list once more. She looked up and caught Susanna studying her. "You did a nice job on Daniel's shirt."

"Thank you. Now that I've bought the Sewing Room, I can make clothes faster. Mrs. Duffey sold me her sewing machine."

She twisted her hands in her lap.

"You really bought the Sewing Room?" Millie asked.

A nervous smile touched Susanna's lips. "I did. Mr. Duffey gave me the keys today."

"How exciting." Millie gave her a big hug. "I'm so happy for you."

Even as she rejoiced in Susanna's happiness, Millie wondered how the widow had been able to come up with the money. Had Levi helped her?

"Thank you."

Millie released Susanna and began gathering up her things. The sun was slipping down, and Levi had mentioned that he was about ready to leave. Other families from town had already packed up and headed back.

She both looked forward to the ride back to the boardinghouse and dreaded it. So much had happened today. He'd kissed her and they'd become solid business partners. Millie wasn't sure how comfortable she felt with Levi now that things had changed between them.

"Would you mind if I ride back to town with you?" Susanna asked, picking up her own blanket and folding it. "Mrs. Westland said I should see if Levi will take me home so that none of the ranch hands will have to take another trip to town, but I thought I'd ask you instead. She really wasn't pleased that I had asked Mr. Tucker to bring me out this morning."

Did she mind? Millie wasn't sure. On one hand, she wanted to be alone with Levi so they could talk about the pictures, but on the other hand she still felt nervous since he'd kissed her. Would he kiss her again if they were alone?

She realized she hadn't answered Susanna. "Of course not. I'm sure it will be fine with Levi, too."

"Oh, are you sure he won't mind? I didn't realize

you came together. I just thought you'd arrived at the same time."

Millie couldn't help but hear the disappointment in Susanna's voice. Was she disappointed that Levi had driven her to the ranch? Or disappointed that he would be with them on the return back to town?

"Won't mind what?" Levi asked.

"If I return to town with you and Millie," Susanna answered.

Millie felt him look at her and saw disappointment in his eyes. Was he disappointed because they wouldn't be returning alone? Or because she'd answered for him instead of letting him have the final say?

"That will be fine," Levi answered. "If you ladies are ready, I'd like to get started back before it gets too dark."

Susanna nodded. "Thank you. I need to get my bags from the house. I'll be living in town from now on." She turned and headed around to the front of the house.

Millie shrugged and followed. Levi fell into step beside her. She whispered out of the side of her mouth, "I'm sorry, Levi. I didn't know what else to say. It was your mother's idea."

He sighed. "I'm sure it was."

She felt the warmth of his hand in the small of her back before he said, "Hold on a moment, I almost forgot something."

When Millie stopped, he reached into her bag and pulled out the copy of *The Strange Case of Dr. Jekyll and Mr. Hyde*. "I promised Hannah she could read it, even though she didn't uphold her end of the bargain." He winked before turning to leave.

She watched him return to the backyard with the book and then proceeded to follow Susanna. Levi Westland was a very interesting and handsome man. Millie couldn't help but like him—as a friend only, of course.

Susanna stood on the front porch with several large cases and a couple of boxes. Millie wondered what Levi would think about packing and unpacking Mrs. Marsh. She giggled. The trip back would be interesting.

Chapter Twelve

Levi listened to Susanna all the way back to town.
She told him how excited she was to be able to have the
Sewing Room and if he chose her as a wife, it would be
another business he could add to his already growing
collection. He noticed Millie sat quietly on the other
side of Susanna.

He'd hoped to sit beside Millie, but Susanna had been
faster. Or maybe Millie had hung back saying goodbye
to Hannah so that the mail-order bride could sit by him.
Thankfully, Susanna's rosewater had evaporated some
and wasn't as overpowering as normal.

"I'm staying at the Sewing Room now," Susanna
happily informed him as they came into town. "I'm not
ready to open for business yet but can live there while
I make more dresses to sell."

He set the brake in front of the store and hopped
down from the wagon. First, he helped Susanna down
and then hurried to the other side to assist Millie. She
was already halfway down so he slipped his hands
around her narrow waist and assisted her the rest of
the way.

A little squeal escaped her throat before her feet touched the ground. "Levi Westland, don't you ever do that again. You scared ten years off my life," Millie scolded.

He leaned forward and whispered in her ear, "Oh good. Now you are closer to my age and we can get married." Levi had the satisfaction of seeing her blue eyes grow wide in the dimming light.

Susanna was already at the door. "Millie, come in and see what I've already done to the place." She lit a lantern from inside the door and led them inside.

If the widow had noticed their interaction beside the wagon, she didn't show it. Levi followed Millie. Shadows flickered about the empty room.

"I've converted the storage room into a bedroom," Susanna said as she opened a door off to the side. "See?"

Levi looked over Millie's shoulder. The light scent of lavender wafted up to him. The room was bare except a small cot and chest. A kerosene lamp sat on the floor beside the cot.

"What do you think? I know it's not much to look at now, but it's a start," Susanna said behind them.

Millie looked about the empty space. "I think you can make something wonderful out of this. Have you thought about ordering a few store-bought dresses to get your business started?"

"I have, but they cost so much I just can't afford them right now." Susanna stood with her hands in front of her. Now she looked a little uncomfortable. It was obvious there was no place for them to sit and she had nothing more to show them.

Millie offered a soft smile. "It takes time to get a business started. Congratulations again on buying your building." She turned to him. "I think I'll walk to the boardinghouse."

He saw the look in her eyes. She expected him to protest. Levi knew it was a test of his will not to tell her what to do. "All right."

With her head held high, Millie walked to the door. "Thank you for showing me your new store, Susanna. I'll be buying dresses from you before either of us knows it," Millie said and then left.

Levi started to follow Millie out the door.

Susanna's voice stopped him. "Levi, can I ask you a question?"

The question ran through his mind: What would she ask? The only way to find out was to consent, so he nodded. Levi really wished Millie hadn't left so quickly.

"I hope you don't think this is improper, but I would like to know what my chances are of becoming your wife." Susanna walked closer to him.

The smell of roses filled the air between them. He wasn't sure how to answer her, so asked for clarification. "What do you mean?"

She sighed. "If you had to choose a wife right here, right now, who would you choose?"

"I'm not sure. I really haven't spent enough time with Emily and Anna Mae." That was a true enough answer without hurting her feelings.

"What about me? Have you spent enough time with me to know if I am possible wife material?"

He hedged. "I think you will make some man a good wife someday." Levi inched closer to the door. He didn't want to hurt her feelings and say he wouldn't be marrying her.

"But not you."

Levi sighed. He'd been doing that a lot today. "Tell me, Susanna. What do you want in a husband?"

Millie held her breath as she waited for Susanna's answer. She'd stopped just outside the store door when she'd heard Susanna ask Levi if she could ask him a question. Millie knew she was prying in their business but couldn't seem to stop herself from listening. Pressing her ear against the wall, she wondered why Susanna hadn't answered.

Susanna finally answered. "I want a man like my Robert. Strong, confident and who will love me unconditionally."

The sound of boots crossing the room filled Millie's ears. Thankfully, Levi stopped before exiting the store. She eased back to the corner of the building. If she listened real close, Millie thought she might hear his reply.

Levi said in a low voice, "Then no, you aren't the bride for me. You see, Susanna, I can't love unconditionally. I'm not sure I can love at all."

The screen door shut behind him. Millie ducked back into the darkness of the building. Poor Susanna. Levi's words must have cut her to the core. She heard him click his tongue and send the horses to the livery.

Millie crept to the window and looked inside. Susanna stood staring at the closed door. The lantern lit her face enough for Millie to see that the widow was smiling.

As she hurried to the boardinghouse, Millie kept asking herself, why had Susanna been smiling? Did she not want to marry Levi? Or had she gotten pleasure from hearing the sorrow in his voice?

The bell jingled over the door as she stepped inside.

Beth came from the sitting room. "I'm glad you are home. How was your day? Did Daniel like his gift? Where is Levi?"

"Let her in here, Beth. The rest of us want to know, too," Mrs. Englebright called.

Millie and Beth shared a laugh. She laid her bag on the entry table and then walked past Beth to the sitting room. Mrs. Englebright was in her usual seat by the fireplace and Mr. Lupin sat on the footstool. Mark was playing with two wooden cars under the piano. She walked over to the sofa and sank into the soft cushions.

"Hello, everyone. Let me answer Beth's questions first and then if you have any you want to ask, I'll be happy to answer them, as well."

Both Mrs. Englebright and Mr. Lupin nodded. Beth sat down beside her on the sofa.

"My day was long but fun. Daniel loved his gift, as did everyone else, and Levi took the wagon back to the livery."

Mrs. Englebright asked, "What do you mean as did everyone else?"

Millie told them about the party and the orders she and Levi had taken for more pictures. She noticed that Mr. Lupin was taking notes in his reporter's pad and wondered if the party would make tomorrow's news. Millie also told the ladies about Susanna Marsh buying the Sewing Room.

"I hate to see the Duffeys leave, but I'm glad someone will be opening the Sewing Room back up." Mrs. Englebright yawned and stood. "I'm tired. I think I'll call it a night."

The bell over the front door sounded, and Beth walked to the door to see who had entered. She called good-night to Levi and then came back into the room. "Mark, it's time we get ready for bed, too."

"Aw, Ma." Mark came out from under the piano.

"Don't sass me, young man." Beth took the little boy's hand and pulled him toward the door.

Millie stood. "I'm ready to head to bed, too."

Mr. Lupin turned the lamp down and followed the rest of them out of the room. Beth stopped and locked the front door before heading to her and Mark's rooms. Millie pulled her bag over her shoulder and proceeded upstairs.

Mr. Lupin stopped her. "Miss Millie, I was wondering if you'd like to go on a picnic with me tomorrow afternoon."

At first Millie didn't know what to say, but reason entered her mind and she answered, "I'm sorry, Mr. Lupin. I really need to get started on these drawings." She patted the bag that held her sketch pad and the paper with her list in it.

He nodded. "I see. Well, you can't blame a man for trying." Then he turned and opened the door to his room.

Millie shook her head and entered her room. First she'd been proposed to, then she'd been kissed, then she'd witnessed Susanna's odd behavior, and now she'd been invited on an outing by a fellow male boarder. She flopped back on her bed and let her hands hang over the edge. What a day.

Levi paced his room. He'd meant to go see everyone when he returned to the boardinghouse, but after speaking with Susanna, he just didn't have the desire to face them all. She'd made it very plain what the brides were looking for: unconditional love.

He couldn't give that. Unconditional love meant that he'd love her no matter what happened. Levi groaned as he pulled his boots off. He couldn't even promise pretend love.

His proposal to Millie had been a flop. He didn't think she was looking for love. Maybe if he gave her more time she'd reconsider his proposal. What he needed was a friend, someone he could talk to about anything. Levi walked to his window and opened it. The sound of the swing squeaking caught his attention.

The wind wasn't up so the porch swing shouldn't be moving. Curiosity got the better of him and he padded out his door and down the stairs to the front. Careful not to ring the bell over the door, Levi eased outside to see if anyone was on the porch.

Moonlight washed the porch revealing Millie. Her legs were pulled up under her and the swing gently swayed. "It's just me, Levi. You might want to oil this thing in the morning."

"I take it I'm not your first visitor?" He sat down on the swing and gave it a gentle push.

She giggled. "No, Beth and Mr. Lupin have both been out to investigate." Millie laid her head back and her hair fell across the railing.

It resembled liquid honey. The desire to reach out and touch it tickled Levi's fingertips. He didn't think she'd take kindly to that so he casually rested his arm along the back of the bench. "Can't sleep?" he asked.

"It was a little warm in my room tonight so I came out for some fresh air." She pulled her legs out from under her and leaned forward.

Her hair spilled over his arm. It reminded him of a silk material he'd touched once as a kid. He missed its softness almost immediately. "You don't have to leave on my account."

Millie swung her legs to the other side and pulled them back up. "I wasn't. Since you are out here, I thought I'd sit where I can face you." She turned her body slightly and did just that.

With her hair flowing about her, Millie looked younger. The ponytail she always wore seemed to add age to her heart-shaped face. She was young enough to want love but didn't seem to crave it like some women her age did. Levi didn't know if she was more mature than most or if she just simply didn't know what she wanted yet.

"You seem to have a question on your lips, Levi." She smiled, and her whole face seemed to light up in the moonlight.

He laughed softly. "I suppose I do."

"Is it a question I can answer?" Fine eyebrows arched upward. He wondered if she'd learned that trick from Hannah.

"Do all women want love when they marry?"

Millie played with the ribbon on her housedress. "I suppose not all of them do."

"What about you? Do you want to fall in love and get married?" He held his breath as he waited for her answer.

She cleared her throat. "If you had asked me that question last summer, I would have said yes. But not anymore."

He looked up at the moon. The stars tried to compete with its light, but failed miserably tonight. Had a boy hurt her? He wanted to ask but didn't.

"Levi, when I was sixteen I wanted Joe Ferguson to notice me so bad that I even flirted with other men to catch his attention, but then one night I overheard my parents talking. My mother had already warned his mother that he was not to try to get too close to me. And that explained why he didn't. She told Papa she had bigger plans for me. It was then I realized how much she controlled my life." Millie stopped talking. She seemed to have realized she'd revealed more of herself than she'd meant to.

His gaze searched hers. "Did you really love Joe?" Levi asked, not liking the idea of Millie being in love with the boy.

A sad smile graced her lips. "I don't think so. I realized that I wasn't as upset about Joe as I was about my mother taking over something that should have been my decision, something big."

Levi nodded. Now he truly understood why Millie hated her mother's controlling ways. "Did you ever confront her?"

Shock filled her features. "No."

"Why not? You don't seem to have trouble confronting people now."

Millie sighed. "She's my mother, Levi. I respect her." The ribbons found their way into her hands and attention again.

Levi reached over and tucked her hair behind her ear so he could see her face and eyes. "You know, I believe you can respect someone and still be honest with them when they hurt you." Levi pushed off the swing. It squeaked as he walked to the door.

The swing swayed and squeaked again. "Levi?"

He stopped and turned toward her. "Yes?"

Millie walked over to him. She reached up and put both hands on his cheeks. She stood on her tiptoes and then slowly her lips came into contact with his. It was a brief kiss that spoke volumes of warmth and caring to Levi.

When she released him, Millie said, "I'm sure there is someone out there who doesn't expect you to love them unconditionally. You just have to keep looking for her." She slipped around him and went inside.

Was she talking about herself? His mind couldn't wrap around anything right now; all he could think of was the soft scent of lavender and the warmth of her soft lips on his.

He smiled.

Millie Hamilton might not know it yet, but Levi felt certain she was the woman for him. They could be best of friends without losing their hearts to each other—at least that was his prayer as he entered the boarding-house.

Chapter Thirteen

Levi wasn't surprised at all to discover that Millie had skipped breakfast the next morning. She was probably embarrassed that she'd kissed him. That kiss had kept him up most of the night trying to figure out how to get Millie to admit that they were good enough friends they could get married and live happily ever after without falling in love.

He picked up his Bible and headed off to church. Sunday was his favorite day of the week, mainly because nothing much was expected of him. Levi hoped Millie was already there so he could sit by her.

"Good morning, Levi." Jonah Richards fell into step beside him.

Levi returned the schoolteacher's greeting. "How are you this morning, Jonah?"

There seemed to be a lively bounce in Jonah's steps. "I'm good. Very good." He grinned at Levi. "I'm moving back to Boston as soon as the school year is out."

They had never been close friends, but Levi could honestly say he was going to miss the schoolteacher. "That's bad news for Granite and its children."

"Nice of you to say, but I'm sure another teacher will come along soon."

That was true enough. Levi's thoughts went to Anna Mae. He was sure she'd like to offer her teaching services to the town of Granite. Levi made a mental note to mention it to her, should he see the mail-order brides today.

They entered the church just as the first song began. Levi looked about the small church but saw no sign of Millie. Disappointed, he took a seat in the back beside Jonah.

From this vantage point, he could see everyone. Two of the brides and his mother sat on the right hand side of the pulpit. He didn't see Susanna in the church. His gaze moved to the left and he saw Beth, Mark, Mrs. Englebright and Mr. Lupin sitting in their usual places.

Had Susanna and Millie made plans to meet during the services? Levi didn't think so. Was Millie still avoiding him because of their shared kiss? Again, he didn't think so. She'd initiated the kiss, not him.

He spent the remainder of the service trying to stay focused on the minister's message. He found it hard to do as his mind wandered off. Where was Millie? Where was Susanna? Why were the ladies absent from services? Was Millie off sketching someplace instead of attending services? If so, could he marry a woman who put off Sunday mornings to draw? The questions jumbled in his mind like sawdust on a damp floor.

Maybe he should focus on Emily and Anna Mae instead of Millie. Even if he married Millie with the understanding it would be in name only, Levi expected his wife to be a God-fearing woman who attended church.

Just before the service was over, the preacher announced that Mr. Richards was resigning at the end of the school year and that the school board would be looking for a new schoolteacher. Levi saw Anna Mae sit up straighter.

When they were dismissed, Levi stood and waited for his mother and the brides to join him. He knew there was no way to avoid having lunch with them today. Levi silently prayed. *Lord, please help me stay focused. Millie seems to occupy my every thought and if I am to choose a bride from one of these two ladies, I need to get to know them better.*

Millie felt horrible. Her nose had finally quit running, but her head throbbed as if a hammer pounded away at it. She slipped into a simple day dress and went in search of Beth.

It was a little after lunchtime so she knew Beth would either be in the kitchen or her private quarters. As she passed the sitting room, she heard laughter. Millie looked in the room and saw Levi sitting on the couch. Anna Mae sat on one side of him and Emily on the other. His mother reclined across from them in Mrs. Englebright's favorite chair, looking very pleased.

She hurried on, not wanting Levi to see her. Millie knew she looked a mess. Her hair stuck out in all angles, her eyes were watery and bloodshot from lack of sleep and her nose was red rimmed from all the blowing it had required earlier.

Thankfully when she entered the kitchen she found Beth sitting at the table looking over a cookbook and Mark playing with a set of blocks at his mother's feet. "I hope I'm not disturbing you," she offered by way of greeting. The hoarseness of her voice and the pain from the effort of speaking shocked her.

Beth looked up. "Not at all. Are you all right?" She hurried to Millie's side.

Mark looked up with a frown on his face. "Have you been crying, Miss Millie?"

Even though it hurt to speak, Millie knew she had to answer. "No. I think I may have developed a spring cold or I've come into contact with something I'm allergic to." Millie felt a little feverish and wished she'd stayed in her room as Beth walked with her to the table.

"Would you like something to eat?" Beth asked. "I have chicken, mashed potatoes and green beans on the warmer."

Her nerves had been so high-strung the night before, she'd skipped dinner and this morning she'd missed breakfast. "Maybe just a few potatoes, thank you." Since they were mashed, she reasoned they wouldn't hurt as bad going down.

"And a glass of iced tea?" Beth asked as she dished up the food for Millie.

"Iced tea sounds wonderful." Millie rested her head in her hands. Having one's elbows on the table wasn't polite, but right now Millie didn't feel very well-mannered.

"Here you go." Beth set the food and tea in front of her. "Is your head hurting again?"

"Yes, but I'm hoping that once I eat it will stop." Millie took a sip from the tea. The cold moisture slid down her sore throat, easing some of the pain but not all.

"Ma? May I go play in the backyard?" Mark asked, watching both women.

"Yes, but stay close to the house."

Mark gathered his blocks. "I will."

As soon as the screen door slammed shut behind the little boy, Beth turned to Millie. "Did you happen to look in the sitting room on your way here?"

Millie nodded and took a small bite of potatoes. They tore down her throat like gravel in a windstorm. She lowered her spoon, swallowed hard and grabbed up her drink.

"Then you know he brought his mother and those two ladies for lunch today." Beth went to the counter and retrieved the tea pitcher.

So Levi had brought them home for lunch. Maybe he'd decided to be sensible and choose a wife from one of the mail-order brides after all. The thought bothered her, but Millie decided she was being oversensitive because she didn't feel well. "That's nice," she answered as Beth refilled her glass.

"You don't really believe that, do you?"

It hurt to talk, but Millie could tell Beth was in a talkative mood. "I do. Levi needs a wife."

"Yes, but why not you? I can see that you like him and he likes you. I know it's not true love now, but after the wedding you'll have the rest of your lives to fall in love."

Millie tried to use as few words as possible. "I don't want to fall in love."

Shock filled Beth's voice and face. "Whyever not?" she demanded. "You are too young to have been hurt by love."

"I don't want anyone controlling my life." Millie took a sip of tea, praying it would ease her burning throat.

"Why would you think marriage is about control?" Beth seemed truly perplexed.

"Because of my parents' marriage."

Beth folded her hands on the table. "Your father is controlling?" she asked, looking sad.

"No, my mother."

Beth's voice went up a notch in disbelief. "Your mother is controlling your father?" she asked. At Millie's nod, Beth continued. "Well, I'm sure it's not unheard of, but it is rare for the woman to be controlling in a marriage." She shook her head.

Understanding and confusion warred on Beth's face. "Are you telling me that your mother controlled you and your father, and that's why you don't want to get married?" Beth refilled Millie's glass once more.

Millie nodded even though deep down it was more complicated than that. She'd used the excuse at first and it was partially true, but the closer she got to Levi the more she realized they could work through her fears of being controlled.

But what she couldn't take back was the fact that she'd burned down Eliza Kelly's home and business and then run. No man would love a coward and an arsonist. Once Levi found out what she'd done, he'd want nothing more to do with her. Millie didn't want a broken heart and she didn't want to see the disgust she knew Levi would feel for her once he found out. The sting of tears burned her eyes.

"Oh, Millie." Beth reached out and took Millie's hands in hers. "Your parents' marriage isn't a reflection of all marriages. Sure, no marriage is perfect, but when two people love each other even the imperfections can be overlooked and oftentimes with just a conversation can be fixed."

Millie knew her friend was trying to help her through

her fear. She offered a smile and another nod. If her throat didn't hurt so badly, she'd explain that it was more complicated than that.

Beth rose from her seat. "I'm going to make you a cup of warm coffee with honey in it. That should help your throat."

"Thank you," Millie croaked out.

While she mixed up the drink, Beth talked. "When my husband and I first married, we didn't know each other at all. I married late in life and thought I'd be an old maid forever. It took a year for me to realize I'd fallen in love with him, that realization came the day I found out we were going to have Mark." She sighed and then continued. "He was a good man who worked hard." She stopped stirring the honey within the cup and looked off into the distance. "Mark has his eyes."

She brought the steaming cup to the table and placed it in front of Millie.

Millie saw the unshed tears in Beth's eyes before she turned away. "You know if you give Levi a chance, I think you'll find he's a good man, too. I'll go get you some powders for your headache." She hurried from the kitchen.

What would it be like to love a man so much that even five years after his death, you still mourned him? Millie didn't know. She didn't think she'd ever know. Even if she did love Levi, burning down Eliza's house had sealed her fate. She'd not ask a man to trust and love her until she'd made things right with Eliza.

Beth returned with the powders. "Here, take these."

"Thanks." Millie took the medicine and grimaced at the pain in her throat. She stood to return to her room. Sleep, all Millie wanted right now was to sleep.

"I'll make you some soup this afternoon. That will make your throat feel better, too. I shouldn't have kept you down here so long." Beth picked up the coffee mug and walked with Millie back to her room.

As they passed the sitting room, Millie heard laughter once more. She was glad Levi was enjoying himself and yet felt alone and left out. Which one of the brides would he choose? Emily or Anna Mae? A tug pulled at her heart.

Beth patted her on the shoulder. "I'm sure he's not having as much fun as it sounds like he is." They continued past the room and started up the stairs. "I really believe, Millie, if you will give him a chance and tell him how you really feel about being controlled, you'll find he will understand and give you the freedom you need." Beth's soft whisper offered comfort.

At the door to her room, Millie turned to her friend. "You don't have to come in with me. I'll be fine."

Beth reached around her and opened the door. "Nonsense, let's get you into bed." She set the warm cup of coffee on the bedside table.

Millie allowed Beth to coddle her. She straightened the bedsheets and then held them back for Millie to get into. Beth fluffed Millie's pillow and felt her forehead. "Thankfully you aren't running a fever."

Beth moved to the window and pulled the curtains closed. "Try to rest. I'll bring you some hot soup and iced tea later." She closed the door behind her as she left.

Millie sank deeper under the covers. Her chest ached. Was it because of her cold? Or was a small part of her heart breaking because she knew there would be no future with Levi?

She closed her eyes and allowed the tears to flow.

The remembered soft words of her mother came to her: *This, too, shall pass.* Yes, but would she come away with a broken heart?

Chapter Fourteen

The month of August slipped into September. Levi could feel the pressure of having to choose a bride. He was one tired cowboy. Entertaining Emily and Anna Mae was hard work. They were both nice women, but they weren't right for him. Levi knew enough now to understand that he'd have to be good friends with a woman to live with her for the rest of his life.

He needed someone with interests similar to his—someone like Millie. After her sick spell, Millie had given him three new drawings to convert into pictures. Nothing more was said about him teaching her how to make the wooden pictures.

She had built some type of wall between them. Millie had been quiet around him but pleasant. They spent most evenings in the sitting room with the other boarders.

Millie continued her drawing lessons with Mark. The little boy proved to have talent of his own. She spent time teaching Mrs. Englebright the piano. But where he was concerned, they were two people living under the same roof, nothing more.

Tonight, Levi felt weary to the bone. He'd just finished helping the Browns finish up their barn, but he pasted on a smile as he entered the sitting room.

He cleared his throat to get everyone's attention. "I have exciting news."

Mark ran to him, his eyes shining. "We're getting a dog?"

Levi ran his hand over the boy's head. He needed to look into getting Mark a pup, but maybe when he was a bit older. "No. Not this time."

"Well, don't keep us in suspense, Levi," Mrs. Englebright chided. "Tell us your good news."

"Not 'my' good news," he drawled. "'Our' good news." He almost laughed out loud at their eagerness to hear something other than the humdrum happenings in their daily lives. "The Browns have decided to have a barn dance next week to celebrate the finish of their barn." He finished with a flourish.

"Oh, I do love an old-fashion barn dance." Mrs. Englebright clapped her hands together, almost knocking the quilt she worked on into the floor.

"Me, too," Beth added.

Mr. Lupin nodded his agreement. "It should be a fun event. One I can cover in the newspaper."

Levi walked over and took Millie's hand in his. She looked up at him with big blue eyes. Her heart-shaped face wore a frown. Still, he pressed on. "Millie, will you do me the honor of going to the dance with me?"

For a brief moment, he saw a flicker of excitement, joy or something happy within her eyes. Just as quickly, Millie shut down the emotion. "I'm sorry, Levi. I don't know how to dance. Why don't you ask Anna Mae or Emily? I'm sure one of them will know how."

He didn't detect any meanness in her voice. Millie simply thought one of the other two women would be better suited for the dance. Levi didn't agree. "I'll teach you," he said, choosing not to comment on the other mail-order brides.

Millie tried to pull her hand from his. "I don't think that's such a good idea. Papa tried to teach me once and he swore I broke his big toe by stepping on it so many times."

Levi laughed. "He just wasn't prepared. Now that you've told me about it, I'll make sure to keep my toes out of your way." He applied pressure to pull her up from her seat.

"Oh, go on, Millie. It will be fun," Mrs. Englebright encouraged.

"Now?" Millie protested. "But there isn't any music."

Mrs. Englebright lay her quilting aside and pushed herself up out of the chair. "This is as good a time as any to practice my piano playing."

She sat down on the bench and began plinking at the keys. Mr. Lupin laughed and walked over to Beth. "Might I have this dance?" he asked.

Beth stood and curtsied. "Why yes, yes, you can."

Levi watched Millie's face as Beth and Mr. Lupin danced about the room. The longing to join them was there in her eyes. He reached down and took her other hand in his.

Millie allowed him to pull her up.

Levi placed her hand on his shoulder and then held the other one tightly. "It's easy, you'll see. Just follow my lead."

She nodded and watched their feet as they moved.

Levi lifted her chin. "Just let me lead."

Millie went stiff.

Beth laughed. "You look like a stone statue I saw at a museum once, Millie. Relax."

Embarrassment and frustration laced her voice. "I'm trying." She stepped on Levi's toe and more laughter filled the room.

She jerked away, stumbling backward. He caught her around the waist and held tight. Millie giggled. "I'm going to fall flat on my face, just wait and see," she said breathlessly, looking up into his eyes. "Thanks for not letting that happen this time."

"Oh, you still might," Levi teased as he lifted her up.

Her features became more animated, and she clutched at his shoulders, but her smile broadened in approval. She trusted him. Happiness radiated from her. He liked that look. A sparkle he hadn't seen before shone in her eyes. He closed his arms around her and pulled her close. Her hair smelled of lavender, a scent he could get used to smelling every day.

"Shall I play a slower tune?" Mrs. Englebright asked.

Levi released Millie a fraction. "No, we'll get this song down first and then move to slower ones."

"I think you just enjoy catching her with those fancy moves of yours," Mr. Lupin teased.

Beth laughed. "Pay attention to your own dance, partner. You stepped on my toe." She playfully slapped him on the shoulder.

For the rest of the evening, Levi showed Millie various dance steps amid laughter and friends. He enjoyed the time Millie spent in his arms, even if it was only in the name of dancing.

As they headed to their rooms, Levi said, "Oh, yeah, Beth, I won't be here for a couple of days."

"Going on a business trip?" she asked over her shoulder.

"Nothing that fun. It's branding time. I'll be out at the ranch if you need me." He hated branding cattle, but new calves had to bear the Westland trademark.

Millie laughed at something Mrs. Englebright said.

Levi knew that over the next few days he would miss her soft laughter. What was it about Millie that so appealed to him? Besides the fact that he found her pretty, charming and engaging. Her presence wrapped around him like a warm blanket, and everything took on a clean brightness when she was near. But unlike the brides, Millie didn't fuss over her clothes, hair or manners. She didn't bat her eyes at him like a mosquito trying to get to the light. She acted like a person with a fully functioning brain. Maybe that was it—maybe she was just wholesome.

Millie missed Levi. She finished sewing up the seam of her green dress and glanced at the sitting room door for the umpteenth time that evening. When was he coming home? She didn't dare ask the other boarders because they would tease her. He'd said that he'd be gone a couple of days and it had been three. Wasn't a couple supposed to mean two?

A yawn overcame her and she covered her mouth with one hand. Millie still didn't understand why her nights had been restless since Levi had gone to the ranch. Maybe tonight she'd get a good night's sleep. She stood. "If you all will excuse me, I'm going to my room."

"Good night, dear. I hope you sleep better tonight," Mrs. Englebright said.

Mrs. Englebright's room was next door to Millie's. Had her moving about during the night kept the older woman awake? "I'm sorry, Mrs. Englebright. I hope I haven't been keeping you awake."

The widow waved her hand in dismissal. "Not at all."

Millie frowned. "Then how did you know I haven't been sleeping?"

It was Mrs. Englebright's turn to frown. "Why, you told me so not more than thirty minutes ago. You must truly be worn-out, dear."

"Oh, I'm sorry. I am." Millie walked to the door. "Good night," she said over her shoulder.

Everyone called good-night to her as she left the room. In the short time she'd been in Granite, the other boarders had become good friends to Millie. She smiled at the thought. They were the closest thing to a family she had here.

"I've missed your smile, Millie."

She felt a lurch of excitement. Had she imagined Levi's voice? No, there he was, right in front of her. He leaned casually against the railing at the foot of the stairs. Millie folded her hands together and let them hang in front of her dress, fighting not to wrap them around his shoulders.

"Levi." She spoke his name eagerly. She'd not heard him enter the front door. "When did you get home?"

"Just arrived a few minutes ago. I wasn't fit for mixed company so decided to go on up to my room to get cleaned up before coming into the sitting room." In his boots, tan shirt and denim jeans, Levi presented the appearance of a hardworking cowboy. He studied her thoughtfully for a moment.

Was it her imagination, or did he seem just as happy

to see her? His dimples flashed as his grin deepened. A lock of damp hair fell across his forehead. Her hand itched to smooth it back into place. Instead, she took a step closer to him and brushed a piece of lint from his shirtsleeve, allowing her hand to rest a moment on his arm. She needed to touch him, to feel that he was really here.

She inhaled his clean, earthy scent. "I'm glad you're back." She withdrew her hand and immediately felt the loss.

Levi pushed away from the railing. "It's nice to be back. Were you headed upstairs?" he asked, moving to the side to allow her to pass.

Realizing that she was staring at him as if he were a painting by her favorite artist, Millie felt heat fill her cheeks. "Yes, thank you." She swept past him, wishing she didn't sound so breathless.

The light treads of his boots on the stairs behind her made Millie hope that Levi was as reluctant as she to end their time together. "Did you finish the branding?" She turned at the pinnacle of the stairs and waited for him to join her.

He stopped on the top step, and they were eye level. Her appreciative eyes traveled over his features, drinking in his nearness. She wished she had the nerve to outline the touches of humor around his mouth and near his eyes. There was inherent strength in his face, bronzed by the wind and sun. He had the arresting dress and confident walk of a businessman and the muscles and tanned face of a ranch hand. And he stared back at her with the same interest she knew he saw mirrored in her own features.

"Just this afternoon."

"I'm sorry. What?" She tried to comprehend what he'd just said.

The beginnings of a smile tipped the corners of his mouth. "I do believe you have missed me, Miss Millie Hamilton." At her look of confusion, he explained. "You asked me if we finished the branding."

She shook her head as she remembered. "Oh, yeah. I did, didn't I?"

"You did." He moved closer to her, and she stepped back, allowing him to join her on the landing.

"Now that I've washed the grime off I'm ready to get back to my workshop." Levi rolled his shoulders as if to get kinks out of the muscles.

Shouldn't he be going downstairs instead of up? Had he missed her as much as she'd missed him? Did he feel that close connection that had drawn her to him the instant she saw him? She took a quick breath of utter astonishment. What was happening to her?

"While you were gone, I managed to get another drawing done." She didn't bother to tell him that the hummingbird had taken longer than she'd planned because her thoughts had kept drifting to him. "I'll give it to you tomorrow morning at breakfast."

He bent his neck from side to side and rolled his right shoulder once more. Grayish smudges laced the skin under his eyes. "Good. I'm looking forward to seeing it."

Millie realized she didn't want to leave him but also that she had no reason to stand on the landing any longer. "Well, if you will excuse me, I'll continue on to my room."

He nodded, also looking as if he'd like to prolong her leaving.

"Good night, then." She turned away.

In a low voice he called, "Millie?"

Her pulse pounded in her ears. It was amazing how much she'd missed the sound of his husky voice. Millie twisted her head to look in his direction. "Yes?"

"After breakfast, would you like to see my shop?"

She saw the longing to spend more time with her in the probing intensity of his gaze. Millie offered him a smile. "I'd love, too. Besides, I do believe you owe me a few carving lessons."

He released a long, audible breath. His lips tilted up in a smile. "Good. I'll see you in the morning." He turned to leave.

Millie stood in the hallway long after he'd left. What was it about Levi that she couldn't resist? So, she'd missed him. Greatly. But that didn't really mean anything, she thought, trying to be rational. She'd miss Mr. Lupin, too, if he were to leave for a few days.

Her inner voice taunted, *Would you really?* She answered herself truthfully. *No, I don't think so.*

Chapter Fifteen

The next morning, Levi felt almost human again. Roping, branding and herding calves weren't his favorite things to do, but he had enjoyed his time with the cowhands and Daniel.

Thankfully, Daniel had decided they were going to sleep on the range until the branding job was done. He'd dreaded spending time with Anna Mae and Emily, but with the men out on the range, he hadn't had to say more than two words to either of them.

Last night when he'd seen and heard Millie leaving the sitting room, he'd been thrilled. It seemed strange to Levi now to realize that the boardinghouse hadn't really felt like a home until she'd moved in.

He glanced across the table at her.

She sipped from her coffee mug, but her eyes were on him. Millie lowered her cup. "Are you ready, Levi?"

He popped the last of his bacon in his mouth, washed it down with coffee and then nodded. "Sure am." Truth be told, he couldn't wait to spend time with her and would have skipped breakfast if she had suggested it.

"Where you going?" Mark asked, looking up from the drawing he'd been working on.

"Levi invited me to come see his workshop." Millie stood and carried her cup to where Beth had gathered their breakfast dishes. "Would you like for me to stay and help you with these, Beth?" she asked, slipping her plate in the hot water.

"No, I can do it," Beth answered and then yawned.

Millie shook her head. "You look tired. I'll stay and help. With my two extra hands it won't take but a moment." She picked up a dishcloth.

Mrs. Englebright stood. "Nonsense. You two head on out. I'll help Beth get this mess cleaned up." She took the cloth from Millie and gave her a gentle shove in Levi's direction.

Levi laughed. "Looks like we are being booted out." He grabbed Millie's hand. "Let's leave peaceably."

"I'm looking forward to seeing where you spend most of your day when you're in town." She quickened her steps to keep up with him.

Levi released her hand and held the front door open. "I haven't been there in a few days and am looking forward to going back to work." He followed her as she walked down the front walk.

Millie studied his features as he held the gate open for her. "When you are on the ranch, do you miss being in town?" she asked, passing by him once more.

"It's strange, but, yes, and when I'm in town I often miss the ranch." He fell into step beside her.

Millie tilted her head to look at him sideways as they walked. "Have you ever thought about living on the ranch and coming into town every day? Or do you prefer living in town and going out to the ranch?"

"I've thought about living out there, but with the ranch being two hours' ride away, it just isn't feasible." He removed his hat and pushed the hair off his forehead. "Besides, none of the mail-order brides want to live on the ranch."

There it was again. That sorrow in his voice, that sound of despair. Millie reached out and touched his arm. "Does it matter that they want to live in town? What about your feelings and where you want to live?" There was a new acceptance between them. Last night seemed to have moved them closer to an understanding. At least she felt that way.

Levi laid his hand over hers. "It matters, Millie. I don't want to force anyone to live where they don't want to." The ease with which he touched her assured her they were in perfect accord.

That he would willingly give up his own happiness for a woman he didn't love shook Millie to her roots. Levi wasn't going to demand that his future wife live on the ranch. He wasn't going to insist he get his way. Was it possible that men and women could be married without one of them always getting his or her way?

"Marriage isn't about always getting your way. Compromise is required," Levi answered her unspoken question as if he'd read her mind or he'd also pondered the inner workings of matrimonial bliss.

"Did your parents have a good marriage?" Millie asked. They stepped upon the boardwalk on Main Street.

Levi nodded. "I believe so. Pa was a tough man but Mother was his match in every way." He patted her hand. "If I have to get married, I'm praying my wife will be my equal in every way, also."

Millie nodded, not sure what to say. She wanted to say she'd marry him but didn't dare. No man in his right mind would agree to marry an arsonist. Millie knew deep down in her heart that Levi wouldn't be a controlling husband, and she envied his future bride.

"Here it is." Levi released her hand and turned to open a door.

She blinked. They'd walked all the way to his store and she hadn't even noticed. Her thoughts had been so wrapped up in his future. A future she had no business thinking about.

He held the door open for her. His shop wasn't very large, but furniture of all kinds sat along the walls and on workbenches in various stages of completion. There was a strong but not unpleasant odor of lacquer thinner and wood polish. "Did you make all this?" she asked, running her hand over the back of a rocking chair.

"Sure did." He pulled his key from the lock and dropped it into his pocket.

Millie admired the workmanship that he'd put into each piece. She could imagine each item in his house. Some woman was going to be very blessed on the day she married Levi Westland. In dazed exasperation, Millie wished she could be that woman, but once again she reminded herself it wasn't meant to be.

She followed him through a doorway into his workshop. Millie saw her drawings tacked on the back wall above a waist-high countertop. A high-back chair sat under it and she climbed into the seat. Pieces of shavings littered the area, but her attention was captured by the discarded attempts to get the drawings on the wood. She picked up one of the pieces and ran her hand over the markings.

"Levi, these are almost as beautiful as the finished one you gave Daniel." She put all the awe and respect she could into her voice.

"Those are just scrap pieces. I will probably use them as kindling this winter." He stood beside her with his arm stretched across the back of her seat. With his free hand he started to toss one of the pieces into the wood box.

She placed a restraining hand on his arm. "Wait." She rescued the piece from his hand. "There has to be a use for these pieces, Levi. Look at them." She held one up between them. Her artist mind could not see destroying anything with such potential. She studied it a moment. "May I have these?" She tilted her head to look up at him.

He shrugged dismissively. "If you think you can find some use for them you're welcome to them."

The main entrance door opened, and Amos called out.

"Back here, Amos," Levi instructed. He dropped his arm from her chair and helped her down.

"Boss, you're not gonna believe this, but you got three more orders on them there pictures while you were gone." His smile was eager and alive with affection for Levi and delight at the news he brought.

"You're pulling my leg," Levi teased.

"No, sir. I sure ain't." He pulled a slip of paper from his shirt pocket, pushing his overall strap out of the way. "Look at this. One is for a raccoon and old Ms. Reinholt wants a sunflower." He paused a moment, his look wavering between excitement and doubt. "The flower might be a hard 'un, for you, boss, it being womany and all." He looked back at his paper, his dark eyebrows slanted in a frown. "And the last one is for a mountain lion." His expressive face changed and became almost somber. "Oh, boss. That's the one I want to see. I hope you work on it first."

Levi's laughter was infectious, and Millie found herself responding with a light chuckle. He caught her by the elbow and pulled her in front of him. "If we can talk this beauty into drawing the pictures first, then we just might get those made in the next few weeks."

Millie watched Amos's eyes widen. "You are the artist, miss?"

A flush of pride filled her. Millie knew that young Amos appreciated the work she'd done and nodded.

The look in his eyes turned to wonderment. "The good Lord sure did load you up with talent, miss."

Millie's heart sang with delight. Someone recognized her talent. After all the years of battling over her "little hobby" as her mother called it, Millie finally felt like someone was taking her art seriously. She took a deep breath but could barely get her voice above a whisper. "Thank you, Amos. Your words mean a lot to me."

He shifted from foot to foot, apparently uncomfortable and finally turned and fled.

"And speaking of your talent, Miss Hamilton," Levi drawled, "I owe you some money."

She followed him to his desk and watched in humble silence as he counted out her share of profit from what he had sold. He folded the money into her hand. Tears filled her eyes.

"Is that correct?" He seemed concerned over her mood.

All she could manage was a nod. How could she explain what it meant to receive payment for doing something she loved? It was the same each time. Satisfaction, contentment and joy all rolled up into one.

Several hours later, Millie and Levi exited his shop. She was thrilled to have spent the morning with him. Levi was a true artist when it came to woodwork. He'd shown her how he transferred the drawings she gave him into wooden pictures.

Millie had never drawn a raccoon or a mountain lion but thanks to the book Levi had given her, she had pictures of them and knew what they looked like.

"Thank you for sharing your morning with me, Levi. I had no idea you were so gifted." She brushed sawdust off her light tan dress. The shavings blended with the material and she wasn't sure she'd removed them all. Millie decided she'd change before going to work today.

"Daniel would say I'm anything but gifted." Levi laughed, taking her elbow and walking with her.

"Then he would be wrong." Millie spoke with a strong suggestion of reproach.

A few days ago, thinking someone didn't believe Levi could be talented would have made her fighting mad. But today she realized that just because someone else didn't believe in your ability to do what you loved didn't mean you weren't talented.

"That's very kind of you to say so, but I wouldn't let on to Daniel that you know he's been wrong before," Levi teased, and the warmth and richness of his voice thrilled her.

They walked toward the general store. Millie planned to buy Mark a few lemon drops. The little boy had been disappointed that he'd had to go to school instead of going with them to the store. Candy would cheer him right up.

A wagon pulled up in front just as they arrived in front of the general store. Anna Mae and Emily waved from the seat. Levi groaned.

"Good morning, Millie, Levi," Emily said as she climbed down from the wagon.

Millie stepped forward to greet them. "What a surprise to see you two."

Levi helped Anna Mae down. He quickly released her and stepped back to stand beside Millie. "Where is your driver?" he asked. "Surely my mother wouldn't have allowed you to come all this way without an escort."

"We sent him home last night," Anna Mae answered. She reached into the back of the wagon and pulled out a straw basket.

Emily walked over to Millie. "Yesterday, Anna Mae and I decided we wanted to come to town. Mr. Jeb drove us in and then rode his horse home, leaving us the wagon to use."

"Are you staying at the hotel?" Millie asked.

Emily smiled. "Yes, but if all goes well Anna Mae and I will be moving into the Nelsons' house in a few hours."

Levi asked, "Is that house for sale?"

"No," Anna Mae said, moving her basket from one arm to the other. "We are going to be what's called 'renters.'"

Aware that they were getting attention from the good town people, Millie asked, "Would you all like to get something to eat?" She indicated they go to The Eating House, which sat next door to the general store.

"Lunch is on me, ladies." Levi led them to the restaurant. He held the door open as the women paraded past him.

"Welcome," Bertha Steward said as she came toward them. "Table for four?"

Millie took on the role of hostess. "Yes, please," she answered for all of them. They followed Bertha to a table in the back.

"We're still serving breakfast if you are interested." Bertha handed each of them a menu, took their drink orders and then headed to the kitchen.

"I didn't realize the Nelsons were renting their house out," Levi said, laying his menu on the table.

Emily looked up from the menu and explained. "Mr. Nelson mentioned to your mother a few days ago that he and his wife planned to move to Austin but that he wanted to keep the house here. She suggested we rent it from him since both Anna Mae and me want to live in town."

"That's Anna Mae and I," Anna Mae corrected softly.

"Anna Mae and I," Emily repeated like a dutiful student, and then she returned to studying her menu.

Millie shared a grin with Levi. Only he wasn't smiling. His forehead was pinched in a frown.

"My mother suggested you move to town?" he asked.

Bertha returned with their glasses and took their orders before Emily answered. "Yes, she's even paying the first three months' rent until we can get jobs and can pay it ourselves."

The scowl deepened on Levi's face.

Millie hurried to ask another question before Levi could express what a meddling mother he had. "So what kinds of jobs are you looking for?"

Anna Mae lowered her tea glass and looked Levi straight in the eye as if daring him to disapprove. "I am going to approach the school board about the teaching position that has recently become available." At his nod of approval, her pretty face softened. "You don't mind?"

"Of course I don't mind. You love teaching—at least that's what I got from the letter you sent."

His dimples made an appearance, and Millie could see she wasn't the only one affected by them. Both Anna Mae and Emily blushed as if his smile were only for them.

Anna Mae sighed. "I'm glad." She leaned forward slightly, looking deeply into his eyes.

The uncomfortable look on Levi's face prompted Millie to ask, "What about you, Emily? What will you look for in a job?"

"I don't know what I'm going to do," Emily said, "I only know how to cook, clean and garden. When you have eleven brothers and sisters, there's not much time for anything else."

Bertha arrived with four plates of scrambled eggs, sausage and hot biscuits. "You might ask Violet Atwood if she needs help. She runs the bakery." She set the food down and waited to see if they needed anything else.

Millie looked at Levi. Didn't he own the bakery, too? She remembered Beth mentioning that she didn't know what she'd have done if Levi hadn't helped her out and that Violet felt the same way. Could Violet Atwood be the same Violet that Beth spoke of? If he did and if she was, Levi didn't own up to it. He simply tucked into his eggs.

"Thank you, Mrs. Steward," Emily answered with a big grin.

"Please, call me, Bertha." She looked the table over. "Do you folks need anything else?"

Again Millie answered for all of them. "This looks great. Thank you, Bertha."

"Welcome. If you need anything else, just give me a call." She turned and left their table.

"If you acquire the job at the bakery and I obtain the teaching job, we'll be able to stay in town longer than three months," Anna Mae said as she buttered her biscuit.

Emily nodded. "I'll go over to see Mrs. Atwood this afternoon." Joy filled Emily's eyes and voice.

"Just think, Levi, with us living in town you won't have to ride all that way out to the ranch to visit us anymore," Anna Mae said.

Millie hurried to finish her meal. Had he been visiting the ranch on a regular basis? Was she just a third wheel sitting at the table? She no longer felt comfortable with the brides and Levi.

When she looked up, he asked, "Are you ready to go?"

Both the other brides looked at them. The expressions on their faces said they suspected more than friendship might be conspiring between herself and Levi. She stumbled over the words. "Yes, I was just getting ready to leave. I'll have to hurry if I'm to make it to work on time."

"I'm ready, also." He turned his attention to Anna Mae and Emily. "Ladies, I'll take care of your meal. It was nice seeing you today."

"Thank you," echoed from both women. Disappointment filled their voices.

Millie allowed him to take her elbow and walk to

the front of the restaurant. "What are you doing?" she hissed out the side of her mouth.

"Escaping."

Millie looked back over her shoulder. Emily smiled and gave her a quick wave. Anna Mae wasn't paying them any attention at all; she was eating.

Maybe since they were moving to town, Anna Mae didn't see her as a threat. After all, the schoolteacher had been the one to point out that they would be seeing more of Levi now. For some unknown reason, Millie sensed that Emily would be happy if Levi chose Anna Mae over her.

Did it bother him that they were in town? Or would he reconsider and agree to see each of them more? Levi had looked a little panic-stricken when Anna Mae had pointed out that he could spend more time with them now.

The sad truth of the matter was that Millie didn't like this new development. Not because she wanted to marry Levi—she didn't. But because that meant he would be getting married soon and their friendship would have to end. Wives didn't usually cotton to their husbands having other women as best friends.

Millie swallowed hard. His best friend? Maybe she was getting too close to Levi. Her feelings for him had certainly grown stronger. Were they feelings of friendship or love?

Both. She let out a long, audible breath of pure frustration. What was she going to do?

Emotions churned within her like sour milk into butter. Her gut ached at the thought that she and Levi might soon lose the delicate relationship they had just begun to develop. Could she continue to be his friend and still keep her heart safe?

Chapter Sixteen

"Do you know the difference between most of us and Job?"

Millie sat forward, eager to hear the minister answer his own question. This Sunday morning service was even better than normal. She enjoyed the preacher's explanation on Job and all the things he'd had to go through. She'd never heard it quite like this before, but it struck a chord in her heart and she knew the pastor was right. Now she waited eagerly for his next words. "The difference is the next verse in our text. Six little words. 'In all this Job sinned not.'"

Millie leaned back in her seat, her mind a crazy mixture of hope and fear. Job. Now there was a man who had lost everything and then been given it back at the end.

She'd wondered if she'd lose everything and go to prison once she confessed to Eliza that she was the arsonist who had burned down her house. Oh, there was a difference between her and Job all right. Job hadn't sinned.

She had. Then sinned again when she'd tried to cover it up. Sorrow gripped her heart.

The pastor's next words caught her attention once more. "Oh, what peace restoration brings. To make things right with God, to settle problems with our brothers and sisters. God restored to Job everything he'd take away and even more. Why don't you ask God to help you, to forgive you so that you can be in full fellowship with Him and others? Let's bow for prayer."

Millie felt hot tears flood her closed eyelids. How wonderful it would be not to have Eliza's house fire hanging over her head. To not be fearful that someone would find out before she was ready to tell.

"Father," she whispered, "I promise I will tell Eliza the first moment I can. Please restore my fellowship with You and help me to be brave when the time comes."

A peace slipped quietly into her heart, and her soul calmed. She knew she'd have to make things right with Eliza, and whatever happened after that she'd leave in God's hands. Millie knew that she wouldn't be able to tell Levi what she'd done, at least not yet.

But since the brides had arrived in town, Millie hadn't had a chance to visit with Levi alone anyway. It seemed that Anna Mae or Emily was always with them.

Millie quickly gathered her things and left the church a little lighter of heart. She swung the picnic basket she carried and hurried to the woods. During her last visit to the woods, Millie had found a small stream that trickled slowly along and wanted to explore the banks a little better. Her mind went to the sketches she could make there.

Just this morning, Mr. Welsh, the town barber, had asked her if she and Levi could make him a wooden picture like Daniel's. She'd assured him they could. He wanted what he called a largemouth bass. Millie knew that was a fish and hoped to see some while at the water's edge.

Through the open church window, Levi watched Millie head across the green grass back to town. Since he'd arrived earlier than her and been cornered by the brides to sit with them, he'd missed sitting with her during the service.

Levi moved down the aisle as fast as the crowd would allow, then through the back door, quickly shaking the preacher's hand. He'd been dodging the mail-order brides all week and just wanted a little alone time with Millie.

He sprinted after her. "Millie!" Levi prayed he wasn't going to draw attention from his mother, Anna Mae or Emily.

She stopped and turned to face him. The smile he'd expected wasn't there, but she waited for him.

As soon as he was close enough to talk to her in a normal voice, he said, "I hope I'm not disturbing you, but I was wondering if you'd like to take a ride in the country with me this afternoon."

She tilted her pretty blond head and looked up at him. "Do you know what a bigmouth bass looks like?"

Her question took Levi by surprise. Was she calling him a bigmouth? Or a fish? Or did she really want to know what a bigmouth bass looked like? And if so, why? Figuring he'd better play it safe, he simply nodded.

"Can you show me one?" Millie stood with both fists on her hips. A wicker basket swung from her wrist. Her curious blue eyes studied his face.

He shrugged to hide his confusion. "Well, we'd have to go fishing and even then I can't guarantee that I'll catch one." She seemed disappointed at his words. Levi rushed on. "But I can try."

She smiled with approval. "All right then. I'll go with you, but you have to go fishing. Deal?"

His mood suddenly buoyant, he shook the hand she extended. "Deal." If she'd asked him to howl at the moon he would have done his best imitation of a wolf.

He knew she had no idea her presence gave him such joy. "All right, but you have to tell me why I am fishing for bigmouth bass."

Levi glanced over his shoulder and saw his mother looking about for him. Fairly certain she hadn't spotted them yet, he turned back to Millie. "I'll go get a wagon and meet you on the edge of town in ten minutes."

She looked at him uncertainly, but then came to a decision and nodded, sending his confidence spiraling upward.

Levi hurried to the livery. The last thing he wanted was to spend another boring Sunday afternoon with his mother and the mail-order brides. Snow snorted in his direction as he entered the barn.

"Sorry, ol' fella. I'm taking the mare today. She pulls a wagon better than you." He already had the mare by the halter and was leading her to the side of the livery where the wagon he'd rented before morning services waited.

What was Millie going on about bigmouth bass for? He didn't mind fishing but hadn't put a pole in the wagon. Where would he find the equipment he'd need to fish? He didn't dare chance running into his mother and the brides at the boardinghouse.

Amos came around the livery with a fishing pole swung over his shoulder. "Miss Millie said I'd find you here." He panted.

Levi stared. "Millie sent you?" he asked, dumbfounded.

"Yep, said you'd need a fishing pole and asked if I had one you could borrow. I told her sure and she told me to bring it here as fast as I could." He handed the pole to Levi. "She also said that if I kept it a secret, you'd pay me." The youth grinned like an ornery mule right before he bit you. Every tooth in his head showed.

Levi laughed. Millie Hamilton was quite a woman. "She was right." He dug in his pocket and handed Amos his payment. "I'd appreciate it if you wouldn't mention this to anyone."

"You got it, boss. See you in the morning." Amos turned to leave but stopped short. "Oh, and be careful with that pole. It was my pa's."

"I will, Amos," Levi promised.

Amos nodded and then left.

Levi put the pole in the bed of the wagon and then hitched up the mare. He took the back roads to the edge of town. A grin split his lips as he realized he was acting much like he had when he had been a boy dodging his mother so he could get out of some chore.

Millie stood in a grove of trees waiting for him. Levi jumped down, took the basket and then helped her up. He looked about to make sure they were still alone.

"I take it we are hiding from your mother?" she asked, scooting over on the seat to make room for him.

He grinned at her. "How did you guess?"

"Oh, after you took off, Amos came running toward me and said Mrs. Westland wanted to know if I knew where you were. I kind of pulled a sneaky on her." Pink filled her cheeks.

Levi set the mare into motion. "What did you do?"

"Well, I asked Amos if he had a fishing pole you could use. When he said yes, I asked him if he would take it to you first and then go find your mother and tell her I said yes, I did know where you were."

Levi groaned. "Then he's going to tell her where we are now."

Millie shook her head. "No, he isn't. I also told him to tell her that I said you were at the livery, but not to tell her anything else he knew. I'm banking on the fact that she will hurry to the livery but you will be long gone and so will Amos."

"But how is he going to explain why it took so long to get back to her?" Levi couldn't wrap his mind around the fact that Millie might have outwitted his mother.

"Oh, that's easy. If she asks, Amos is to tell her he went to make sure you were still there." A smile split her lips and the pink ran high in her cheeks.

Levi tossed his head back and laughed with joy. Together, he and Millie had saved him from another Sunday afternoon spent in the sitting room at the boardinghouse answering endless questions. Millie's giggle blended with his laughter, and they headed down the road.

"Where are we going?" Millie asked once they quit laughing.

"To the ranch. We have several fishing holes there."

Millie looked about them. "I can't believe you are going to the ranch while your mother is searching for you in town." Her expression was one of disbelief, but her beautiful blue eyes danced merrily, and a hint of humor tilted the corner of her mouth.

"Desperate times call for desperate measures. Sometimes a man has to run for his life."

"That sure is the truth." Millie knew too well about desperation and running.

"Where were you headed when I stopped you?" Levi guided the buggy around a muddy spot in the road. Deep ruts had kept the water from draining, and Thursday's rain still sat in the low areas.

Millie played with the folds of her dress. "There is a spring in the woods."

"You went that deep into the woods?" Levi tried to keep his voice calm. If she was talking about the stream he thought she was, Millie had ventured way too far into the woods. Hadn't she heard him when he'd told her about the mountain lions?

She met his gaze. "Yes, and I didn't run into any mountain lions, rattlesnakes or black bears."

The challenge in her eyes said he had no business telling her where she could go or what she could do. Levi remembered his father once telling him and Daniel, "Boys, when it comes to a woman pick your battles carefully." This was one time he intended to do just that.

"I'm glad." He turned his attention back on the little brown horse's back. "Why am I fishing for a bigmouth bass?"

Millie laid her hand on his arm. Heat filled the spot where she touched him. "Thank you for not scolding me. I'll be careful in the woods. I promise. As for why you are fishing, well, Mr. Welsh asked if we could make him a picture using a bigmouth bass. I told him sure, but I have no idea what one looks like."

Levi laughed. "I see. Well, let's hope we find one or I might have to get out one of my fishing books and show you."

"You have a fishing book?" She removed her hand from his arm.

He missed her nearness, but today he just felt happy, and spending time with Millie gave him so much joy that Levi laughed again. "Yes, doesn't everyone?"

Millie grinned. "No, I don't think I have that one on my bookshelf." She looked up at the sky. "Levi, are those dark clouds coming this way?"

Dark clouds were coming in fast. Spring storms were not uncommon in Texas, but they could be deadly. He estimated they were a good hour still from the ranch. "It looks that way."

Her voice became small as she stated, "In New Mexico, we can see clouds like that but not get one drop of rain."

"I wish that were true here." Levi slapped the reins over the mare's back to get her going a little faster. "We might be able to avoid getting wet if we head for the house."

Lightning flashed across the sky, and a few seconds later thunder rocked the atmosphere. Millie jumped. "We hardly ever see lightning like that." She eased closer to him on the bench.

Levi raised his arm over her shoulders and hugged her close. "You don't have to worry. We'll find shelter soon." He prayed it was the truth.

Millie remained silent, but her hands clenched so tight he could see the nails biting into her palms. Lightning and thunder chased each other across the skies and with each boom, she quaked a little harder.

Once, when the lightning touched a tree near them, she cried out, then nervously bit her lip. He'd never met anyone who feared storms and wasn't sure how to comfort her.

"Sing with me, Millie."

"What?" He could barely hear her voice above the noise of the storm.

"Sing with me." At her look of disbelief, he explained. "It will calm the horse so that she doesn't bolt." He hoped she didn't know horses or she'd recognize right off that the mare was too old to bolt and had weathered much worse storms than this. But if he could get her mind off the storm, he could calm her fears. He waited for her to nod.

He began in a robust voice, "On Jordon's stormy bank I stand and cast a wistful eye." She joined him, singing harmony, her voice shaking, but they finished the song and started on another. "I will arise and go toward heaven." She laid her head against his arm—whether to hear him better or for comfort, he wasn't sure, but it felt good and right.

They arrived at the ranch as the first drops of rain hit the ground. A burst of lightning lit up the front yard. Millie squealed.

The front door burst open, and Daniel rushed out to meet them. Hail dropped from the sky, creating marbles of ice under his feet. Daniel held his coat over Millie's head and herded her toward the house.

"I'll put the horse and buggy in the barn," Levi called after them.

Millie's fearful voice called back, "Please hurry."

He hated hearing the sound of trepidation that came from her and wished the little mare could take care of herself. Levi pulled the scared animal by its harness toward the barn.

Jeb met him halfway. "I'll take care of her, Levi." He grabbed the mare.

"Thanks." Levi spun on his heels and raced to the house. He wanted to check on Millie. He'd never seen anyone that afraid of storms. It had broken his heart to see the terrible tenseness in her body and the anxious look on her face.

The rain and hail pelted him as he ran across the yard. He hurried to the kitchen, where he found Millie wrapped in a blanket, huddled in a chair. She shivered as if she'd taken cold, but he knew she'd only been in the rain for a couple of minutes.

Daniel stood beside her chair looking worried. "I need to get back upstairs with Hannah. She hasn't been feeling good today."

Levi waved him away. "Go on, I'll take care of Millie." If anyone had told him a year ago that both he and Daniel would have women who needed them, Levi felt sure he'd have laughed.

Take care of Millie. The words grated on Millie's nerves. She didn't want to be weak. She didn't want someone to take care of her. Still, when the thunder shook the house, she cried out and grabbed Levi's arm.

"Easy, Millie, it's just thunder. It can't hurt you in the house." He scooted his chair close to her and wrapped his arms around her shoulders.

Millie hated this weakness. She leaned her head against his shoulder. "I know, but storms have always scared me."

The sound of boots bounding on the stairs sounded

almost as loud as the thunder had earlier. A few seconds later, Daniel went past the doorway. They heard the front door slam and knew he'd run out into the rain.

Concern filled Levi's voice. "I wonder where he's going in such a hurry."

Millie patted the arm that held her tight. "Maybe he forgot to do something in the barn."

"Maybe." Even to himself, Levi's voice sounded doubtful.

The front door slammed open, then shut just as forcibly. Millie eased out of his arms, and he sat forward, both of them looking intently at the kitchen doorway.

Daniel appeared within seconds. His face ashen, his breaths came in ragged gasps. Levi experienced a dull ache of foreboding. He'd only seen that kind of fear in Daniel's face once, the night their sister had died.

"What is it, Daniel? What's wrong?"

Daniel opened his mouth to speak, but no sound came forth. He rubbed his hands down his pants, then tried again. In a low and tormented voice, he told them, "I think Hannah is losing the baby."

Chapter Seventeen

Levi's chair crashed behind him as he jumped to his feet, the noise shattering the last of Millie's hard fought for calm. "I'll go get the doctor." His voice broke with huskiness.

Daniel shook his head. "I just sent Tucker after him. Boil water. We might need it." He started toward the stairs then turned back to them. "And pray. Please." His earnest eyes sought each of theirs and seemed to plead for help.

The blanket slipped from her fingers as Millie stood and started toward him. "Is there anything I can do?" she asked, knowing in her heart they were all helpless if God didn't intervene.

"No, just help Levi." Daniel left. His boots pounded up the stairs as he hurried back to Hannah's side.

Levi pulled pans down and began filling them with water from the water bucket. Next, he added wood to the stove and started a fire within its belly.

Millie set Levi's chair upright. "It will be hours before Doc arrives. It might be too early to start the hot water," she advised. Her gaze moved up to the second floor where she knew Hannah was fighting to keep her baby.

Levi placed the pans on the stove top. "True, but we might need the water before he arrives." He turned to face her.

Millie saw his hand shake as he put it in his pocket. Levi was scared. His eyes clung to hers, analyzing her reaction, uncertainty in their dark depths. She didn't know if he was trying to see if she needed comforting or if he himself was looking to her for comfort. She dropped her gaze to the floor.

Levi moved to the window and stared out into the storm.

Thunder boomed, but it didn't seem nearly as scary to Millie now. All she could think about was Hannah and her unborn child.

Hannah couldn't be more than four months along, but Millie had seen the excitement and heard Hannah and Daniel discussing names. Hannah loved her baby as much right now as if it were already in her arms.

"Millie, will you join me in prayer for Hannah and the baby?" Levi turned from the window, his hand outstretched.

She crossed the room and stood in front of him. Levi took both her hands, his thumbs smoothing the backs of them in a comforting motion. He leaned forward until their foreheads touched, his warm breath against her face. He prayed for Hannah and the baby.

Millie forgot about the raging storm. She focused on God and Levi's prayer to their Heavenly Father. In a voice that wavered once or twice, Levi asked that God's will be done and that God protect Daniel's heart should they lose the child. He finished, and Millie added a whispered amen. He didn't move away, so Millie tilted her face toward his.

She saw the need, the anguish, and in an instinctive gesture of comfort she wrapped her arms around his waist and laid her head against the taut smoothness of his shoulder. He pulled her close. She felt his chest heave a jagged breath. They stood together for a brief moment. Both received strength and comfort. Then he released her slowly, placing both hands back in his pockets.

Levi turned back to the window. He'd regained control of his emotions.

As the storm raged outside, Millie and Levi waited in silence. Feeling jumpy from both the storm and the waiting, she picked up the picnic basket Levi had set beside their chairs. "Would you like to eat something while we wait, Levi?" It wasn't hunger that drove her to ask, but she felt it was something to do to keep their hands busy.

"No thanks. I'm not hungry."

Millie pulled her sketch pad and pencils from the basket and then returned it to the floor. She placed her art supplies on the table. Still needing something more to do, she asked, "How about a cup of coffee? I could make a pot and you can take a cup up to Daniel, as well."

He stared at her for a moment and then nodded his consent. He bowed his head and continued in a low voice, praying for Daniel and his small family.

Thankfully, the storm's intensity had lessened and she began to feel useful again. Millie had never cooked in the Westland kitchen but soon had the coffee brewing. Its rich aroma filled the room. When it was ready, she poured two cups.

Levi hadn't moved.

"It's ready," she said in a soft voice.

Levi turned from the window. He walked to her and took both of the cups from her hands, then leaned in and gently kissed her cheek. "Thank you." He left the room.

Millie touched where his lips had caressed her skin. Why had Levi kissed her? Didn't he realize that by doing so he only made it harder for her to resist him?

She couldn't quite put her finger on just when it had happened, but their relationship had shifted from friends to something a bit deeper.

After he'd given Daniel one of the cups of coffee, Levi stood outside his brother's old bedroom door. Thankfully, Hannah had been visiting their mother when the labor pains had begun. Never in his life had he felt so helpless. Levi couldn't even begin to imagine what Daniel must be going through. How could a man see his wife in pain and know that the life they had made together was possibly dying right in front of them and they could do nothing to stop it?

His mind flashed back to the sermon on Job the preacher had preached earlier. How had Job lost it all and still been able to say, "The Lord giveth and the Lord taketh away. Blessed be the name of the Lord?" Levi didn't know if he had that kind of faith or not.

The doctor and Levi's mother arrived, and with their arrival, the storm ended. They immediately went upstairs and for the next hour Levi busied himself with feeding the animals, filling the wood box in the kitchen and carrying fresh water. Still there was no news.

Levi returned to the empty kitchen and began to pace the floor. He'd expected to find Millie waiting for him there. Where had she gone? He'd left her alone while he found things to keep him busy. Levi realized he'd been an insensitive oaf. After she had comforted him in the sweetest, most caring way she knew how.

Millie slipped quietly back into the room. She sat down at the kitchen table. Her eyes looked a bit puffy and tired. Had she been crying?

He needed to make amends and sought in his mind the best way to do just that. Levi studied her carefully. Her sketch pad rested in front of her, but she wasn't working on anything. He pulled out the chair across from her and sat down.

"Millie, I'll be happy to take you back to town if you'd like me to." Levi took her hand that lay on top of the sketchbook and measured it against his, then entwined their fingers together. She made no effort to remove her hand from his.

She shook her head. "Thank you for the offer, but I can't leave until I know that Hannah is all right." Millie gently squeezed his hand and offered him a soft smile.

They sat in silence, each lost in their own thoughts till Bonnie Westland entered her kitchen looking aged and tired. If she thought it strange that her son was holding hands with a female guest, she didn't let on; she sat down at the head of the table and sighed. Levi hadn't seen his mother look so drawn since the day his father had died.

"Would you like a cup of coffee?" Millie asked, releasing Levi's hand to stand.

"That would be nice."

Millie went to get his mother a fresh cup. She filled

it and then placed the hot coffee in front of Bonnie. "I'll be right back with the cream and sugar."

When she returned, Bonnie asked, "Millie, would you mind getting a cup for the doctor, too? He'll be down in a moment."

"Of course not." Millie turned to do Bonnie's bidding.

Levi watched his mother's hand shake as she added sugar to her cup. He waited, knowing that she'd say what needed to be said once Millie was reseated.

Dread filled him. Somehow he knew what she was going to say. Levi tried to think positive for a moment. Daniel and Hannah could have more children. They would get to spend more alone time together before starting a family, get a few more things finished or caught up on.

He also was smart enough to know that they would grieve together and either grow closer or be torn apart. Having seen the love between them he felt certain they would work through this tragedy and come out stronger than ever. As it had with Job, time and the good Lord would heal all things.

He watched his mother take a sip from her coffee. A tear slid down her cheek. Levi felt a lump seize his throat. He could not stand to see a woman cry, especially one as tough as the one in front of him. Levi reached out and placed his hand over hers.

Just as he'd thought, when Millie rejoined them at the table, Bonnie said, "Hannah lost the baby." She took several deep breaths and got her emotions under control, even though a few rebellious tears trickled past her defenses.

Levi released a pent-up breath he'd been holding. He

patted her hand. She was handling things just fine; she wouldn't need his help. His relief was short-lived when he looked at Millie.

Her elbows rested on the table, and both hands covered her eyes. Her shoulders shook, and he knew tears filled her hands, even if he couldn't see them.

Deep pain twisted his gut. Uncertainty gnawed at him, making the sourness in the pit of his stomach worse. He didn't know how she would feel about receiving comfort in front of his mother. Yet he longed to return the favor she had granted him earlier by taking her in his arms.

Levi returned his attention to his mother and asked the only thing that came to mind. "How is Daniel doing?"

"He's being strong for Hannah." His mother took a long drink from her coffee and then straightened her spine. "Millie, you are welcome to stay in Levi's old room tonight. Levi, you'll stay in the guest room."

Millie removed her hands. Tears marred her pretty features, but unlike his mother she hadn't bothered to wipe them away. She gathered her composure about her like an iron mantle. "Thank you. Is there anything I can do to help?"

Levi glanced between the two women. Though sorrow filled his mother's eyes, when she looked at Millie he saw something else. If he wasn't mistaken, there was a glimmer of respect in her eyes. "No, thank you, dear."

The doctor chose that moment to enter the room. "I've done all I can for her, Bonnie. Make sure she takes the sleeping powders tonight. Tomorrow will be soon enough for her to face her sorrows."

Millie picked up the additional coffee mug and

stepped forward. "Sir, I've poured you a cup of coffee." She handed the cup to him.

"Thank you. Miss Hamilton, right?"

She offered him a watery smile. "Yes, sir. I'm Millie Hamilton. But please call me Millie."

He sighed tiredly. "Drop the sir, and I'll call you Millie."

"Yes…"

"Doc. Just call me Doc."

A bittersweet smile filled her eyes. "Yes, Doc."

He gulped the coffee then the doctor set his cup down. "I'll be heading on out."

Bonnie snapped out of her stupor. "You'll do no such thing. It's late and the road is pure mud. Unless you have patients waiting for you, you'll be spending the night here."

He raised a bushy eyebrow. "How can a man refuse such a sweet invitation?" He picked up his cup and took another drink.

His comment brought a grin to Bonnie's sad face. "You'll be bunking with Levi. Son, please show the doctor to his room. I'm sure he's tired."

Levi stood. He didn't want to leave Millie. Just being in the same room with her made him feel better, but Levi knew it would be best for all involved to do as his mother said.

He turned to the doctor. "Sometimes it's easier to simply surrender. I think this might be one of those times."

The older man nodded. "Agreed. However, I want to check on my patient one more time before retiring."

"I understand. Our room is across the hall from Daniel and Hannah's," Levi answered, walking to the door with the doctor.

Just before they left the kitchen, he turned to look at Millie. Her eyes were gentle and contemplative as she returned his gaze. She managed a tremulous smile and a softly whispered, "Good night, Levi."

As he started up the stairs he heard her begin to hum one of the songs they'd sung during the storm. He didn't know which of them she was trying to comfort right now, but he did know the moment was theirs alone. They had a story between them that bound them together. He liked it.

A little while later, Millie met the doctor at the top of the stairs as he left Hannah's room. "Doc, do you think I could speak to Hannah? And if so, would you ask her if that would be all right? I don't want to intrude if she doesn't want to see me right now."

"I think that's a great idea. I'll ask her."

He disappeared a moment into Hannah and Daniel's room, then reappeared and held open the door. "She's just taken a sleeping powder so don't be too long."

Millie nodded and then entered the room. She took in the scene before her, her heart racing in her chest. Daniel lay on top of the covers with Hannah's head on his chest. A tiny candle burned on the chest of drawers against the wall. An open window allowed cool air to stir across the covers. Millie had never felt more like an intruder in her life. She turned to leave.

"Millie?"

She twisted back around to find Hannah beckoning to her. Daniel slipped off the bed and offered Millie his place. "Stay with her till I get back, please." At her nod, Daniel closed the door gently, leaving them alone.

Millie eased down on the bed beside Hannah and looked into eyes heavy with grief. "Oh, Hannah, I am so sorry." She brushed Hannah's hair back and wiped the tears that silently streamed down her face.

Hannah hooked her arms through Millie's and they lay looking at each other. Millie sensed that Hannah needed her presence, not small talk.

"I must look a mess." Hannah smiled. Her lips trembled, but the flow of tears had stopped.

"You look beautiful." Millie waited, feeling inept, yet happy to be there. Hoping to help. "Are you going to be all right?"

Hannah gave a short laugh. "Health wise, yes. Doc says I'm healthy as an ox. That we should be able to have many more babies, Lord willing." She looked at Millie and whispered, "Heart wise, I'm not so sure."

Millie was at a loss for words. She wanted to help her friend but didn't know how.

Hannah swallowed then smiled ruefully. "I dreamed of holding this baby, of nursing him. I was getting used to the idea of three of us instead of two."

Millie teased gently, "Of sewing booties and washing out stinky diapers?"

Hannah chuckled. "Yes, even stinky diapers."

"How is Daniel?"

Hannah sighed. "He's a wreck. He prayed for God to save the baby and then was angry at God when He took the baby home. I told him it was dangerous to be that way so he apologized to God. Then he apologized to me, and then he told Doc he was sorry. Doc had no idea what he was talking about because he hadn't even arrived when all this took place. So then Daniel was mad at Doc."

Millie couldn't help it. She laughed out loud and was rewarded by Hannah's soft chuckle. When they stopped laughing, Millie smiled at Hannah and said, "He loves you so much."

"I know." Hannah picked at imaginary lint on the blanket. "You know what, Millie? I think this was good for us. Not that losing the baby will ever be anything but a great loss, but I felt Daniel's love like I've never felt it before. And he wanted the baby, too, Millie. Not for some stupid old challenge his mother made, but for the two of us. Does that make sense?" She didn't even wait on Millie to respond. "It's as if we are now bonded even more. Like we have experienced something that was only between us." She smoothed the covers between them. "I love him so much. I know this sounds silly, but he's my hero, like the heroes from the books I so love to read."

What would it be like to have a man love her like that? And to love him in return? Levi's face came to mind. Millie sat up, then went to the dresser and picked up Hannah's brush. "Are you allowed to sit up? If so, I can brush out your hair."

"Yes." Hannah flipped back the covers and eased to a sitting position on the side of the bed. "By the way Doc talked, I can ride a bucking horse in a couple of weeks." Hannah's dry sense of humor and natural sarcasm had kicked in.

It was then Millie realized her friend would be just fine. She gently pulled the brush through Hannah's hair. Millie braided it in a single braid. Hannah yawned, and then in a few moments yawned again.

"Okay, sweet friend, I think you're ready for sleepy town." Millie settled Hannah back under the covers and heard her soft snores before she could place the brush back on the dresser.

The door opened, and Daniel walked in. He looked at his wife, then looked at Millie in wonder. "Did I hear her laughing?"

"Yes, she was laughing."

"If she was laughing, then she is going to be okay, right?"

"I think so. She will have sad days, but time will heal her loss and she will move on. I've never known Hannah Young to mope around. I doubt being Hannah Westland has changed that." Millie offered him a teasing smile.

He grabbed her hand and shook it awkwardly. "Thank you for talking to her."

"But I mostly listened…" Millie felt sure Daniel didn't even know when she left. He had already gone to his wife before she'd finished her sentence. As she prepared for bed, she whispered a prayer heavenward. "Lord, please, please, allow me to experience that kind of love in my life."

Chapter Eighteen

Levi wouldn't dare say it out loud, but he felt happy and relieved to be back in town. It had been five days since Hannah had lost the baby. She seemed almost back to normal. Before they left the ranch Hannah had managed to come downstairs with a little help from Daniel and see them off. She'd given Millie a fierce hug, and to Levi's jaw-dropping astonishment, Daniel had hugged Millie, too.

His brother and Hannah seemed to be taking their loss as well as could be expected. God surely had applied the Balm of Gilead to their sorrowful hearts.

Even his mother had hugged Millie and thanked her for all her help over the past few days. Something had changed between the two women. Bonnie Westland now treated Millie like a daughter instead of an intruder, and for that Levi was thankful.

He stood at the bottom of the stairs waiting for Millie to come down. Tonight was the barn dance and he'd gone out of his way to provide her with an evening she'd never forget.

This was their first outing alone in almost a week.

He'd rented Mr. Meriwether's carriage in hopes that Millie would enjoy riding the short distance in style. He wore a new pale green shirt Susanna had made him at his request. He'd seen Millie sewing up her new dress and had wanted his shirt to match the grass-green color.

As if on cue, Millie appeared at the top of the stairs. She placed her hand on the banister and looked down at him. He felt a ripple of excitement. The very air between them seemed electrified.

He swallowed hard, unable to manage even a feeble hello. Finally, he simply nodded and she descended the stairs. Millie seemed to be in slow motion, careful not to trip on her dress. The hunter- and grass-green material floated about her, making her look like a princess to him.

It wasn't a real fancy dress, nor a ball gown, but on her it looked elegant. And she looked radiant. Tonight she'd pulled her hair into some kind of fashionable style, which surprised him. Millie wasn't one for keeping up-to-date with the latest hair styles. Had she done so to please him?

Levi finally found his voice and could speak again. "You look lovely." Huskiness filled his voice and he wondered briefly if he was coming down with something. He took her hand and helped her down the remaining stairs.

"Thank you." An escaping strand of blond hair fell over her forehead, and she swept it back into place. "You look nice, too." Millie sounded shy and unsure of herself. Was she nervous with him?

On the night Hannah had lost her baby, everything had changed between them. They'd grown closer and talked freely on the few occasions they had been together. Yet at this moment, she seemed to have built a wall between them.

"Shall we go?" He extended his arm to her.

Mrs. Englebright stepped off the stairs behind Millie. "You kids enjoy yourselves tonight."

They said their goodbyes and headed out the door. The chaise carriage waited in front of the house, drawn by two black horses. Amos sat on the wagon's side seat while Levi hurried to the carriage door and held it open.

Her palm felt warm against his as he helped her into the wagon. Levi missed that warmth the moment she released his hand. He slapped the top of the carriage, then swung inside and closed the door.

The interior darkened, leaving him feeling lost. The horses lurched forward, throwing him off balance. He landed beside her with an *oomph* sound. As he settled beside her, Millie finally spoke in a soft voice. "Levi, this carriage is a bit extravagant, isn't it?"

"A little, I guess. I borrowed it from Mr. Meriwether. He's English and was happy to loan it to us this evening. I thought we could arrive in style." Why was he rambling like a rusted saw?

"But what if the mail-order brides see us arrive like this? Won't they think we are courting?"

Levi struggled to maintain an even tone. "You mean we're not?" he teased halfheartedly, wanting more than anything for her to say, "Yes, we are courting." He couldn't give her his heart, but he could give her his friendship and protection. So why shouldn't they court?

"No, we are only friends. Remember?" Millie lifted her chin and boldly met his gaze. He was caught off guard by the determination in her voice. "I don't want the mail-order brides or anyone else to think otherwise."

Her manner irked him, and he allowed his annoyance to show. "Are you sure that's what you want, Millie? Just to remain friends? We can still be friends and be married." He wished the carriage weren't so dark so he could see her expression better. "I thought things had deepened between us. Can you seriously deny you have feelings for me?"

He heard her soft sigh and felt her sit up straighter on the seat. "Levi, I'll admit that something has changed between us, but it doesn't matter. I still can't marry you." Was that a catch he heard in her voice? Or wishful thinking on his part?

"Can't? Or won't?" Levi was more shaken by her refusal than he cared to admit. He knew his voice held the anger he felt, but he couldn't help it. It was as if he were trying to draw a different response from her. To make her admit she cared. He sought to erect a wall of defense around his heart.

"I don't have a choice, Levi."

"What does that mean, Millie? Are you secretly married to someone else? Betrothed? What?" Levi came to an abrupt halt.

What was he doing? Had he gone mad? His intention had been to show her the best night she'd ever had. How could he have gotten so far off base? In the dusk of the carriage, he saw the anxious look on her face and knew he had hurt her. But her refusal simply to let people think she cared for him hurt, too.

She didn't answer, and the silence between them grew tight with tension. He could feel the tenseness in her body posture but he couldn't or wouldn't take back his words. Why couldn't she see that a marriage between them would be the best solution? It dawned on him it was the solution to his problem, not hers.

The carriage slowed to a stop. Masking his inner turmoil with a deceptively calm voice, he spoke. "All right, I'll dance with the brides and you can dance with whomever you wish. I'll try and stay out of your way."

She rested her hand on his arm. "Levi, please don't be like that. Please, for tonight, until we can talk this out, can we be friends?"

Pride kept him from answering her.

Amos opened the door of the carriage. Levi turned to help her down and she curved her hand along his jaw before settling it on his shoulder.

He felt weak and vulnerable in the face of his emotions for this woman. Emotions he continued to deny, too. He didn't want his heart broken and she didn't want to get married. What were they doing?

She turned to him with a sad smile. Millie leaned close enough to him to whisper so that Amos wouldn't hear. "Friends only. Nothing more. You are going to have to choose one of the other ladies as a wife."

A pain filled his chest like nothing he'd ever experienced. Levi realized he'd only thought his heart was breaking when Lucille had tossed their engagement back in his face. He'd been wrong. This pain was the true feeling of a broken heart.

Levi followed her toward the barn. Light and music flowed from the interior. He knew she cared for him, so why did she fight marrying him? Surely it wasn't just because of her controlling mother? It was then he realized, that while they were in the carriage, he'd hit on the fact that Millie Hamilton had a secret.

For the rest of the evening, Levi watched her and

wondered what she was hiding. She seemed to have as many dance partners as he did. He danced with Emily, Susanna and Anna Mae several times each. The ladies also danced with other men, but just when he thought he'd head over to the punch bowl, one of them would be waiting for the next dance.

Lucille Lawson whirled past him and smiled. She was on the arm of the banker's son and seemed quite happy. The truth of the matter was Levi was pleased for Lucille. The old hurt was gone.

When the song ended, Levi applauded with the other dancers and then turned to his current dance partner. "Thank you for the dance, Anna Mae. I am in need of a glass of punch. Would you like one?"

She opened her mouth to reply but was interrupted as the music started again, and Mr. Lupin stepped forward. "May I have this dance?" he asked.

Anna Mae looked confused. "I guess I'll pass on the punch, Levi, and dance with Mr. Lupin."

Levi nodded and watched as they walked to the dance floor. He gazed about the barn in search of Millie, but he didn't see her in the crowds or on the dance floor. His throat was parched so he headed toward the refreshment tables.

Susanna's voice reached his ears. "How serious is your relationship with Levi? If you're not interested in him as a husband, would you please step aside so that Anna Mae or Emily will feel free to pursue him? Right now, you two seem to be together and neither of them wants to come between you. But if it's just friendly, well, then he'd be a great catch for one of them. I'd pursue him myself, but I've already come to the conclusion that he isn't for me."

Levi stopped in his tracks. He ducked behind a stack of hay bales and listened.

Millie's sweet voice answered the other woman. "Oh, what makes you think Levi will be a 'great catch' for one of them?"

Susanna laughed. "His family is the wealthiest in the area. Didn't you know?"

"And that's what makes him a 'great catch'?" Millie's voice held an edge to it, and he wondered if she was irritated or simply interested in what the other woman had to say.

He almost chuckled out loud. A great catch? Him? If those women really knew him, they would run screaming in the other direction. He left his socks turned inside out, forgot to empty his shaving water most mornings and on cold winter days, had to be forced to get out of his nice warm bed.

Susanna's voice dropped and Levi strained to hear. "His father left both Levi and Daniel large trust funds and whichever man wins the ranch will be even wealthier. Just think, Millie, a girl would never have to struggle financially again."

"It may surprise you to learn that I'm not interested in the Westlands' wealth. Levi and I are good friends. We were friends before you told me this, and we will be friends until the day he marries regardless of what he's worth financially." From the closeness of her voice, it sounded like Millie had moved closer to him, but he dared not peek from behind the hay bale.

He heard her dress rustle away once more. "If you will excuse me, I see Emily and need to speak to her."

Levi chanced a glance around the hay bales. Susanna was gone and he could see Millie stomping off in the opposite direction. What had she meant, until he got married? He'd never thought their friendship would end when he chose a bride. Why must it end?

His chest felt as if something heavy sat on it. Distractedly, he ran a hand across his heart in an effort to ease the pain. He didn't want to lose Millie or her friendship. What was he going to do?

The music and fellowship continued around him—happy voices, teasing and laughing—but Levi heard none of it. Strange and disquieting thoughts raced through his mind.

The fact that his emotions were so out of control bothered him the most. How had his heart gotten involved? When had everything about Millie become more important to him than his own well-being? And just now he'd learned that unlike Lucille and Susanna, Millie didn't care about the Westland fortune.

But could he trust Millie with his heart? Apparently not. She insisted that they would never have any other relationship beyond friendship. He knew with sudden clarity that he wanted more than that from her.

He came to the edge of the dance floor, where Millie spun around in the arms of another man. He wanted to demand that she dance with no one but him. She looked up into the face of the man dancing with her. Joy bubbled in her laugh and shone in her eyes.

Levi couldn't stand seeing her in the arms of another man. Before he knew what he'd done, Levi found himself on the dance floor stopping beside the man. He tapped him none too gently on the shoulder. "May I cut in?"

Irritation radiated from the man. He didn't like the interruption of his dance with Millie. Levi noted it, but it didn't matter one whit to him what the other man thought. Reluctantly the gentleman stepped aside.

Millie placed her hand in his. The music changed from fast beat to a slow tempo. When she stepped close and laid her head on his shoulder, the barn, the dancers and everything else completely disappeared.

Levi inhaled her scent and brushed his lips across the top of her silky hair. He felt her take a deep, unsteady breath; then she stepped back in his arms. Her lips formed a soft and loving curve, and her rounded blue eyes stared up at him full of questions.

"You're no longer angry with me?" When she spoke, her voice was tender, barely above a whisper, but he heard her. He, on the other hand, could not utter a word past the rioting emotions in his heart. He answered her the only way he could at the moment. Levi pulled her close, so that her head rested over his chest, and let his heart speak for him.

The rest of the evening passed in a blur. He lurked on the outskirts of the barn, dancing only with Millie when the opportunity presented itself.

Levi searched his heart and questioned his thoughts and intentions. He avoided the other ladies and the mail-order brides. There was no interest in him for the other women so why waste his and their time?

Still, he had to ask himself if he could trust Millie not to break his heart. She was still running from something, but what? They were alike in this also. Much like her, he'd been fearful to trust another person with his well-being.

Levi realized that he'd been making decisions based on past hurts. Not once had he asked God to be in control. How foolish.

He did what he should have done in the first place. Levi slipped out of the barn and walked to the carriage. He climbed inside, welcoming the darkness, and bowed his head. It took him a moment to gather his thoughts. With a heavy heart, Levi prayed.

"Lord, please forgive this foolish man. I should have come to You for guidance instead of trusting my own emotions." He took a deep breath—this part was the hardest. He didn't want to allow God to make this decision for him but pressed on knowing it was the right thing to pray. "Father God, I trust You so I'm coming before You now with these questions. Should I continue to pursue Millie? Or start looking closer at the other three brides?"

Chapter Nineteen

The next morning, Millie gathered up her sketch pad and headed to the woods. She stopped in the kitchen long enough to tell Beth where she was going and to grab a hot buttered biscuit.

"Will you be back in time for services?" Beth asked.

Millie pushed the back door open. "Yes, I just need some alone time to think and pray."

Beth scooped fried potatoes into a bowl. "About Levi?" Levi had left the dance early, instructing Amos to take her home when she was ready.

"Among other things. Thanks for the biscuit. See you at church." Millie hurried out the door before her friend could ask any more questions.

It had been a full, busy week since Levi had stopped her from exploring the stream she'd discovered in the woods. If she hurried she might be able to find it again before church, explore a little and maybe even sketch an outline of its banks. Millie set off into the woods at a brisk pace, loving the feel of the cooler morning air.

Going farther than she'd ever gone before, she followed the sound of running water. The birds in the trees twittered back and forth as if they didn't have a care in the world. It was a happy sound and she wondered how long it had been since she had laughed spontaneously. If only she could feel that free.

She had to admit that her heart ached each time she'd seen Levi dancing with another woman at the barn dance. She'd experienced a gamut of perplexing emotions. Confusion that her response to him went directly against what she spoke out loud, and then extreme happiness when he singled her out for dances. It had hurt that he'd left early and left her well-being in the hands of another.

Millie sat down on a rock under a large oak tree. She took a deep breath and tried to relax. What did it all mean? *I love him.* The words whispered through her mind.

She spoke the words tentatively as if testing the idea. "I love Levi." Millie could no longer deny that she loved him. It felt good; it felt right. Being in his arms and feeling his heart beat under her cheek had brought the truth of her feelings for him to the surface. If only she could tell him how she felt.

In her heart, Millie recognized the truth and knew he'd never be controlling like their mothers. But even so, because of the issue of her being an arsonist, she couldn't let him know her true feelings.

Even if he could accept that she had burned down another woman's house and then run away, Levi had vowed never to give another woman his heart. So where did that leave them? She fought hard against the tears she refused to let fall.

She opened her sketch pad and began drawing the outline of the river. Millie wanted Levi's love, not just friendship. She wanted it all. The happy home, children, a husband who adored her and one she could please.

"Stop it, Millie." She spit out the words impatiently. What good was it doing her to focus on those things? She couldn't tell him about her past, and he couldn't bring himself to love again. They were definitely at an impasse.

Millie pushed thoughts of Levi to the back of her mind. It was time to focus on something else, like making things right with Eliza Kelly. Thanks to the sales of her drawings and Levi's pictures, plus the money she'd made working with Beth, Millie felt sure she had enough saved to give Eliza at least a little money to help replace her home and business.

How much would Eliza demand from her? Millie didn't know, but she knew, whatever the price, she'd pay it. She raised her head and looked out across the small stream.

Momentary panic swept through her heart as she thought about returning to Cottonwood Springs. She'd have to tell the U.S. marshal everything.

Would he throw her into jail? What was the punishment for what she'd done? Her thoughts began to torment her. She forced herself to settle down and ignored the fact that her hand shook as she attempted to shade in the drawing of the stream.

Millie closed her eyes and prayed. *Lord, I'm real scared. I know I have to face up to what I've done, but I can't do it alone. If I am to go to prison, like Peter and Paul, I ask that You be with me.* She realized comparing herself to the disciples was a little farfetched but also knew God would understand what she meant. She opened her eyes.

A deep purring sounded over her head. Millie looked up into the tree branches and saw the biggest cat she'd ever seen. Its yellow eyes watched her every move, much like a barn cat would watch a mouse. Icy fear twisted around her heart. Her entire body began to shake.

Levi entered the woods determined to talk to Millie.

His chest tightened when he arrived at the log where she normally sketched. As he'd feared, Millie wasn't there. Where could she be? He searched his memory for something, anything, that might give him a clue to her whereabouts. Nothing came to mind.

Levi started to sit down when he heard the mountain lion's scream. It sounded like a cross between a cat's purr and a deep growling sound.

His blood ran cold. Fear and anger knotted inside him. Why hadn't she listened to him? Fearful images built in his mind. Panic forced him into a run.

Where was Millie? He followed the sound. Each step that brought him closer to the mountain lion caused his heart to pound and his stomach to churn.

What if Millie wasn't even in the woods? He would be walking into a lion's snare for no good reason. Unarmed and with no other means of protection. Still, Levi pressed on.

The big cat sounded off the loudest purring roar that he'd ever heard. Levi noted that the birds were no longer singing in the trees. His breath came in short gasps, and his chest felt like a volcano that might erupt at any moment.

He crouched closer to the ground as he neared the sound. He recognized the sound of a hunting cat. The mountain lion continued growling deep in its throat and hissed as if warning something or someone to stay away from her, all the while giving Levi the impression that the lion was on the hunt.

That meant the cat would not easily give up its prey. How he hoped it had found another animal for its supper and not Millie.

He heard water trickling and knew he was close to the stream. Levi wanted to call out for Millie but didn't dare. If the mountain lion wasn't aware of either of them, he didn't want to draw her attention.

Just when he'd decided Millie wasn't around and he should turn back, Levi's felt a chill race down his spine.

Millie crouched beside a large rock, her large eyes focused fearfully up in the tree above her head. His gaze followed hers and his heart stopped beating.

The cat was one of the biggest he'd ever seen in these parts. Tawny in color, she looked to be about six feet long and if he was to guess, she weighed somewhere between seventy and one hundred pounds.

His knowledge of the animal scrolled through his mind, and he tried to plan a strategic defense. His dad had taught Levi and Daniel early in their lives that mountain lions use their claws as hooks to hold their prey till they could administer a lethal bite. If he could somehow avoid those claws, they might stand a chance, but he knew it would be a slim chance by far.

He looked around for a tree limb or big rock, anything he could use as a weapon. The mountain lion jumped from the limb and landed a few feet away from Millie.

Levi gave no thought to his own safety. He ran forward and placed himself between Millie and the cat.

He hunched down ready to come under her belly should she leap toward them. *God, please keep us alive,* he silently pleaded.

Millie whimpered behind him. It broke his heart that he couldn't turn around to offer her comfort, but to do so would mean his death for sure. In a soothing voice, he said, "Millie, don't panic. Just stay put."

The big animal bared her stained teeth at him and growled lower in her throat. She swiped in his direction with her big paw. Thankfully, she was too far away to reach him.

Millie gasped.

Levi swallowed. If the mountain lion chose to move closer and swat at him, her claws would rip right through his flesh. He heard Millie's skirts rustle behind him and prayed she wouldn't do anything foolish.

In the distance the sound of another cat sounded off. Levi prayed it was calling to its mate. He continued to stare at the big cat as she answered the call. With one final hiss, the mountain lion turned and ran into the underbrush.

Levi backed up until he could feel Millie at his back. He kept his gaze glued to the spot where the big cat had disappeared. "Millie, we have to get out of here. Back up slowly."

She kept her hand on his back but did as he requested. Levi's heart felt as if it were going to burst through his shirt. The blood pumping through his veins echoed in his ears.

"Do you think we are safe yet?" Millie whispered. Her hand trembled against his shirt.

"We won't be safe until we are out of these woods," Levi responded. He turned around and pulled her against his side. Then with the speed of a threatened man, Levi rushed them through the woods.

The cat was probably long gone, but they weren't out of the woods. Until they were, Levi wouldn't drop his guard. Millie sobbed at his side. He could feel her pressing as close to him as she dared and yet all the while her wide eyes scanned the trees above their heads.

They burst through the trees and into the open meadow between the businesses and the woods. Millie collapsed against him, and sobs shook her whole being. She repeated over and over, "I'm sorry, Levi. So sorry."

He thought she might be in shock but had no clue what to do about it. Following his instincts, Levi scooped her up into his arms and carried her to the boardinghouse. He felt her face press into his shoulder and her tears seep into his shirt. She breathed in shallow, quick gasps.

When he arrived at the boardinghouse, Beth and Mark sat on the porch swing. Beth took one look at them and came running out to meet them. She opened the gate and he slipped through. "Is Millie all right? What happened?"

Millie burrowed deeper into Levi's shoulder. A fresh whimper issued from her throat. He wasn't sure if she was still frightened or simply embarrassed.

Either way, Levi was worried. "Help me get her to her room. I'll explain everything there."

Beth nodded and raced ahead of him to open the door. "Mark, stay out here on the porch and play. I'll be back in a few minutes," she instructed as she closed the door behind them.

Levi carried Millie up the stairs. He cuddled her close and whispered softly that everything was fine now, she was safe. With each step a sixth sense troubled his mind. How long had she faced the cat? His heart had all but stopped in his chest when he'd seen her. How had she managed to stay still and not run? Would she have nightmares about it?

Her body had not stopped trembling in his arms. At the top of the stairs, Beth hurried around them. She pulled a ring of keys from her apron pocket, found the one that matched Millie's door and opened it. "Set her on the bed, Levi."

Levi carried her to the bed but she wouldn't release her hold around his neck. Millie raised her head and begged. "Please don't leave me." Her face was as white as any whitewash paint he'd ever seen. Tears slipped down her cheeks. Levi gulped hard, trying to keep his own emotions in check.

He sat down on the edge of the bed and cuddled her close as if she were a frightened child. Over her head he mouthed to Beth, *Go get Doc.*

Beth nodded and slipped out of the room. She closed the door behind her. The sound of her feet running down the short hall and stairs echoed in the silent room. Millie's whimpering was the only sound left.

His arms tightened around her, and he gently started rocking her, like one would a child. Levi kissed the top of her head and murmured, "Shh, you're safe now. I won't let anything happen to you."

Levi's whole body suddenly felt engulfed with weariness and despair. He could have lost her. The very light of his life and she could have been snatched away in a brief moment of carelessness. He wanted to shake her for scaring him so, yet he found his arms tightening around her in hopes of offering comfort instead. It felt right to hold her in his arms, even if she had gone suddenly very still.

A few minutes later, Beth arrived with the doctor. "What happened?" the doctor demanded.

Levi spoke in a soft voice. "I found her in the woods with a mountain lion hanging above her on a tree limb. It didn't attack her, but I think she's in shock from the scare."

The doctor nodded. "Beth, would you get me a glass of water and a spoon?"

Beth nodded and then hurried from the room once more.

Millie had calmed down but still clung to Levi like a frightened child.

The doctor knelt down in front of them and looked into Millie's face. "How long has she been like this?"

"I don't know how long the cat had her trapped, but she got hysterical once we were out of the woods. I picked her up and carried her here. It's just been within the past few moments that she's gotten this still." Levi cradled her close against his chest, still unwilling to release her.

Beth arrived with the water. The doctor opened his bag and measured out some type of powder. He mixed it with the water.

Kneeling once more in front of them, the doctor ordered in a firm voice, "Millie, drink this."

Slowly, she did as he said. Her hands shook so hard as she tried to take the glass that finally the doctor pushed her hands away and held the glass to her lips himself. Millie scrunched up her nose at the taste but did as he ordered and drank the whole glass.

"Now, Levi, lay her down on the bed. That will help her sleep."

He didn't want to release her but knew it was for the best. Levi gave her a gentle hug and lightly kissed her forehead as he laid her down on the soft mattress.

The doctor stood by the door, holding it open. "If you two will excuse us, I'd like to examine my patient." He shooed Beth and Levi from the room.

Chapter Twenty

Millie woke from her drug-induced sleep with fear, stark and vivid, shivering through her. One hand lashed out, the other covered her head as she rolled into a crouched position. As she came fully awake, instinct caused her to search the hidden areas of the darkness of her room. Pure relief slowed the pounding of her heart, but in a small defensive gesture she pulled the covers up to her chin and quietly waited as her mind and body became oriented to the fact that she was safe and in her room at the boardinghouse. It was silly, she knew, to be looking for the big cat to jump out at her, but she couldn't help it.

Why hadn't she listened to Levi? He'd warned her that mountain lions roamed those woods. After this experience, Millie felt certain she would never enter the woods alone again. She lay there, her mind congested with doubts and uncertainty, wearied by the choices she'd made.

She'd learned today while staring into the face of death that there was nothing like a good scare to help get your priorities in order. Just a few days ago she had settled it in her heart that she would return to Cottonwood Springs and make things right with Eliza. Now, that decision seemed urgent. She had to make things right as soon as possible. Millie knew she would soon be leaving Granite and returning to Cottonwood Springs.

Just the thought of leaving Levi caused disturbing quakes in her stomach, which chose that very moment to growl with hunger. The desire to get up and find food struck her, but so did fear that something was lurking in the shadows.

Millie was sick and tired of fear keeping her from living life. No more. Never again. She gritted her teeth and pushed back the covers. She pulled a light day dress over her nightgown.

Creeping down the stairs, Millie felt like a little girl sneaking down to the kitchen. She held a lantern out in front of her to light the way. What must Levi think of her after the way she'd behaved today? She felt her face flush in the semi-darkness. It was a humiliated, deflated feeling.

Levi had been there when she needed him most. Fear had held her captive, but Levi had faced the mountain lion head-on and protected her from its massive claws and teeth.

She closed her eyes and swallowed hard. She could still see his protective stance. If the cat had jumped him, he would be dead right now but instead, his strong arms and soothing words had penetrated that wall of fear and kept her from becoming totally lost in darkness. It was a selfless act. He had put her safety before his own. He had unlocked her heart and soul; how could that not affect her?

Millie cut two slices of bread from the loaf and then

discovered a block of cheese in the icebox. She made herself a sandwich, filled a glass with water and then walked to the front porch.

At first she didn't want to leave the safety of the house. What if a mountain lion rested on the porch, waiting to jump on her? Millie took a deep breath and faced that fear.

She stepped through the door and into the night air. The lantern filled the porch with light. She set it down, and then gently shut the door, not wanting to wake Beth or the other boarders.

The porch swing swayed in the evening breeze. Millie stopped. Her heart beat with fear within her chest. She closed her eyes and reminded herself that she was safe.

Was it her imagination or could she also detect a hint of earth and sawdust in the air? Millie felt his presence long before she actually saw him. Her gaze searched the porch for Levi.

He stepped from the shadows. His husky voice filled with warmth and concern. "Good evening, Millie. Are you feeling better?"

Immediate calm soothed her nerves at the sight of him. "Yes, much, thank you." She walked to the swing, needing to sit down. Her legs had the consistency of pudding. At least it felt that way to her.

Levi picked up the lantern and set it on the porch railing. "I'm glad. I've been worried." His dimples and teeth flashed in the pale light.

"I'm sorry I worried you."

He walked over and sat down beside her. "We've had quite the day, haven't we?" Levi ran his hand through his tousled hair.

Millie nodded. She felt heat fill her face, knowing she'd been the cause of his stressful day. "I really am sorry, Levi. I promise never to go into the woods again." She gave an involuntary shudder.

He reached across and took her hand. "Don't be sorry. I hate that you were in danger, but something good came out of this."

"It did? For the life of me, I can't imagine what." What good could have possibly come from her being trapped by a mountain lion and his having to rescue her?

He seemed to struggle inwardly, then arrive at a decision. When he next spoke it was in a determined voice. "Millie, I didn't think I would ever love again after Lucille broke my heart. But seeing you and that mountain lion today, well, it made me realize just how much I love you." He gave her hand a gentle squeeze. "I love you, Millicent Hamilton. More than I've ever loved anyone in my whole life."

Levi looked deeply into Millie's eyes, praying she could see the love shining within his own and would be willing her to accept and return it. In frustrated concern, he watched her eyes fill with moisture. Great drops welled up within her blue depths and rolled slowly down her cheeks. She pulled her hand from his and stared down at the porch.

When she finally spoke, her voice held a strong suggestion of reproach and something close to desperation. "Why did you have to tell me that? You know I can't return your love."

"I don't understand why not." Levi sighed with exasperation. "I thought you knew by now that I am nothing like your mother, that I'd never hurt you."

Her shoulders shook. "Oh, Levi, it isn't that." She wiped at her cheeks, but the tears continued their steady flow downward. "You wouldn't feel that way if you knew what I've done."

Levi scooted closer to her. All he wanted to do was wrap her in his arms and assure her there was nothing that would stop him from loving her. Following his instincts, he reached for her.

Millie leaped off the swing. Her sandwich made a soft plopping noise as it hit the porch. "No." She held her hands out in front of her as if to ward him off. "Don't touch me. This is too hard as it is."

A tumble of confused thoughts and feelings assailed him. How could he help her? What could she have done that was so horrible she felt it made her unworthy of his love? Levi had no intention of relenting or taking back his declaration of love. He already knew he'd stand by her no matter what. He tried to maintain an even tone. "Tell me."

She stepped backward and stopped only when she touched the porch railing. Millie took a deep breath and sighed. She acted as if the whole world rested on her slim shoulders. "I ran away from home, Levi."

He hated seeing her look so frail, as if she would shatter if the wind blew. "Yes, you told me that. Your mother is overbearing and you wanted to get away from her, pursue your dream of becoming an artist."

"That was only part of why I left Cottonwood Springs." She sobbed and covered her face. "You won't understand. I can't bear to see the loathing in your eyes when I tell you."

Levi stared at her, completely tongue-tied. Didn't she understand that he could never hate her? He would never judge her that harshly. All he wanted was to take her in his arms and comfort her, to reassure her. He opened his mouth to explain, but she cut him off.

"I'm an arsonist." Though she lowered her hands and lifted her chin, he could tell she wasn't looking at him but over his head at the roof. "I burned down Eliza Kelly's home and dress shop and then I ran away." Her body trembled. "I know it was wrong and I plan to return to Cottonwood Springs and make things right. I plan to pay Eliza back."

Levi stood. He took a step toward Millie, but she shimmied to the side and hurried to the door. If only Millie would look at him, Levi felt sure he could convince her to let him help her.

The tears had stopped, but in their place he saw defeat, and a woman facing the harsh realities of loneliness and life. "Please understand, Levi. I can't love you. I can't love anyone. I have no idea what the U.S. marshal will do to me when I turn myself in to him. What I do know is that I can't expose someone I love to that kind of existence. I just won't do it. That would kill me." Millie grabbed the door, wrenched it open and hurried inside.

If he hadn't been so emotionally wrung out, Levi would have smiled. So that was her big secret. Burning down Eliza Kelly's house and business had to have been an accident. He couldn't bring himself to believe otherwise.

If Millie Hamilton thought that would stop him from loving her, she had another think coming. His determination settled like a hard rock in his chest. He would be the winner in this game of love.

Millie wasn't aware of what she had let slip, but he

had heard it loud and clear. He clapped his hands together and headed to the stable. There was no way he could sleep tonight, and the sooner he straightened things out, the sooner he could claim Millie as his own.

He barely refrained from whistling as he saddled Snow and headed to the ranch. Millie's words wrapped themselves around his bruised heart in a silken cocoon of joy. *I can't expose someone I love to that kind of existence.* She loved him.

The door slammed back against its hinges and Millie almost fell off the swing. Mark ran down the porch steps, shooting his pretend gun at his imaginary mountain lions.

Ever since he'd heard of the cat in the woods, the little boy had been playing hunter. "Careful, Mark," she exclaimed in irritation as she jumped to her feet.

Her annoyance increased when she found that her hands were shaking. She'd like to blame her skittishness on her run-in with the mountain lion, but her new resolutions for her life demanded that she face realities.

The truth was she was hurting and confused.

Her mind could not comprehend how a man could proclaim his love for her with such intensity one day, and then simply disappear from her life without any warning the next.

Three days. Three long, lonesome days Levi had been gone and no one knew his whereabouts. Just that his horse, Snow, was missing from the stable.

She entered the house and wandered restlessly through the downstairs rooms. Millie tried to force her emotions into order. Strange and disquieting thoughts

had been her constant companions since waking up and
not finding Levi anywhere in town.

Had he gone for the marshal himself? Was he so dis-
gusted with the secret she'd revealed that he couldn't
face her? She was an arsonist. What did she expect? No
one would ever love her. She didn't even love herself.
Her misery was so acute that it was a physical pain. She
ran up the stairs and flung herself down onto the bed.

One thing had been constant in her life and that was
prayer. Millie started at the beginning and poured her
heart out to the One who'd always loved her no matter what. She admitted her weaknesses, begged God to
help her; and when she finished the tears were gone as if
swept away by an onrushing wind. A sense of strength
had come to her and the despair in her life had lessened.
She felt reassured and comforted.

No matter the outcome, she would do what was right,
because she was a child of the King and children of
the King were subject to a higher power and their lives
needed to reflect the beliefs and rules of that Kingdom.
She would have the backing of her Father, and if she
had to spend time in jail, He would be with her like He
had been with Paul and Silas in the Bible.

And if He granted her desire for love, then that would
be an even greater blessing and one she would receive
with a thankful and humble heart, for she loved Levi
with every fiber of her being.

Millie started down the stairs and the door slammed
against the hinges again. She opened her mouth to scold
Mark, but the person standing in the doorway was a
good bit taller and made Millie's heart lurch up into her
throat. When he spotted her at the top of the stairs, he
sprinted up them two at a time till he stood beside her.

Levi grabbed her hands, then rushed into speech so fast she couldn't understand a word he said.

"Levi, slow down. I don't know what you're saying." He had the audacity to laugh, and she straightened herself with dignity.

"My precious Millie, don't you dare stiffen up on me. I have good news."

She interrupted impatiently. "Where on earth have you been, Levi? I searched everywhere for you."

His eyes studied her with curious intensity. "You did? You missed me?"

"Of course I missed you. You tell me you love me and I tell you why you can't ever love me, then you disappear. I felt…" She foundered before the brilliance of his look.

"You felt what, Millie? Don't stop now." His voice simmered with barely checked excitement. His whole being seemed to be filled with waiting and his steady gaze bore into her with silent expectation. His invitation to share her heart with him was hard to resist. Her resolve began to melt, and she tentatively tested the waters with her true feelings.

"I felt totally alone."

Before she finished speaking she was in his arms, wrapped so tightly she could barely take a breath. Her senses leaped to life. Dare she have hope?

With obvious reluctance, he moved her away from him and motioned for her to sit with him on the top stair. Still, he took her hand and entwined their fingers, his eyes on her face.

"I went to the ranch. I've had three days of talking things out with Daniel and Hannah. Hannah needs to go home for a visit to Cottonwood Springs, and Daniel has agreed to take her. They want you to go with them. Of course, I'll be going, too, and we will face the marshal together." When she started to protest, he placed a gentle finger across her lips. "It's all worked out, Millie. I will not let you go alone. Hannah and Daniel will be our chaperones until we arrive and then I plan to ask your father for your hand in marriage. Whatever happens, we will, with God's help, conquer it and our love will keep us strong." He tipped up her chin and his head descended slowly. "Because I do love you, Millie, with all my heart and soul."

His lips claimed hers. Millie's happiness knew no bounds. Levi said he loved her. He'd promised to travel with her and be beside her come what may. She lifted her arms and put them around his shoulders.

Chapter Twenty-One

Millie's hands shook. She was almost home. She twisted them in the folds of her dress. Levi reached out and captured them under his own. The gentle squeeze he gave them was meant to assure her all would be well. It amazed her that he was so attuned to her feelings. He continued to focus his attention on Daniel and their conversation but had instinctively known that she was fretting.

They'd grown closer on this journey back to Cottonwood Springs without feeling the pressure of others always watching them. Hannah and Daniel were with them most of the time, but something about getting away from the mail-order brides and Levi's mother made them both feel more at ease.

In Denver, Colorado, they'd stepped off the train expecting to have to rent a buggy for the rest of the journey, but were pleasantly surprised to learn that the stage now ran all the way to Cottonwood Springs.

Only one other passenger traveled with them. Millie had listened to his talk of bringing the railroad through to Farmington until the man had become bored with his own voice and leaned his head back for a nap.

Her gaze moved out the window. A beautiful river ran alongside the road. Cottonwood trees lined its edges and she knew they were almost to the only home she'd ever known, until the day she'd answered Levi's letter. Normally the sight of the river and trees would have calmed her, but not today.

Today she'd face her parents, but in all honesty, Millie expected that for the most part it would be a joyful occasion. What she dreaded was facing Eliza Kelly and Seth Billings, the U.S. marshal. Just thinking about it caused her heart to pound in her chest and her stomach to roll. Nauseated, she pulled her gaze back inside the stage.

Hannah rested with her head against her husband's shoulder. She looked peaceful as she slept. Color filled her cheeks, but the trip had taken its toll on her. Unaware at how close they were to Cottonwood Springs, Levi and Daniel were discussing the next cattle run. None of her companions realized just how stressed she felt.

The possibility of going to jail frightened Millie more than she'd let on to any of them. Levi glanced in her direction and winked. The dimple in his cheek flashed when he smiled.

He took her hand and pulled it into the crook of his arm, covering it with his own. He answered Daniel but gazed only at her. His look spoke to her, saying, *It will be all right. I'm with you.*

If it hadn't been for him, Millie felt sure she would have gone running back to Granite, Texas, after the first night on the trip. He'd teased and laughed with her, all the while pulling information about her childhood from her. Millie had learned more about him, too, and what she'd learned, she loved. Now, a week later, they were pulling into town.

As the stage slowed, Hannah sat up. "Are we here?" She smoothed down her hair and pressed at the wrinkles in her dress with her palms.

Millie nodded. Her ponytail brushed her back. Unlike Hannah, she'd chosen to wear a simple brown dress and pull her hair up in her normal style. She and Hannah had become even closer on this trip home, but Millie was still her own woman and refused to gussy up since she didn't want to draw attention to herself.

Levi leaned over and whispered in her ear. "Almost there. We can do this together."

When the stage came to a complete stop, the railroad man was the first to disembark. Loud cheers greeted his arrival. Millie wondered what the hoopla was about but couldn't find out until everyone had exited the stage before her.

Daniel followed the railroad man and then helped Hannah. Levi followed Hannah, and then he turned to take Millie's hand in his. The cool air felt good on her flushed cheeks. Her gaze scanned the faces of the excited people who circled the railroad man, but she didn't see her parents. Relief and disappointment hit her hard. It was foolish to feel this way since they didn't know she would be arriving.

A squeal to her right had Millie turning. She watched as Eliza Kelly and Rebecca Billings hurried to Hannah. The three women hugged and laughed.

Levi and Daniel were helping the driver unload their bags. Millie felt alone in a sea of people. She looked about for her old friend Elizabeth Miller and her best friend, Charlotte Walker. They stood on the sidelines watching the railroad man.

As if she sensed Millie looking at her, Charlotte turned in her direction. Her eyes grew wide and she spun away. Elizabeth watched her friend leave and then looked at Millie. A frown marred her pretty face.

"Millie Hamilton! I am so glad to see you." Eliza Kelly grabbed Millie by her arm and pulled her away from the crowd.

Once they were out of earshot, Millie blurted, "I burned your house down and I am so sorry. I didn't mean to do it." Tears filled her eyes and she wept.

Eliza pulled her into a hug. "I know, Millie. Charlotte told me shortly after you left. Honey, I'm not angry at you. If anything, I am indebted to you and need to thank you."

Millie pulled back and felt a warm, strong chest against her shoulders. Just to be sure, she glanced back and up. Levi grinned down at her. She turned her attention back to Eliza. "Thank me, Mrs. Kelly?"

A warm chuckle slipped past Eliza's lips. "Yes, thank you." She held up her left hand displaying a beautiful ring that caught the sunlight, casting rainbows of color about. "I'm Mrs. Hart now." She turned and grinned at a big man who stood a few feet behind Eliza. "Jackson, come meet Millie Hamilton. Millie, this is my husband, Jackson Hart."

Jackson stepped forward and offered her his hand. "Nice to meet you, ma'am."

Confusion filled Millie at the twist of events. Eliza wasn't upset with her for burning down her house and business, and she had married the large blacksmith in Millie's absence.

Levi gently gripped her shoulders. She felt him squeeze as if reminding her that she wasn't alone.

Millie reached out and shook Jackson's hand. "I'm glad to meet you, too." She wasn't sure that those were the right words, but at the moment it was all she could think of to say.

Jackson nodded and returned the handshake. His gaze moved behind her as he released Millie's hand. Again, Levi gently squeezed her shoulders.

"Oh, I'm sorry. Mrs. Hart, Mr. Hart, this is Levi Westland." Millie felt Levi's warmth as he reached around her and shook Jackson's hand and nodded to Eliza.

"Now that the formalities are out of the way, why don't we all become friends and simply use our given names?" Eliza looped her arm into Millie's and pulled her away from Levi's grasp. "I'm dying to know about your adventures while you've been gone." She looked pointedly at Levi.

Millie saw that they were following Daniel, Hannah, Rebecca and Seth. Her heart skipped a beat knowing that the marshal was going to want to know what had happened at Eliza's store. She looked over her shoulder, searching out Levi. He and Jackson were talking quietly but staying close enough that she could reach back and touch him.

"I can't tell you how happy Rebecca and I were to see you and Hannah step off that stage," Eliza exclaimed.

Millie wanted to stop them from walking but knew she'd only draw more attention to herself. So instead she leaned close to Eliza and said, "I don't understand why you aren't angry with me for burning down your house and store." She searched Eliza's face.

Eliza rested her head against Millie's. "Believe it or not, your burning down my house was the best thing that's ever happened to me."

"But why?"

"Because if you hadn't, I probably would never have married Jackson. You did me a great service by burning the place down. I can't thank you enough."

Millie's head hurt. It spun with the knowledge that Eliza wasn't angry with her but genuinely happy. Her gaze moved to the wide-shouldered marshal. "What about the marshal? Is he going to arrest me?" Her voice caught in her throat.

Eliza raised her head. "Of course not."

Relief hit Millie head-on. She wanted to weep with happiness, but because that was all she'd done since setting foot on New Mexico soil, Millie chose to smile instead. "Oh, thank you. I feel so foolish."

"Don't. We all make mistakes and it looks like the young man behind us is pretty happy that you found him. Are you married?"

Millie gasped. "No, and I'm not sure I want to get married."

Eliza stopped and looked at her. Questions shot from her eyes, but before she could ask them, Millie heard her father's voice.

"Millie! You're home!" He rushed forward and grabbed her.

Compared to Levi, Millie's father was a small man. She held him close and inhaled the fatherly scent she'd missed so much. She was home. "Papa."

He held her out at arm's length and examined her.

A proud smile touched his lips. "Your mother insists you come home right this moment. She has been worried sick about you."

Millie nodded, aware the rest of their party had stopped and returned to stand about them. "Papa, I want you to meet Levi and Daniel Westland. I believe you know Miss Young. She's now Mrs. Daniel Westland."

While he shook hands with Levi and Daniel, Millie wondered why her mother hadn't come to meet her. Was she angry that Millie had run away? Or was this just her first step at trying to regain control over her again?

She'd been so deep in thought that she almost missed her father's words to Levi. "Charlotte Walker said Millie had come home with a man. Why don't you join us, Mr. Westland? I believe you and I should have a talk." He raised his eyebrows at Levi, much like he'd done to her when she was a small child and had been naughty.

"Papa!"

Her father ignored her and motioned for them to follow him.

Levi grinned wickedly and raised his eyebrows like her father had, only he gave his a little wiggle and winked. He placed his hand in the small of her back and gave her a gentle shove in her father's direction.

The cad. He had no idea what they were in for, but she did, and dread filled Millie at the thought.

An hour later, in the privacy of her parents' home, Levi faced Millie's father. "I know you are upset, Mr. Hamilton, but you have to believe that I love your daughter."

"I found out from my daughter's own lips that you are not married and that you have been living under the same roof for months." Mr. Hamilton's nose turned red with anger.

Millie hadn't handled the situation very well at all. When they'd arrived at the house, Mrs. Hamilton had her leg propped up on a cushion on the sofa. She claimed it could be broken, much like her heart. The woman should be in plays, she was so dramatic.

While Millie apologized for running away, Mrs. Hamilton had sniffled into a handkerchief, but no tears leaked from her blue eyes. If anything they danced with happiness. No wonder Millie wanted to get away from the woman.

And when Mrs. Hamilton learned they weren't married she demanded that they get married and had proceeded to send Mr. Hamilton out for the preacher. Levi had been surprised when Millie's father turned to do her bidding.

That was the final straw for his sweet Millie. She stood up straight, pulled her shoulders back and, while staring her mother in the eyes and in anger, said it would be a cold day in Florida before she'd marry the likes of him.

Levi had to admit that had stung somewhat.

Still, he knew she was angry with her mother and would reconsider once she'd gotten over being mad at her mother who still was trying to control Millie's life. At least he hoped so.

"It's a boardinghouse, Mr. Hamilton. There are six of us that live there, so it isn't like we aren't chaperoned."

"Why haven't you asked my Millie to marry you if you love her?" Millie's father demanded.

Levi wanted to laugh but knew Bart Hamilton

wouldn't appreciate the gesture. "I have asked her, several times, in fact. And she's turned me down."

Bart sat down with a frown. "Why?"

He shrugged. If Millie wanted him to know, she'd tell him. "You'll have to ask her."

Confusion laced Bart's face and he shook his head. "I could have sworn that girl loves you." He looked up at Levi. "Are you going to ask her again?"

Levi rubbed his chin. "No, the invitation is out there. If she wants to marry me, she'll have to let me know."

Bart frowned. "I don't know if that's such a good idea. Millie is the child of my heart, but that girl is stubborn, like her mother."

He couldn't disagree with Millie's father more. As far as he could see, Millie was nothing like her mother, but Levi was wise enough not to comment. "If she does change her mind, do we have your blessing?" he asked instead.

For the first time since they'd arrived at his house, Bart smiled. "You most certainly do. I know Millie loves you, too."

The smell of roast and potatoes filled Millie's senses as she entered the kitchen. She frowned when she realized it was her papa pulling dinner out of the stove instead of her mother. "Hello, Papa."

He turned to face her. "Feeling better?"

Millie felt like a heel for running out of the house the way she had, but her mother made her so mad. Why couldn't she leave her alone? Why did she feel her hand had to be in everything Millie did?

"A little."

He nodded and pointed at one of the kitchen chairs.

"Please have a seat. Dinner won't be ready for a little while. I want to talk to you about that Westland boy."

Hearing her father refer to Levi as a boy almost brought a smile to her face. Levi was anything but a boy. She sat where her father had pointed and crossed her arms. "I'm not going to marry him, Papa, and Mother can't make me."

Bart sat down beside her. "Why not? I can tell you love him."

Tears filled Millie's eyes, and she fought not to let them fall. This was her papa; she'd always been honest with him. "I do, but I'm also afraid."

"Why do you fear him? Has he hurt you? If so, I will see that he never leaves Cottonwood Springs." The threat hung in the air between them. Her father looked like a mighty warrior who was about to take on the Goliath in her life.

Millie reached across the table and covered the fist that rested upon it. "Oh, Papa, it's nothing like that. Levi would never hurt me on purpose."

The anger seeped from him and was replaced with confusion. "I don't understand, then."

She sighed. "I believe Levi loves me now, but what if he marries me and then decides he doesn't love me? I won't be in a loveless marriage like you and Mother."

Her father's jaw dropped. The hurt look in his eyes was almost her undoing. Then, her papa transformed into a powerful, strong man. He straightened his shoulders and stared her straight in the face. "Millicent Summer Hamilton, I love your mother very much and she loves me. Our marriage is far from loveless." Truth shone from his eyes as he challenged her to deny what he'd just said.

"But Papa, she bosses you around just like she does me. I can't believe you married her when she acted like that. Surely after getting married Mother changed."

He cut her off. "Of course she didn't change. Your mother has always been strong and protecting in her love for both of us." His gaze softened as he studied her face. "You really have believed that your mother didn't love us?"

How could bossiness and controlling someone be love? Millie saw the love in her father's eyes when he spoke of Mother and she understood. Except when it came to Mama and how Millie truly felt. She loved her mother, too, but couldn't stand the way she treated her.

It was his turn to reach out to Millie. "Millie, it's because your mother loves us that she is, in your words, bossy. What you call bossy, she calls love. Your mother lost three babies before you were born and two more after. You are the only child God allowed to remain in her care. She takes that responsibility very seriously."

Millie had never known her mother had lost three babies before she was born. She put herself in her mother's place. It was no wonder her mother guarded her from all harm.

Understanding and newfound appreciation for her mother consumed Millie. Her mother wasn't trying to smother her or enjoy being in control; she simply loved too strongly. Millie smiled at the thought. She'd rather be loved too much than not enough.

How many nights had she lain awake resenting her mother? A sob tore at her throat. "Oh, Papa, I've been so wrong."

He came around the table and pulled her to her feet. Papa's strong arms wrapped around her shoulders, and he hugged her. "Yes, but now you know and will treat your mother in a more caring manner."

Millie nodded. "I will try."

Bart chuckled. "You sound so much like your mother." He hugged her for a few seconds more and then set her back from him. A teasing light filled his eyes. "And for your information, your mother does not boss me around. She likes to think she is in control and I let her think that. It gives her pleasure and because I love her, it gives me pleasure also."

Millie realized she'd misjudged her mother and father's relationship. Was this a sign that she was maturing herself? Or was she simply a daughter finally comprehending what love truly meant?

"Thank you, Papa."

He nodded. "Now, don't you have a young man to go find? I like him and wouldn't mind having him for a son-in-law."

Millie nodded. "After what I said to Mother in front of him, he may never speak to me again."

Her father cupped her face in his rough hands. "He loves you. That trumps any ill-spoken words you may have said. Now go to him and say yes to his marriage proposal."

She prayed her father was right. Millie wasn't so sure. In anger she had told her mother she would never marry Levi. Had he taken her words seriously? Where was he now? She stepped out onto the front porch.

Panic gripped her at the thought that she might have lost him forever. Where had he gone after she'd fled her parents' house? Her heart raced. *Oh, Lord, please help me find him.*

The thought came to her that Daniel would know

where his brother could be found. Last time she'd seen Daniel and Hannah they had been headed to the marshal's house.

Millie picked up her skirt hem and ran to Rebecca and Seth Billings's house. She frantically knocked on the door several times.

Seth came with the speed of a snail to the door. Millie figured he was used to people banging on his door. As soon as it was opened enough for her to speak, Millie asked, "Is Levi or Daniel Westland here?"

"No, they were headed to the livery. Levi's saddling up and leaving town. Didn't you know?"

Headed home? Her hand went to her chest as the pain of loss cut through her. She'd really done it this time. A tear trickled down her cheek. An absurd question entered her mind: When had she become such a crybaby? She swatted away the tear.

Seth cleared his throat. "Shouldn't you be going to the livery to stop him?"

Stop him? Could she? Millie didn't take the time to answer Seth; once more, she picked up the hem of her dress with both hands and took off at a run.

She ran into the dark barn that served as the town livery. It was open at both ends, and when her eyes adjusted she saw Daniel and Hannah standing at the opposite end. If they were still here, maybe it wasn't too late.

Millie ran to them. Her side ached and her breath came out sounding like a broken-down windmill. "Where is Levi?"

Daniel pointed down the street. He looked shocked to see her.

Levi rode a big paint horse. His shoulders swayed in the saddle as he left town.

Whatever dignity Millie may have had fled. She couldn't let him leave with her heart. Millie chased after him, screaming, "Levi! Levi!" *Oh, Lord, please make him stop. I can't bear to lose him now.*

He turned in the saddle. When he saw her running toward him, Levi stopped the horse. He looped the reins over the horn and swung from the saddle. Concern laced his beautiful green eyes.

Millie couldn't stop. All she wanted was to be close to Levi. He held her heart; he was her heart. She threw herself into his arms. "You can't leave, Levi."

Levi caught her up and swung her around with a laugh. Millie held on for all she was worth.

He stopped swinging her and allowed her feet to touch the ground once more. "Why not?" The love in his eyes spoke volumes.

"You haven't married me yet."

Levi leaned forward and for her ears only asked, "Is it a cold day in Florida?" he teased.

Millie remembered her words to her mother. She'd been wrong to say them, she'd been wrong to judge her mother and she'd even been wrong in judging Levi based on how her mother made her feel, but now wasn't the time to go into that. They were standing in the middle of the street with the whole town looking on.

So, taking a page from her mother's book, she grinned back and whispered, "I'm not sure. Are you willing to wait for a Florida weather report to find out?"

He tossed his head back and laughed. "I wasn't leaving town forever, Millie, but I'm glad you chased me down." At her confused look, he laughed again.

Millie slapped him on the arm and hissed, "Levi Westland! That isn't funny."

Once he could control his laughter once more, Levi looked her right in the eyes and said for the whole town to hear, "You're right! We've got a wedding to attend."

Millie didn't protest as he scooped her up in his arms and kissed her in such a way that she forgot about the crowd watching them, their meddling mothers and the other mail-order brides. All she cared and thought about was Levi, his love for her and how wonderful their lives were going to be.

Epilogue

"What do you mean they were born at the same time?"

"How could that be?"

Levi and Daniel asked the doctor in unison. Bonnie Westland stood with her mouth hanging open. Daniel raked his fingers though his hair.

Levi could sense the struggle going on in Daniel's mind. He wanted his wife to be okay and he wanted to keep the ranch he loved as his home.

Then the strangest thing happened. He stood frozen in place and watched his mother throw her arms around the doctor's neck and thank him through the sobs that racked her body.

Finally getting control of her emotions, Bonnie Westland turned to face her sons. "Boys, I know I have done you both a great disservice, but I did it to help you, not hurt you in any way." She pulled at the handkerchief Doc placed in her hands.

Had their mother gone mad? Was she finally losing all her senses?

She ignored their confused looks and continued.

"Starting the contest was wrong. But I did it for your own good. You see, I wanted you to experience love. I didn't want you to be alone like I was after your dad died."

Some of the old spark came back into her eyes. "But you boys were muleheaded and wouldn't go looking for wives like most young men do." She heaved a big sigh. "So I took matters into my own hands and made sure you didn't do something stupid like a marriage of convenience just to get this ranch. That's why I added the extra ultimatum for it to be the first grandchild born."

She walked to Daniel and placed a hand on his chest. "Can you forgive me, son?"

Daniel looked as if a mule had kicked him in the head and he'd lost all sense of what was going on. He stared at their mother as if she'd sprouted wings.

When he didn't answer, she looked at Levi, a pleading expression on her face. "You both can have the ranch. Or you can buy each other out. I don't care. I only wanted you to know love in every way. Love of a good spouse and love of a child."

Thankfully, Daniel snapped out of his stupor. He and Levi exchanged looks of pure amusement and relief.

Their mother wore a look of pure confusion. "What am I missing, boys?" She addressed them now as if they better answer her or suffer the consequences.

Levi should have known the humbleness in his mother wouldn't last long. He took great pleasure in telling her. "Mother, I gave Daniel full rights to this ranch several weeks ago. Millie and I will continue to live in town."

Huge tears rolled down his mother's cheeks, and she

gathered her sons as close as she could get them. They returned her hug with smiles on their faces.

"Umm." The doctor cleared his throat to get their attention. "I hate to break this up, but your wives would like to see you."

Levi and Daniel raced up the stairs. They shared one more grin before stepping into their wives' rooms.

Levi closed the door softly and entered the dimly lit room. Millie held their sweet daughter in her arms. A tender smile graced her beautiful face as she beckoned him to come closer. Levi eased onto the bed beside her.

He held his finger close to the tiny balled-up fist that rested outside the blanket. His little girl latched on tight to both his hand and his heart.

Levi pulled Millie close, careful not to hurt her. In awe, he said the first thing that came to his mind. "You're both so beautiful. How can I be so blessed?"

Millie laughed softly. "We are the ones who are blessed." She eased the baby into his arms.

He slid back against the headboard, with his newborn princess in the crook of his arm and a beautiful mail-order bride resting against his shoulder. Levi silently prayed a prayer of thanksgiving that God had protected the woman he loved and the daughter who had already stolen into his heart.

His wife's easy breathing also had him thanking God for a meddlesome mother who had, with a contest, helped him to find the perfect love.

* * * * *

Dear Reader,

Hi and thank you so much for picking up *His Chosen Bride*. I fell in love with Levi while writing, *Taming the Texas Rancher*. He gave his brother such a hard time over his mail-order bride that I got to thinking Levi needed a mail-order bride of his own. At the same time, his mother whispered in my ear that she had already sent off for three of them for him. Imagine how surprised I was, and I'll be honest, I thought it was kind of funny. Poor Levi. Then Millie decided she'd come to Granite, Texas, too. *His Chosen Bride* was born, and I had the best time juggling all these people. I hope you enjoyed their story and will watch for the other mail-order brides' stories.

Please visit my website at www.rhondagibson. net to get updates on this and other books. I love hearing from readers so feel free to contact me at rhondagibson65@hotmail.com or write me at P.O. Box 835, Kirtland, NM 87417.

Warmly,

Rhonda Gibson

Questions for Discussion

1. Millie ran away from home. Have you ever run away from home? Or a problem? Why?

2. Millie learned that facing our problems gives peace where strife used to live. If you ran away from home, did you return? And if so, what was your family's reaction? And how did it make you feel?

3. When Levi discovered his mother had invited three more mail-order brides to Granite, Texas, he felt overwhelmed. Have you ever had someone put you in a situation where you felt overwhelmed? Please explain the situation.

4. Both Millie and Levi felt they had manipulative mothers. Have you ever felt one of your parents was manipulating you? If so, how old were you and what was the situation?

5. Millie had a dream of becoming an artist and opening up her art gallery. Have you ever had a dream and someone told you it was impossible? What did you do?

6. Levi didn't want to get married because he was afraid of having his heart broken again. Have you ever felt this way? If so, what did you do to overcome those feelings?

7. Do you think Levi and Millie's mothers really loved them? Why or why not?

8. What did you think of the way Millie and Hannah handled the "which baby came first?" question?

COMING NEXT MONTH FROM
Love Inspired® Historical

Available June 3, 2014

LONE STAR HEIRESS
Texas Grooms
by Winnie Griggs

Ivy Feagan is headed to Turnabout, Texas, to claim an inheritance, not a husband. But when she meets handsome schoolteacher Mitch Parker on the way to town, will she become both an heiress and a wife?

THE LAWMAN'S OKLAHOMA SWEETHEART
Bridegroom Brothers
by Allie Pleiter

Sheriff Clint Thornton is determined to catch the outlaws threatening his town. When his plan to trap them requires conspiring with pretty settler Katrine Brinkerhoff, will this all-business lawman make room in his life for love?

THE GENTLEMAN'S BRIDE SEARCH
Glass Slipper Brides
by Deborah Hale

When governess Evangeline Fairfax plays matchmaker for her widowed employer, he agrees on the condition that she give him lessons in how to court a lady. Soon Jasper Chase longs to focus his newfound courting skills on Evangeline!

FAMILY ON THE RANGE
by Jessica Nelson

Government agent Lou Riley thought of his housekeeper Mary as a sister—until now. As they work together to save an orphaned child, will they find that love was right in front of them all along?

LIHCNM0514

REQUEST YOUR FREE BOOKS!

2 FREE INSPIRATIONAL NOVELS
PLUS 2
FREE
MYSTERY GIFTS

Love Inspired.

HISTORICAL

INSPIRATIONAL HISTORICAL ROMANCE

YES! Please send me 2 FREE Love Inspired® Historical novels and my 2 FREE mystery gifts (gifts are worth about $10). After receiving them, if I don't wish to receive any more books, I can return the shipping statement marked "cancel." If I don't cancel, I will receive 4 brand-new novels every month and be billed just $4.74 per book in the U.S. or $5.24 per book in Canada. That's a saving of at least 21% off the cover price. It's quite a bargain! Shipping and handling is just 50¢ per book in the U.S. and 75¢ per book in Canada.* I understand that accepting the 2 free books and gifts places me under no obligation to buy anything. I can always return a shipment and cancel at any time. Even if I never buy another book, the two free books and gifts are mine to keep forever.

102/302 IDN F5CN

Name	(PLEASE PRINT)	

Address		Apt. #

City	State/Prov.	Zip/Postal Code

Signature (if under 18, a parent or guardian must sign)

Mail to the **Harlequin® Reader Service:**
IN U.S.A.: P.O. Box 1867, Buffalo, NY 14240-1867
IN CANADA: P.O. Box 609, Fort Erie, Ontario L2A 5X3

Want to try two free books from another series?
Call 1-800-873-8635 or visit www.ReaderService.com.

* Terms and prices subject to change without notice. Prices do not include applicable taxes. Sales tax applicable in N.Y. Canadian residents will be charged applicable taxes. Offer not valid in Quebec. This offer is limited to one order per household. Not valid for current subscribers to Love Inspired Historical books. All orders subject to credit approval. Credit or debit balances in a customer's account(s) may be offset by any other outstanding balance owed by or to the customer. Please allow 4 to 6 weeks for delivery. Offer available while quantities last.

Your Privacy—The Harlequin® Reader Service is committed to protecting your privacy. Our Privacy Policy is available online at www.ReaderService.com or upon request from the Harlequin Reader Service.

We make a portion of our mailing list available to reputable third parties that offer products we believe may interest you. If you prefer that we not exchange your name with third parties, or if you wish to clarify or modify your communication preferences, please visit us at www.ReaderService.com/consumerchoice or write to us at Harlequin Reader Service Preference Service, P.O. Box 9062, Buffalo, NY 14269. Include your complete name and address.

LIHI3R

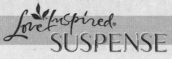
The marshals are closing in on the illegal adoption ring, and Serena and her partner Josh must team up to bring it down for good.

Read on for a preview of the exciting conclusion to the **WITNESS PROTECTION** *series,*
UNDERCOVER MARRIAGE by Terri Reed,
from Love Inspired Suspense.

U.S. marshal Serena Summers entered three-year-old Brandon McIntyre's room with a packing box in hand. Her heart ached for the turmoil the McIntyre family had recently suffered. Danger had touched their lives in the most horrible of ways. A child kidnapped.

But thankfully rescued by the joint efforts of loving parents and the marshal service.

The McIntyre family no longer lived in Houston. The U.S. marshal service had moved them for a second time when their location had been compromised.

Only a few people within the service knew where Dylan, Grace and the kids had been relocated.

Serena and her partner, Josh, were among them. It was their job to pack up the family's belongings and forward them through a long and winding path to their final destination.

Serena's fingers curled with anger around a tiny tennis shoe in her hand.

So many deaths, so many lives thrown into chaos.

The thought that someone she had worked with, trusted, had stolen the evidence and had been leaking information to the bad guys sent Serena's blood to boil.

If her brother were alive, he'd know how to compartmentalize the anger and pain gnawing at her day in and day out.

But Daniel was gone. Murdered.

A sharp stab of grief sliced through her heart. Followed closely by the anger that always chased her sorrow.

"Hey, you okay in here?"

Serena glanced up at her current partner, U.S. marshal Josh McCall. He'd taken off his navy suit jacket and rolled the sleeves of his once crisp white dress shirt up to the elbows. His brown hair looked like he'd been running his fingers through it again, the ends standing up. She'd always found him appealing. But that was before. Now she refused to allow her reaction to show. Not only did she not want to draw attention to the fact that she'd noticed anything about him, she didn't want him to think she cared.

She didn't. Josh was the reason her brother had been alone when he'd been murdered.

Turning away from Josh, she said briskly, "I'm good."

Taking the two ends of the sheet in each hand, she spread her arms wide and attempted to fold the sheet in half.

"Here," Josh said, stepping all the way into the room. "Let me help."

He reached for the sheet, his hands brushing hers.

An electric current shot through her. She jerked away, letting go of the ends like she'd been burned. "I don't need your help."

His hand dropped to his side. "Serena." Josh's tone held a note of hurt.

Glass shattered.

Someone else was in the house.

Pick up UNDERCOVER MARRIAGE by Terri Reed, available June 2014 from Love Inspired® Suspense.

SPECIAL EXCERPT FROM

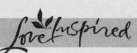

*Now that an Amish widow's daughters have all married,
is it time for her to find her own happily ever after?*

*Read on for a preview of
HANNAH'S COURTSHIP by Emma Miller,
the final book in the **HANNAH'S DAUGHTERS** series.*

Hannah was so shocked by Albert making such a public
show. She had never been a flighty goose, prone to light-
headed nonsense, but suddenly she felt positively giddy.
Why had Albert bid on her picnic basket? People would be
gossiping about it for months.

Just behind her, her sister-in-law Martha remarked
sharply in *Deitsch*. "Has Albert Hartman lost his mind?
What does he want with your basket?"

Even Anna, her sensible daughter, was shocked. "You
can't share supper with Albert. He's Mennonite, not one of
us. How would it look?"

Hannah's sense of humor surfaced, and she barely stifled
a most improper response. Anna was right, of course. She
should have been put out with Albert for getting her in
this pickle, but all she could think of was how much more
enjoyable sharing supper with him would be than eating
with Jason Peachy. She wouldn't have to listen to talk of
the price of pork or of Jason's plans for a new sty. She and
Albert would sit with her family, and he could tell them
about the imminent arrival of the alpacas.

Shyly, carrying Hannah's basket in both hands, Albert
walked toward her. Hannah smiled at him. She would not
provide the gossips more to whisper about by acting as if
she had something to hide.

"What have you done, Albert?" she teased. He grinned, and she decided that he really did have a very pleasant face.

"I hope I didn't upset anyone's buggy, but…" He glanced over his shoulder and lowered his voice conspiratorially. "And I hope Jason doesn't take it to heart, but I didn't get any lunch today, and…and I thought that a homemade supper made by Hannah Yoder was just what I needed."

She arched one eyebrow. "How did you know I made the food inside? It's my mother-in-law's basket."

He grimaced. "Your foster son, Irwin."

"I was afraid of that. Shall we join the family?" She motioned toward her daughter Anna. "She and her family have laid their picnic supper out in the shade on the far side of the schoolhouse."

"I'd like that," Albert agreed.

*Will Hannah and Albert's courtship
be allowed to flourish?*

*Pick up HANNAH'S COURTSHIP
to find out.*

*Available June 2014
wherever Love Inspired® books are sold.*

Love Inspired®
SUSPENSE
RIVETING INSPIRATIONAL ROMANCE

Hometown secrets

Was the explosion that took the lives of Sarah Russell's parents an act of murder? Her teenaged daughter thinks so and is determined to seek answers in their sleepy small town. Sarah fears her daughter will uncover a secret she's not ready to share: everyone—including Sarah's daughter—believes the girl is Sarah's kid *sister*. Even the child's father doesn't know the truth. But as Sarah reunites with Nick Tyler to look into the mysterious deaths, she knows she'll have to tell him—and her daughter—the truth. Yet someone wants to ensure that no one uncovers *any* long buried secrets.

COLLATERAL DAMAGE
by
HANNAH ALEXANDER

**Available June 2014 wherever
Love Inspired books and ebooks are sold.**

LIS44599